I0654504

The Rebel Christian Publishing

Copyright © 2022 Valicity Elaine

All rights reserved. No part of this publication may be reproduced, distributed, or transmitted in any form or by any means, including photocopying, recording, or other electronic or mechanical methods, without the prior written permission of the publisher, except in the case of brief quotations embodied in critical reviews and certain other noncommercial uses permitted by copyright law. For permission requests, write to the publisher, addressed "Attention: Permissions Coordinator," at the address below.

Kindle Vella ASIN: B0B4D5WKR4
ISBN (eBook): 9781957290188
ISBN (Print): 9781957290195

This is a work of fiction. Any references to historical events, real people, or real places are used fictitiously. Names, characters, and places are products of the author's imagination. Inclusion of or reference to any Christian elements or themes are used in a fictitious manner and are not meant to be perceived or interpreted as an act of disrespect against such a wonderful and beautiful faith.

Cover image provided by Shutterstock
Artist: Momentum Ronnarong

The Rebel Christian Publishing LLC
350 Northern Blvd STE 324 – 1390
Albany, NY 12204

Visit us: http://www.therebelchristian.com/
Email us: rebel@therebelchristian.com

This book was originally published as an episodic story on the Kindle Vella platform. It has been modified and formatted for your enjoyment. Original author's notes can be found at the very end of the book. Please enjoy **Clipping Thorns** and take the time to leave your thoughts and opinion in a review on Amazon, Goodreads, and Bookbub. Thank you!

Series Order

Other Books by Valicity Elaine:

I AM MAN series:

Cross Academy series:

To Jesus Christ

Clipping Thorns

Withered Rose Book II

By Valicity Elaine

A Rebel Christian Publishing Book

A note from the author
*** Warning ***

If you read Book I in this series (*Withered Rose*) then you already have an idea of what you are getting into. While this is certainly a work of Christian fiction, I will not make the claim that it is a 'Clean & Wholesome' story.

There are no graphic scenes of sex, no foul language, and no graphic gore. However, the story does follow a young couple involved in the **mafia**. Rosa and Amory are not in a warm and welcoming environment, they are immersed in darkness, death, and sin. The objective here is to demonstrate a dependence on God, even in the most brutal of places.

Our protagonists are married, so I did not shy away from depicting their encounters. However, I am still a Christian author, and I do believe there are certain lines that should not be crossed in Christian fiction. Everyone has a limit; unfortunately, those boundaries can be different for some or others. This is why I have taken the opportunity to warn you before the story begins.

Readers may find some content to be sensitive/triggering, such as abuse, gang violence, manipulation, human trafficking, etc. This book is best enjoyed by mature Christian readers ages 17+

Please continue at your own discretion.

Enjoy a free sample of Book III, Starting Over, at the end of the book.

Be the wife he needs you to be…

—Christina Jäger

One

Nona hits hard. My jaw aches as she lands a terrible left hook to my face. My head whips to the side and my mouthpiece flies out as I spin and fall to the ground. I don't know how long we've been going at it, but I've only been able to land a hit on her once.

I hear her light footsteps as she shuffles closer, probably to kick me in the ribs, but Adella's voice stops her. "Enough, Nona."

I groan and roll onto my side, tapping the mat to let them know I've surrendered the match. I hear someone sigh in disappointment, but I don't care. Every part of me hurts. I have a black eye, a swollen lip, and I'm sure Nona's just given me a bruise on my cheek.

It's been two weeks since I walked out of Amory's home. Two weeks since I signed those papers of annulment. Two weeks since my life changed forever. Moving in with Grandpa Jamie was my only option—it wasn't a bad choice at all; he offers a lot more kindness and protection than my brother Gio does, but he also offers tough love.

One thing my grandparents made clear when I arrived on their doorstep was that I would earn my keep and I would learn my place. In the German mafia, learning my place meant doing as I was told and obeying Amory's every word. But here in the Willis Stronghold, where my grandmother is queen of the kingdom, learning my place means learning how to stand side by side with royalty.

"There's a war coming, you need to be ready," Mama Monique had said after showing me my new bedroom. She'd placed a hand on her hip and used the other to brush a loose, grey curl from her face. It was then that I'd noticed how toned her arms looked in her designer blouse. She was clearly an older woman, but nothing about her physique looked aged or worn.

"You will begin training with Adella. She runs her own kickboxing gym."

I'd frowned at this. "I don't want to learn how to fight."

Mama Mo' had laughed. "You won't be learning how to fight. You'll be learning how to defend yourself."

And so, here I am. Kickboxing training twice a day, two hours per session, five days a week.

My cousins, Adella and Nona, were once my blushing bridesmaids at my own wedding months ago. I never would have guessed their warm hugs and gentle touches could so easily become quick punches and deadly kicks. Then again, they both have killer bodies—that has to come from more than just eating salad and taking strolls through the park.

Adella squats beside me and brushes my dark hair from my

face. "You did better today, Rosa."

"Are you kidding?" Nona laughs, unwinding the tape from her knuckles. Della never lets us wear gloves or shoes. We fight in nothing but our underwear with taped knuckles. I don't even get to put on sweat-shorts. I'm just thankful I own more than one sports bra, despite the fact that I never workout.

Nona looks strong and confident in her white sports bra and matching boy shorts. I can count her abs as she laughs again and says, "I just knocked her down for the third time."

Della rolls her eyes. "And she didn't tap out until the third time." She looks down at me again, a very proud smile on her face, even though I know my performance was pathetic. "You lasted a minute longer than yesterday's session."

"Which puts her at a full two minutes on her feet," Nona teases.

I remember Nona being the nice cousin and Adella being the critical one. But that had been when we were cousins who only shared girl talk and candy. Now we're women—mafia wives preparing to go to war beside our husbands or defend the territory they leave behind. We aren't whispering secrets in my living room anymore; we're training for the fight of our lives in Adella's gym.

This is her haven. This is her kingdom. Mama Mo' might be the Queen of the Bronx, but in *Finesse Fitness*, Adella reigns supreme. Maybe that's why she's calmer than Nona now, or maybe it's because I'm lying on the floor in my underwear with bruises on my face. Either way, I'm more than grateful for the hand Della extends when she helps me to my feet and slaps my

3

butt.

"Give me four laps around the gym and then hit the showers."

I begin a slow pace around the track that encircles the entire gym. It's a quarter of a mile per lap so I'll be getting in a mile once I'm finished. Nona flies by me, her bare feet slapping the track with each step. Normally, I would push myself to try to keep up with her, but I'm sore and achy and just not in the mood. I've been getting my butt handed to me every day, twice a day, for two weeks now. After a while, it starts to get to you.

I won't say I've given up. But I've certainly considered it.

And then I think … What will I do after I give up?

My grandparents took me in, but they won't have a problem kicking me out if I don't cooperate. Jameson and Monique Willis are not doting grandparents who bake cookies and spoil their little grandkids. They are mafia bosses, leaders of the gang that runs the Bronx—also called, the Willis Stronghold.

Ten years ago, New York City defunded its police department and fired half the force due to the dramatic shift in their payroll. Since then, the mafias of the City have taken over and now rule the Big Apple through violence and oppression. Police are on their payroll and justice is in hiding.

Each borough is owned and operated by a different gang. The Stronghold rules the Bronx under Jameson Willis, Manhattan is held by the Italian mafia under my older brother, Giovanni De Luca Jr., Queens is ruled by the Spanish mafia under Emilio Moreno, Mikhail Volkov runs the Russian mafia out of Staten Island, and my father-in-law, Uwe Jäger, is the Jägermeister of the German mafia in Brooklyn.

Well … Uwe is about to become my former father-in-law now. I'm married to his oldest son, Amory Jäger, but after things blew up between the Hunters of Brooklyn and the Wolves of Staten Island, Amory decided to have our marriage annulled so he could form an alliance with the Morenos.

The whole situation is as painful as it is complicated. But the point is that I was forced into a marriage with a man I hardly knew, and the day I found it in my heart to love him, I was suddenly forced out of that marriage. I thought maybe it was an opportunity from God. I had already tried to escape New York and the mafia once before, but I know God has plans for this place and for my soon to be ex-husband.

Father Serrano, my spiritual advisor, told me he believed God wanted to use me to draw Amory closer to Him. So that God could use Amory to destroy the mafias of New York from the inside out. But now Amory and I are getting a divorce. How will God use either of us?

Maybe Father Serrano got it wrong… I sigh as I begin my final lap around the track. *Or maybe there's still a chance.*

Whatever the case, I've got more immediate things to focus on right now, like my best friend's wedding. I'm related to the Willis Stronghold through my deceased mother—Laura Willis—but I'm also connected to the Italian mafia through my deceased father, Giovanni De Luca Sr. My best friend is the daughter of the current Italian underboss and she's getting married soon.

Olivia's wedding should have happened around the time I got married, but her arrangements were delayed by all the drama that went down with Gio kidnapping me from Norman, New Jersey and forcing me to marry Amory. Now, I guess things are back on track.

Last I checked, Olive was engaged to Marco Segreto, the General in charge of Harlem. He's a successful mafioso but he's also old enough to be my father. I know Olive doesn't love him at all, but she's a far more committed mafia princess than I ever was. She's ready to marry Marco, despite his age, his looks, and his rumored cruelty. But it isn't like she has much choice.

Since Olivia is my best friend, she came under suspicion after my escape from New York almost a year ago. My father and brother likely suspected she'd helped me, even though she didn't, so they set her up with this arrangement to shame her family and punish her. Olivia has accepted her fate with an air of dignity which I envy.

I went into my marriage kicking and screaming—I'd refused to let Amory even touch me until the day he ended things. That was when I'd stripped down and offered myself to him, finally realizing that I was in love with him.

Too little too late.

Now, I've got to watch my best friend walk down the aisle to marry a man who will never appreciate or love her. All while knowing I'd stupidly ruined my own marriage to a man who *did* love me and appreciate me.

I wonder when Amory and his new Spanish fiancé will tie

the knot. I wonder if he will give her the wedding night he'd promised me.

I can be gentle… He had said in a voice that'd left me weak in the knees.

I can take it slow… He'd looked at me like I was the only woman in the world.

I shake my head as I finish my last lap and grab my water bottle. Adella dismisses me with a slap to the butt; I immediately slip back on my sweatpants and t-shirt so I can go home to shower. I just want to stand under the steaming water and let it drench me until I'm red and wrinkled. I need something to distract me from the pit of grief left gaping in my heart.

This is why I never complain when Nona hits too hard or when I feel like I've broken a bone. The pain is horrible, the bruises are severe, but they're nothing compared to what I feel inside. Bones will heal, bruises will fade. But nothing can mend my broken heart. Especially when I played a role in breaking it.

The pain is a distraction. But it's only twice a day for a few hours. When I'm left alone to my thoughts and my emotions, I fall into the dark parts of my mind that whispers blame against me. Tells me this is all my fault, and that Amory is better off without me.

The only thing that gives me solace is the memory of that day; Amory's last words to me. How he thought he didn't deserve me. How he believed he was helping me by ending our marriage.

Amory loved me. He truly did.

A small part of me believes he still does, which gives me hope that things will work out in my favor. It's been two weeks since I signed the papers—enough time for the courts to have noticed my 'mistake.' If I'm fortunate, my little typo should have bought me at least another month of paperwork before things are finalized. That's enough time to convince my husband that he was wrong.

He did deserve me—we deserved each other. We'd been brought together by God. And it was never part of His plan for us to split up or for me to escape New York again. I don't care about the coming war; I am fighting my own battle right now. And I intend to win, even if it means fighting dirty.

Two

I'm standing between my cousins Morgen and Conrad in matching suits with matching ties. The room is stuffed with Germans, all hushed to a quiet murmur as we watch the bride walk slowly down the aisle. She looks beautiful. Any man in the room could admit that—even me. But I'm not interested in this. I don't want to be here.

The whole thing reminds me too much of my own wedding, and the fact that I'm here at another one just a few months later makes me sad. The only thing that eases the discomfort is the look on Petra's face as she catches her groom, Eike, smiling at her. They take hands and stand before the Priest when she reaches the end of the aisle. Those two were made for each other. I'm positive their marriage will turn out much better than mine did.

At the thought of my failed marriage, I glance out at the audience in search of my new fiancé. Petra and Eike moved up their wedding after the war officially began last week. Shots were fired between a group of Russian bar hoppers and some off-duty German security guards near the east side of Brooklyn. No deaths or injuries, but the panic that came after sent everyone into a frenzy. Petra, my little cousin on my mother's side, decided to move up the wedding date by four months. Eike, who's madly in love with Petra, didn't have any arguments about it so the date was set, and everything was thrown into place. My family even found room to squeeze in a seat for my new fiancé. Eliana Moreno, oldest daughter of Emilio Moreno—capo of the Spanish mafia.

She looks beautiful and daring, wearing an all-white gown to another woman's wedding. But my family took the insult in stride, wisely choosing not to respond to her blatant disrespect. We can't respond to any of her taunting right now. We need the Morenos and everything they have to offer—men, weapons, intel. All of that will come at the cost of my hand in marriage, but it's a deal I'm ready to take. It's a deal *I* put together.

My chest clenches as Eliana catches me staring and offers a sultry smile. I don't miss the way she shifts in her chair, slowly arching her back so her full breasts poke out more. It's a subtle movement but I can't ignore it even if I want to—especially not with the way she winks at me and catches her bottom lip between her teeth.

Eliana is an absolute vixen.

I would know. I've been sleeping with her since before all this went down. Her father has no idea. *No one* has any idea or else she'd be shipped off to Spain as punishment and I'd be fighting a war with the Morenos for breaking the virtue of a mafia princess.

In this business, women of Eliana's stature are expected to remain virgins until marriage. It's an old-fashioned tradition, but it's been a contractual clause in our arranged marriages for generations. Virtue is valued in the mafia. Loyalty is demanded. Respect is owed—not earned.

Sleeping with Eliana was not a mistake. We had a fling months before Rosa came along, but it was never romantic. I gave her good sex and she gave me good intel on her father's business. It was Eliana's information that laid the foundation for many of the deals I made with her father. And it was Eliana's whispers that convinced her father to ally with my family in this war.

So long as I end my marriage with Rosa. The princess of the Italian mafia.

Despite being absolutely in love with Rosa, I accepted Emilio's deal and got engaged to his daughter. Shockingly, I haven't touched her since before I first got engaged to Rosa. Months ago. It isn't that Eliana isn't sexy. It isn't that I don't feel anything about the way she licks her lips before I glance away and focus on Petra now. It's just that ... I don't love Eliana.

I love Rosa—love her so much that I value keeping her alive and safe over keeping her by my side as my wife. I value her beliefs as a Christian more than my code as a mafioso. I value the way she views sex. How she thinks of it as a sacred act, the ultimate demonstration of love and passion. Not some dirty act of perversion, just two people getting off before falling asleep.

I had that sort of raunchy relationship with Eliana for months, and I don't miss it. But I had only a glimpse of joy with Rosa, and I can't stop thinking about it.

I never even touched Rosa. I didn't get the chance to make love to my own wife, but I'd rather be with her right now than have Eliana blowing me kisses across the room. I don't know if this is truly what it means to love someone or if I've actually gone mad. But something must be done. Because I can't take the stress, the pressure, or the aching pain anymore. I'm tired.

But I don't get to be tired. I'm Amory Jäger, underboss of the German mafia. Hunter of New York. And this is what I have to do to keep my family's legacy alive. And … to keep Rosa alive. Because loving her from a distance is better than losing her altogether.

I smile and clap as Petra and Eike kiss and then hold hands for photos. They are man and wife now. Soon, it'll be my turn to do this all over again. I am not excited.

At the reception, I busy myself with a bottle of whiskey. I've been doing that a lot these last few weeks. The alcohol doesn't help. It doesn't do anything but burn. But if I didn't have this bottle in my hand, Eliana would make me hold hers. She's been all over me since the ceremony ended, clutching my arm, whispering in my ear. She even backed me into the wall and tried to kiss me when we were alone in the hallway.

Once the reception doors opened, I quickly took her

around for introductions. She had an attitude about it, but she met her match with Christina Jäger, the woman who married the Jägermeister and gave him two (horrible) sons. A smile claims my whiskey-soaked lips as I lean back in my chair and watch them chat from across the room. I can see the stiffness in Eliana's jaw as she nods at whatever my mother is saying. The expression on her face is neutral but her eyes are filled with anxiety—she's probably realizing how much of a mistake it is to marry into this family. Rosa had learned about our insanity, but she'd still gotten on well with Petra and Christina, had even made friends with the wife of one of my cousins. Too bad I'm having our marriage annulled.

That thought leaves a bitter taste in my mouth. The whiskey burns worse than it ever has as I swallow it down, and I feel my stomach churn in agitation. I can't remember the last time I ate anything. The horrible nausea that floods me is a desperate plea for food. I stand and stumble my way to the buffet; an array of German foods sits on display—some traditional, some just favorites of Petra and Eike.

I pile a load of wedding noodles onto a plate and eat half of it right there with the serving fork. One of the guys in charge of the buffet gives me a frown, but it's quickly wiped away when he recognizes who I am. He even offers me a napkin once realization sets in.

I smile and take it, swaying as I'm hit by another bout of nausea. The wedding noodles are good, but they're too rich for my empty stomach. The whiskey threatens to claw its way back up my throat. Before I can stop myself, I lurch forward with a gag, making the buffet guy lean away with a frightened look on his face.

"Sorry," I mumble, setting down my plate and tripping away.

At this point, I'm positive I'm drunk. I think it's official— I am *that* guy. The one who can't make it through a wedding without half a bottle of booze in his system.

I remember my own wedding, and how drunk I'd been sitting next to Rosa. She couldn't even look at me back then, let alone sleep with me. I had tried my hardest to seduce her, but she wouldn't give in. Which only made my attraction to her grow deeper. Between the whiskey at the wedding and the champagne I'd found in our hotel room, I think I went through a bottle and a half of alcohol that day. I'm about halfway there now, but I'm too sick to go on.

I push my way through the crowd of my own family members and trip into the hallway for some fresh air. It isn't until I'm panting and wiping sweat from my forehead that I realize how much cigarette smoke and body odor was stuffed into the reception hall. Technically, the banquet area is supposed to be a smoke-free location, but my father's best friend—Klaus Brandt—owns the place, so we can smoke wherever we want.

I catch another whiff of smoke as the doors to the hall open once again. This time, the smell is mixed with elegant perfume. I'm not surprised when I glance up to find my fiancé standing before me.

"Eliana," I say slowly. My eyes drink her in; long legs

crawling from beneath a white gown that hangs helplessly from her slender shoulders. Eliana is almost as tall as me, a model if I've ever seen one—and she knows this. Her eyes narrow, but her lips stretch into a gorgeous smile. She is deceptively innocent, like an imp with angel wings. Her olive skin seems to glow behind the curtain of dark hair that falls like silk around her body. Her hair is so long, I'm sure she could sit on it, and I can't help staring as it sways around her hips. She sashays toward me, and the motion almost makes me sick. I'm too drunk to handle any interaction with Eliana right now.

It was stupid of me to cuddle up with a bottle of whiskey while she chatted with my mother. Now my defenses are lowered. My self-control hanging by a thread. I can feel myself giving in before she's even made an offer.

"My love," her voice comes out like a purr. "You look sick."

"I was just going to the bathroom."

"I'll take you."

Before I can stop her, she grabs my hand and tugs me down the hall, but I know we aren't going to the lavatory. We end up around the corner with my back against the wall as she trails kisses along the line of my jaw. I turn my head away when she tries to kiss my lips.

"Playing hard to get?" she whispers.

"I don't want to do this."

The skin between her eyebrows bunches together as she frowns at me, but before she can speak, someone clears their throat behind us, and we jump apart in shock.

It's just Douglass, my personal guard and driver.

I smile at him, relieved that he found me, but my smile doesn't last long. Douglass isn't German—he's one of the men we hunted down and forced to join our gang six years ago when he was just a teenager. I took him under my wing and practically raised him into the man he's become. Taught him how to survive in the German mafia, and the biggest lesson he learned was to keep a low profile.

Douglass only comes around when he's got something important to tell me.

I untangle myself from Eliana and straighten my shirt. "What is it?"

Douglass glances between us and then says slowly, "Your father wants to see you."

Uwe Jäger, boss of the German mafia. The Jägermeister. My own father.

I wouldn't say I hate the guy, but I don't enjoy being around him. Even so, I am his underboss so I know whatever's going on must be important if Vater needs to see me in the middle of Petra's wedding reception.

I nod at Eliana. "Take her back inside. I'll go find my father."

Douglass hesitates. When he casually rubs his chin, I realize what he means and start rubbing at my own. Eliana left her lipstick along my jaw, where she'd been kissing me.

I give him a nod of thanks and turn to leave.

The wedding reception is being held in one of Klaus's hotels. It's a fancy place called German Grande, rivaling the Trump Tower in extravagance, and charging double their rate per room. Klaus keeps the penthouse for himself, but I know he lets Vater use it for his mistresses when my mother starts giving him grief about it. So I take the elevator to the top floor and am not surprised when I hear my father's voice drifting down the hall as I near the double doors leading to the penthouse.

I don't bother knocking, but I stop in my tracks when I push the door open and find Emilio Moreno inside with my father. For a heartbeat, I think he's here because he's found out I deflowered his little girl months ago. And then I worry if he caught me with Eliana in the hall downstairs, but the way he's frowning doesn't seem so personal. In fact, he actually gives me a tight smile as I step into the room and shut the door behind me.

"Amory," his use of my first name catches my father's attention, but he keeps talking before Vater can comment on it. "We have a problem, son." Again, his term of affection makes my father squint between us.

Emilio and I are something like friends. We are closer than any of the other mafia bosses and have had very positive and beneficial dealings with each other. When my men captured and tortured information out of a Russian grunt, I sold that intel to him in exchange for a raw shipment of cocaine. The drugs went to Rosa's grandfather—King Jameson Willis of the Bronx—so I could win his approval of our marriage. It's ironic that it's Emilio who ended up ruining that marriage by forcing me to marry one of his daughters. And even more ironic that I've been sleeping with his daughter behind his back the entire time.

I have to force myself not to smile at that thought.

"What's the problem?" I ask. The news of an issue instantly sobers me up. I'm no longer swaying on my feet, and I feel well enough to ignore the pangs of nausea that hit me every so often.

Vater glowers at the coffee table in the middle of the large living room. The entire penthouse is pearly white and gleaming with sterling silver finishes. I almost have to squint when I gaze down at the little table, it's polished so brightly it reflects every bit of light in the room.

"I don't understand…" I begin, but my voice trails off as I move closer. There's a stack of very familiar papers resting on the table.

Papers of annulment.

"That little mix-breed played us!" Vater turns red as he yells. "The paperwork was sent back to us this morning. I can't believe this!"

"Can't believe what?" I ask.

Emilio steps forward and points to the dotted line where Rosa signed her name—and her fate.

"The social security number and the date of birth listed on these papers match with Rosa De Luca."

"Then what's the problem?"

He presses his lips together tightly before answering, "She signed her name as Rose Lucas."

My heart stops long enough for me to clutch at my chest. Pain shoots through my core and I even gasp from the jolting shock of joy, relief, and fear.

Rosa signed the wrong name on the documents. That means our marriage has not been annulled. We're still married. And we'll remain that way until we file the papers all over again.

I glance at Emilio to see if he noticed my bewildered smile. Both him and Vater are still frowning at the stack of papers, as if their anger could somehow change Rosa's signature to the right one.

"So, what does this mean?"

"It means she will have to file the paperwork again," Vater spits.

"It also means your marriage to my daughter will be delayed."

I hope he can't tell I'm thrilled by this.

Emilio sighs and the air in the room suddenly feels heavy and dense. "I cannot supply you with aid in this gang war until you have married Eliana."

Now all the negative aspects of the situation hit me. Hard. Yes, I'm still married to my wife—to the woman I love. But our marriage could end up costing lives. It could end up ruining this family and maybe even endangering Emilio's family.

"Fix this, Amory!" Vater yells. He pounds his fist on the countertop where he stands in the open kitchen. Vater loses his temper quite easily, so I'm not impressed with his outburst, but I do understand the weight of the situation.

I have to get Rosa to sign the documents again. Which

means I'll get to see her in person.

I know Emilio is looking at me, I know Vater is watching me from across the room. But I don't let their stares stop me from smiling. It's only been two weeks, but I've missed my wife…

I'm looking forward to seeing her again.

Three

Olivia is glowing. She takes Marco's arm as he guides her from St. Joseph's Cathedral, her long train trails behind her for another ten feet. Olive's father spared no expenses on his daughter's wedding. It's likely his way of trying to make up for the man she had to marry. Marco Segreto isn't a poor choice, he's just old and has a reputation for being cruel. But I'm confident my best friend can handle herself. I've convinced Adella to let her take lessons with us starting next week. I don't think things will ever get physical between Olivia and Marco, but I want her to be prepared.

I can't help thinking of Christina Jäger and how she'd been dragged away by one of her husband's guards in a room full of people. She had shrieked and cried for help the entire time. No one had intervened, not even Amory.

The memory sends a chill up and down my spine, but I ignore the discomfort and focus on Olivia. Her dress is slim and elegant, much like her, and leaves her looking breathtaking with its lace accents and plunging neckline. When I first saw her, I thought the dress might have been a little too scandalous—especially since she has a *very* generous set of knockers—but with her short hair curled up and decorated with a crown of pink roses, she looks like an angel. Even Marco can't keep his eyes off of her, he takes every chance he gets to glance her way or place a possessive hand on her lower back.

I'm so happy for my best friend. Standing beside her for the wedding photos is a dream come true. She was my matron of honor when I married Amory, I wasn't surprised at all when she told me I'd be hers. We were both forced to marry men we didn't know or want to be with, but things seem to have turned out okay. For one of us, at least.

Olivia was happy for me when she found out Amory had the marriage annulled, and then I broke down in tears and she almost started crying too. She hadn't realized I'd developed feelings for him. Neither had I. Until it was too late. But I'm not giving up. I can't.

Amory and I made a promise to fight for our marriage. I don't care what happens or what contract he's signed, I intend to keep my promise. I'm strong enough to do it now. I haven't been training with Adella for long, but this isn't just about me being able to take a punch, it's about my mental and emotional fortitude as well.

When I first returned to New York, they called me the withered rose. I'm not that anymore. I've been replanted. I've grown up. I will always be a rose, but now I'm a fresh new flower—one with thorns.

After the wedding photos, I help Olivia to her dressing

room and pour her a glass of water from the pitcher left at her station. Her father rented out one of the hotels Marco runs, I know he got it at a discount, but I'm still impressed with the fresh bouquet of roses, the expensive bottle of champagne left on ice for us, and the free bottles of perfume given to all the bridesmaids.

"You're doing great," I tell Olive, dabbing her forehead with a cloth. Her makeup still looks great, but her forehead looks shiny from sweat.

Olivia hits me with a radiant smile. "It's all so romantic, isn't it? I can't believe I just got married!"

"You did it!" I squeal, holding both her hands.

Her smile fades. "Rosa, you can come stay with us—"

I shake my head before she can even finish. "I'm not going to be a burden to anyone else."

Olivia has been trying to convince me to move in with her since the war started. So far, the shots have only been between the Russians and Germans, but no one is convinced the rest of us are safe. Even Papa Jamie has reinforced the borders of the Bronx, and Gio has double the men on duty for Olivia's wedding today. We're all scared. But he seems the most spooked. I want to say he's just protecting the Garden, but I know my brother. He's always been a confident man— overconfident, if you ask me. But this fear seems overwhelming. Like he isn't afraid of the war overtaking us, he's afraid of someone coming after *him* specifically.

Since the first shots were fired on the eastside of Brooklyn, he's tripled his own security and won't take meetings with anyone outside his inner circle. He wouldn't even let me come over for dinner the other night, and when Olivia went to present a gift of honor to him for supporting her marriage as the don of our mafia, he told her to leave the present with a guard. He's so paranoid, I'm surprised he decided to actually attend the wedding.

Olivia squeezes my hand and I realize I've been staring into space. "Well," she says with a smile, "you're always welcome."

"I promise I'm safe with my grandfather."

"I know," she whispers.

In the silence that follows, I sneak a glance in Olive's mirror to check my own makeup. Adella decided to go easy on me this last week; she didn't let Nona hit me in the face during our sessions, so I'd look pretty and elegant at the wedding. Instead of bruised and deranged like I normally look. The black eye I had before is gone, but the bruise on my cheek has only faded somewhat. I had to apply more blush than normal to fully cover it, but I'm sure no one has noticed it yet.

Olivia nudges me with her elbow and smiles until her cheeks turn pink. I can't believe how excited she is about this, but I'd rather have her smiling all day than weeping in my arms at the thought of going off on a honeymoon with Marco.

"Are you ready to dance?" I say, thinking of my first dance with Amory. It was such a disaster, but now the memory makes me smile. I'd give anything to replay that day and make everything right. But I'm glad I'm here now. My struggles so far have only made me stronger.

Olivia starts to shimmy at her reflection in the mirror. "I'm gonna tear that floor up!"

I snort.

"What?" she says with a self-conscious smile. "This could be the last night we get to celebrate like this. Who knows what'll happen tomorrow?"

She's right… The war could overtake us all at any moment. The Garden is already damaged, some say beyond repair.

I squeeze her shoulder. "Enjoy yourself tonight."

"You, too!" Olivia shifts in her chair to face me. "Promise me you'll dance, too."

"I—uh—I …" I honestly hadn't planned on staying for much longer. I love Olivia and I'm so happy for her, but this atmosphere is starting to weigh on me. It all reminds me of everything I had with Amory and how much it sucks that it's suddenly, inexplicably over.

I can't say any of this to Olive, though. I don't want to make her sad and reveal that her best friend is abandoning her on her special day. Instead, I say, "I don't have anyone to dance with."

Her jaw drops. "Are you kidding me? You're Rosa De Luca! And you're absolutely gorgeous! I saw so many guys checking you out."

I didn't.

"Really?" I ask politely.

She nods so emphatically her crown of roses shifts on her head. I fix it for her as she says, "Of course I did! But you know who stared the longest?"

I shrug.

Olivia grins and lowers her voice, even though we're the only ones in the room. "Aldo."

I suppress a groan. Aldo Romano is Olive's older brother. He's twenty-seven and crazy hot, and high-ranking enough that my father had once hinted that we'd be paired together once I finished college. But I never graduated. And I've honestly never been interested in him.

None of that has ever deterred Olivia, however. She's been trying to hook us up since I turned fourteen. Aldo was twenty-one at the time, by the way.

In his defense, Aldo's never looked at me with any more interest than I've looked at him. But that might have been because I'm seven years younger and have never been old enough for him to take seriously. But now I'm twenty and everything's changed.

I sigh. I am totally not ready to step out and try dating again. But this is my best friend's wedding and I want to make her happy. If Olivia can smile after being married off to a man like Marco Segreto, then I can make it through one measly dance with her admittedly sexy brother.

"Fine, I'll tear up the floor for one song only," I tell her with a grin.

Olivia crushes me in a hug.

We find our way back to the bridal party so we can enter the reception hall. Everyone has been waiting but no one complains too much, one of the perks of being best friends with the bride. I pass Olivia her bouquet and dab at her stubbornly shiny forehead with a tissue once more before she takes Marco's arm and starts the procession.

Incidentally, I've been paired with Aldo in the party. He's one of Marco's groomsmen and has been my partner for the whole event so far. We walked down the aisle together and posed like a couple for the group wedding photos. I honestly hadn't noticed him much until now.

I smile up at him as we start walking into the hall. "Excited?" I say.

He quirks a dark eyebrow and leans down so he can hear me. I catch a whiff of his masculine cologne and try not to let it affect me. "What'd you say?"

The cheering from the hall gets louder as Olivia and Marco enter. We're the next ones inside, so I can barely get my voice loud enough without shouting at Aldo. Instead of trying to speak, I just take his arm and lean my head against his shoulder. Aldo pats my hand and then guides me to our spot where we wait for the MC to tell a joke and then announce that dinner can begin. We find our seats and I sit with a sigh, Aldo leans over with a question in his eyes, but Father Serrano takes the mic to lead us all in prayer before the food is served.

When the old Priest is finished, my eyes meet with Aldo's once again. They're green just like Gio's, with flecks of gold sparkling through them. I can't help but smile when I catch his gaze.

"You were trying to tell me something," he says, leaning closer.

"I was only asking if you were excited."

He smiles, eyes quickly scanning the rest of me. The bridesmaid dresses are just as racy as Olivia's gown; a gentle shade of lavender with a sweetheart neckline that shows off my cleavage. The dress goes past my knees, but there's a split all the way up my right side so you can see up to my upper thigh.

Aldo's eyes seem to ride curves I didn't even know I had as he drags his gaze up my body to my face again. "I'm very excited," he says in Italian.

We eat in relative silence, watching the crowd and exchanging small talk. Mostly, Aldo just complains that his workload has doubled since I went to Jersey. I feel embarrassed for a moment, but then he says something that catches my attention.

"Your escape made things difficult for us, but not much worse than they were before."

I look at him with my brows knit together, trying to understand what he means. Aldo catches my expression and then waves me off. "I mean, we're not broken beyond repair."

"But business is bad." I can't stop myself from thinking of the conversation I overheard between Amory and his cousin Conrad before he had our marriage annulled. Conrad had mentioned Amory taking over a bunch of failing businesses.

Aldo studies me a moment before he forces a smile and says, "Rosa, it's a wedding. Don't you know it's bad luck to talk business here?"

I give him an equally forced smile and stuff wedding cake into my mouth. I don't believe in luck. And I'm not fooled by

Aldo's charming smile. It seems the entire Garden of Manhattan is withered, and I'm starting to think Giovanni has something to do with it—more than my great escape ever did.

But Aldo is right, it may have nothing to do with 'luck,' but it is rude to discuss business while Olivia twirls like a princess on the dancefloor. Marco handles her delicately, almost like he's afraid of breaking her, but their performance is heartwarming, and I can't stop myself from smiling as I watch.

When the music changes from the sappy love song Marco picked out to a more upbeat groove, Aldo touches my shoulder. "Should we join them?"

I nod and take his hand.

Aldo is a great dancer. He moves smoothly and never lets me feel awkward, not even when I accidentally trip and step on his foot. We go through three different songs before I try to break away, but that's when the DJ decides it's time for another slow song.

Panting, Aldo pulls me closer and says in my ear, "One last dance."

It's hard to resist him when he's being so charming, holding me like we're in love, making me miss the husband I barely got to know

I must miss Amory more than I think … as I step into Aldo's arms and glance over his shoulder, I swear I see him in the crowd. I want to say my eyes are playing tricks on me. I want to say the feeling of Aldo's warm hands on my hips is making me dizzy with desire. But I would know those stormy grey eyes anywhere. I would recognize his strong jaw and his sharply focused gaze. And I would never miss the way he so easily finds my gaze, locks eyes with me, and then coolly walks away.

"Amory…" I whisper.

Something tugs at my elbow, and I realize I've pulled away from Aldo. He's staring at me in shock, undoubtedly confused as to why I suddenly walked away from him.

My heart breaks a little at the sincerity in his eyes as he says, "Rosa?" but I don't have time to pity him. I need to get to my husband.

"I'm sorry," I say, tugging my arm away as I turn and leave.

Four

I don't look back as I push through the crowd. I don't want to see the look on Aldo's face, but I also fear I'll lose my resolve if I look away from the door I saw Amory leave through.

I feel like I'm losing my mind. There's no way the German underboss showed up at an Italian wedding unnoticed. Then again, Amory was once best friends with Giovanni. And they'll still have business with each other until our annulment is finalized. I suppose it wouldn't be too farfetched to imagine him showing up to pay his respects. It could be taken as an act of goodwill on Amory's part—extending an olive branch in the midst of war.

When I push through the door, I take a deep breath and freeze in place.

The hallway is empty.

But I won't let defeat get to me just yet.

Without thinking, I start down the corridor as quickly as my four-inch heels will allow. Just as I pass the turn for the restrooms, I see him.

Amory is leaning against the wall, his hands in his pockets, hiding in the shade of the bathroom alcove. I can't stop the gasp that escapes me, and I curse myself for the tears that immediately well up in my eyes. I don't want him to see me crying, but I won't ignore the way I feel. It was that shyness—that fear of exposing myself to my own husband—that got us in this situation in the first place. I won't make that same mistake again.

"Amy," I whisper, stepping closer.

He turns and casually walks deeper into the little hall. I follow him without hesitation. There's a set of lounge chairs around the corner, by the entrance to the men's and women's lavatories. I expect to find him sitting in one, but as I turn the corner, I am suddenly grabbed by my arm and jerked to the side.

I react faster than I mean to and end up jabbing my perpetrator in the chest with the heel of my palm.

Amory stumbles backwards and bucks his eyes wide open. "Sheesh, Rosa," he says, grabbing his chest.

I squeal and cover my mouth. "I'm sorry! You scared me!"

"What's gotten into you?"

"You tried to snatch me up!"

He laughs, still rubbing at the spot where I'd hit him. "I tried to pull you into my arms." His strong arms open wide, welcoming me. "For a hug."

I hesitate. *Is this really my husband?*

A frown works its way over Amory's full lips, and he drops his arms. "Where'd you learn that?"

"Adella's been teaching me," I say with a proud smile, but it doesn't last long. I actually meant to hit him in the throat, but Amory's over six feet tall and I'm an inch shy of five feet. I'd have to aim at the sky to get to his throat, but I think my older cousin would be proud of my reflexes. It's only been three weeks since we started, but my hard work is already paying off.

Amy steps closer. "Rosa, I don't have much time."

"What are you doing here?"

"I came to talk to you."

"At Olivia's wedding?"

"I couldn't find any other way to contact you. Giovanni won't answer my calls and your grandfather keeps telling me you're unavailable."

Everyone knows it's only a matter of time before each gang is dragged into this war. But Grandpa has made it more than clear that he wants to stay out of it for as long as possible. The best way to do that is to mind our business—which means no communicating with rival gangsters. Especially ones you're in love with.

The look on Amory's face is difficult to name. Hurt? Confusion? Anger? He seems to frown down at me as he asks, "Did you tell Jameson you don't want to speak with me?"

"Is that what Papa Jamie told you?"

He makes a face at the nickname but answers with a slow nod. "It doesn't matter now that I'm here."

"What is it, Amy?"

He runs his hand through his hair and looks at me fully, his grey eyes trailing from my head to my toe. Then he turns away like it pains him to speak his next words. "The annulment papers, Rosa. You signed the wrong name."

My heart skips a beat. I did sign the wrong name, hoping the mistake would cause the paperwork to be sent back and re-filed—giving me more time to sort things out with my husband. I'm ecstatic that it actually worked, but I'm still not sure how Amory feels about it, so I don't speak for a moment.

His sharp grey eyes lock on me when he looks up. "You have to fill everything out again."

For a moment, I can't speak.

In my head, he was supposed to rejoice that we had a second chance. He was supposed to be thrilled that I hadn't broken our promise, that I'd fought for our marriage. Instead, his face is unreadable, just as it was the day he passed me the pen and told me to sign on the dotted line.

I ball my hands into fists and lift my chin. "I'm not filling anything out."

"Yes, you are."

"No, I'm not," I snap.

"Rosa, the Hunters will lose this war if we don't get aid!" He takes a large step toward me, immediately closing the space between us. "Do you want me to fight the Volkovs alone?"

"I want you to fight them with me by your side!" I nearly yell.

Amory looks shocked, but the emotion passes quickly. When I blink, his face is back to its usual passive expression, though I can see the way his jaw seems to tighten.

"I'm not signing any more papers," I say sternly. "I didn't want to sign the first copy."

Amory's face pinches in anger and he opens his mouth to say something rude, but his phone chimes and cuts him off. He hisses out a nasty string of German words before he yanks the phone out and then curses in English.

"I've got to go," he says stiffly. "But I'm not done with this conversation."

"I am," I say with a huff.

His eyes seem to drill holes into me. "Rosa—"

"You're wasting time you don't have if you think you can convince me to sign the papers."

To my shock, a smirk stretches over his face. "You really don't want to let me go, do you?" he murmurs, coming even closer. He's hovering over me now, making me shrink before him.

There is a weighty silence that stretches between us. The air is tense, and my body feels stiff, like a light wind could knock me over. I don't know what Amory wants from me right now. He's just standing there staring down at me; the full intensity of his stormy gaze almost makes my knees wobble. There is a heat exuding from him that I cannot understand, like there is only one thought on his mind, but he won't dare speak it aloud.

What does he want? I wonder as his eyes narrow on my face. His grey gaze drags down the length of my dress, pausing briefly on the split up my thigh. He's so close, I can smell his cologne. I can reach out and touch him if I want, but I know any contact right now would send me over the edge. If he hugs me, I won't let go. If he kisses me, I won't stop him.

But the silence and his nearness are making me nervous. What does he expect me to do with him standing so close—climb him like a flagpole and claim my prize at the top?

I almost shake my head at myself. I need to get it together.

"Do you still want me?" Amory asks in a low, buttery voice.

My heart flutters and my ears burn in embarrassment. Of course I still want him. I never stopped wanting him. The annulment was his idea, not mine. But I'm too afraid to say that—at least in so many words. Instead, I muster the courage to whisper, "We both promised to fight for this marriage."

Amory finally steps away, taking the storm of emotions with him. "This is me fighting."

"Fighting to walk away."

"Fighting to keep you alive."

"Amy—"

His phone buzzes again, this time I grunt in annoyance, and he sighs tiredly. "I've got to go, Rosa. How can I contact you again?"

Amory had to sneak his way into Manhattan to see me. God knows what my grandfather will do if any of his men catch him trying to slip into the Bronx. He's an underboss in a rival mafia. He's locked in a war with the Russian gangs of Staten Island. Visiting me could end up costing him more than he's willing to give.

But no one said I couldn't find my way to him.

I take a breath. "I'll contact you."

Amory raises a single brow. "How?"

"I'll come to your house." I shake my head. "I'll come *home*. Tomorrow night."

He doesn't question it. With a nod, Amy leans down and brushes a kiss to my forehead. It's a quick little peck that shouldn't even mean anything, but it nearly takes my breath away. I'm dizzy with emotion when we leave the alcove side by side, but the sight of Eliana Moreno standing in the corridor slaps me back to sobriety.

I stop walking dead in my tracks. "Why did you bring her to my best friend's wedding?" I don't bother hiding the growling snarl in my voice.

Eliana's voice is just as nasty. "Because I am his fiancé, and he wants me by his side."

"I told you to wait in the car," Amory bites out.

She ignores him and takes a step toward me. "I am tired of you coming between us."

I take a step too, unfazed and unafraid. "*I* am Mrs. Jäger. *You're* the one coming between *us*."

Amory gets between us and pulls Eliana out of my face. She stumbles in her heels but doesn't lose her footing. She also never takes her eyes off me, not even when Amy starts cursing in German and yelling at her. After releasing a string of foul words, his phone chimes again and he nearly throws it at the wall.

"*Behave*," is the last word he says to Eliana before stepping away.

We spend a few moments staring at each other in silence. The hatred between us is palpable, but I fight against it. Eliana and I don't know each other. I know she's supposed to be my husband's new fiancé, but, technically, we have no reason to feel such animosity toward one another. As far as I know, this marriage is a contractual arrangement. It isn't something she wants any more than I did when I first got engaged to Amory.

Unless …

I squint at Eliana, overcome with shock as I realize what's going on now.

"You actually want to marry him," I whisper.

She nods slowly. "Of course I do."

"But why? Why do you want him so badly?"

"Because I'm in love with him. I know him more intimately than you ever have or ever will."

My eyes widen at the true meaning in her words. "You've slept with him."

Eliana takes a step. "That's right." Up close, I realize just how tall this woman really is. She towers over me and looks down the barrel of her nose as she says with a Spanish accent, "I had your husband before you did." She lets that sink in. "I know him in ways you never will."

What a low blow…

Eliana's laughter sends chills over me, it's like the sound of shattering glass—loud and piercing and painful. She reaches out and gently strokes my cheek. "I know what makes him moan. I know what leaves him short of breath." She drops her voice to a whisper, leaning closer. "I know how to finish him in just ten—"

I slap her.

My hand whips out before I can stop myself. The sound of it echoes through the entire corridor, louder than my pounding heart. Eliana's head snaps to the side, her curtain of dark hair flying up around her. I can see the print of my hand on her cheek when she turns back to look at me.

We're both shocked and speechless, but she comes to her senses before I do. Her lips pull back into a snarl and her eyes turn to orbs of fire burning in her face as she raises her hand, but she never gets to strike back. Amory is there, grabbing her arm and pulling her away with a hiss.

"What is going on?" he snaps at us both.

I stare at him with my mouth open and my eyes wide. "I didn't mean to—"

"She hit me!" Eliana screams. Some stragglers from the reception glance up to stare at the scene, it won't be long before we attract too much attention, but Eliana doesn't care. She twists her arm free from Amory's grasp and shouts, "Why are you just standing there! She just struck your fiancé!" She jabs a manicured finger at me. "Hit her back!"

Amory steps into her face. His voice is low, and his eyes are filled with rage. "Be quiet, Eliana," he says darkly. "If you speak again, you will be sorry."

Eliana turns and glares at me, then she shoots a horrible look at Amory and storms off. I don't allow any joy or relief into my heart. Amory might have threatened Eliana, but he hasn't exactly taken my side.

I can barely meet his eyes as I mumble, "I'm sorry."

He shakes his head. There's still plenty of rage in his eyes, but it isn't as much as when he was glaring at Eliana. "What have you done?" he says slowly.

Eliana had been out of line. She'd been rude. She'd been disrespectful. But she didn't deserve to be slapped—and even if she had, no one had the right to deliver the blow. Not even me.

She's the oldest daughter of a mafia boss, that makes her a princess of equal standing to me. Hitting her would have gotten anyone else killed on the spot. But since I'm the offender—another mafia princess—that slap can only be taken as a declaration of war.

Amory knows this, which is why he shakes his head and takes a step back, his eyes filled with a mix of emotions I've never seen him express.

Worry. Anxiety. Fear.

"What have you done?" he says again.

"What have *you* done?" I snap. "You've been sleeping with her all along!"

His face pales and his eyebrows shoot up. For a moment, his mouth just hangs open and no words come forth. When he does gather himself enough to speak, his phone buzzes again, and he grinds his teeth together. Grey eyes glance at the screen before he takes a deep breath and pinches the bridge of his nose, but I'm the one who gets the last word.

"I'll see you tomorrow night. Then we can discuss everything."

I turn and walk away, headed toward the reception, without looking back.

Five

My hands are shaking so badly, I can't even finish my tie. It's been days since I went to see Rosa in Manhattan and she still hasn't come over like she promised. Every night since then, I've gone through the same routine, preparing myself for her anticipated visit.

Right around five, I finish up my business, then I head home and place a special order with my personal chef. He remembers all of Rosa's favorite foods, so I get him to prepare a feast each night. I hop in the shower while he cooks, find something nice to wear once I'm finished, and then I sit and wait for the bell to chime.

It never does.

It's night number four and I'm starting to wonder if Rosa was just pulling my leg at the wedding. If she'd only been saying what she thought I wanted to hear. If maybe this was her way of getting revenge for what I did to her almost a month ago.

The pain is still raw. I can still see the tears in her eyes as she sobbed. I can still hear her pleading with me to stay. To make things right between us. I can still see her body, when she'd undressed right in front of me and offered herself for my enjoyment.

It had taken strength I didn't know I had to shove her away and leave. And now she's coming back. Or at least that's what I hope.

There could be a number of reasons why she hasn't shown up yet. It might have been difficult to sneak away. She might not have access to a ride all the way to my side of Brooklyn. She might even be having second thoughts.

Whatever the case, I need Rosa here—even if it isn't for selfish reasons like trying to seduce her all over again. I don't even know why I'm trying with the fancy dinner and the new tie. She's coming here to sign new annulment papers, not to have a steamy date night. But even though I know what must be done, I can't stop the inkling of hope from pouring into my heart. I can't stop myself from wondering what could happen if I play my cards right.

Destruction. That's what could happen.

If Rosa doesn't sign the papers this time, I will lose aid from the Morenos, and I'll have to fight this war alone. Which means it'll be a race against the clock to see how long it'll take Mikhail Volkov to put a bullet in my brother's head and then my own for trying to protect him.

It isn't even that the Volkovs are so much bigger, stronger, or richer than us. It's that they're more motivated, which obviously gives them an edge. The Volkovs will not stop until they have their revenge, or they no longer exist. Neither option is good for us, because it will take everything we've got to get rid of them. And some.

We're at war because my little brother Wolfgang beat a Russian woman so badly that she went into a coma and nearly died. It also doesn't help that Wolfgang has been on Mikhail's radar for four years now. Ever since his fiancé died under suspicious circumstances, the Russians have had it out for us. I don't blame them. Sofia Volkov was Mikhail's oldest daughter. She had been a beautiful woman full of love and joy and laughter, all the things my brother didn't deserve.

Wolfgang killed her with his bare hands. And I helped cover it up.

With some assistance from Giovanni, we covered up the murder and made it look like a robbery gone wrong. Gio was supposed to destroy all the evidence, but when his sister ran away and the Italian mafia nearly crumbled, Giovanni threatened to use the evidence to expose me to the Russians if I didn't agree to marry Rosa.

You already know our marriage didn't last long. What you probably don't know is that I don't want the annulment any more than Rosa does, but it has to happen or else I'll die at the hands of Mikhail Volkov.

I sigh as I give up on the tie and sit on the edge of my bed. I start rummaging through my bedside table in search for the clip-on I know I have somewhere in there, but the first thing I see when I open the drawer is a King James Bible. I know it's Rosa's because I don't own a Bible. I used to read it on an app on my phone before Rosa left, but after the annulment, I deleted it and haven't looked back.

For reasons I can't explain, I reach for the Book and sit with it in my lap for a few silent moments. I don't open it. I don't read it. I just stare at the cracked leather cover and run my fingers over the dry ridges. I'd had all of Rosa's things sent over to Jameson's Palace when she moved out, but I hadn't known the Bible was in my drawer until now. *She must have left it on purpose*, I realize, *for me.*

Rosa is a devout Christian—so devout that she refused to sleep with me because she thought it would be wrong to share her marital bed with a sinner like me. I almost laugh at the memory of all the times she'd blushed and shied away whenever I'd tried anything sexual with her. One time, she even lied about being on her period just to get away from me. It had been frustrating at the time, but when Mikhail declared war and I realized her grandfather and brother would not stand as my allies until we consummated the marriage, my frustration turned to understanding.

I refused to buy allegiance using Rosa's body as payment. It's a decision that cost me the aid of two powerful gangs, but I won't change my mind on that. I don't share Rosa's beliefs or her views on sex, but I deeply respect them, and I won't do anything to ever try to change them.

In fact, it's Rosa and her faith that's been slowly changing *me.*

I remember sneaking away to read passages of the Bible I barely understood when we were still together. Mumbling the scriptures aloud, trying to force myself to understand. At the time, I'd only read the Word because I was trying to understand my seemingly insane wife. But now, as I stare down at the old leatherbound Book, I realize there was more to it than that.

I … miss reading the Bible. I miss hearing and watching Rosa pray, even though I never understood why she did it or if anyone was even listening. I miss having someone who cared enough about me to be concerned for my eternal soul. Even though I'm still not sure if I have one—if a soul really exists.

Rosa believes in souls. And she wanted to save mine. That's why she left this Bible here, an echo of her concern left in our home. I squeeze the Book in my hands, unsure what to do with it. I should read it, but the thought summons a sudden charge of pain deep inside. *What's the point?* I ask myself. I had only started reading for Rosa's sake; once she signs the papers again, I'll be with Eliana, and I won't need the Bible or prayer or anything else Rosa brought into our marriage.

Eliana isn't religious. That much was obvious the first time we slept together. And the second and the third, and every other time since then. But I hadn't opened my bedroom to her because of her spiritual beliefs, I'd taken her to bed because she was sexy and willing. And now, for reasons I can't even understand, I don't want to marry the woman.

She's still sexy and she's still willing. But I don't want her anymore. I want Rosa. My wife. Even though she never wanted me until it was too late. Even though she may never want me again.

I remember her last words to me at the wedding reception. How angry she had been after finding out about my relations with Eliana. She had to know she was the only virgin between us, but I suppose knowing your husband had other women and actually meeting the other women face to face are two different things. Their encounter had ended in a slap fight and would have gotten worse if I hadn't intervened.

The only reason the whole thing hasn't dissolved into an all-out gang war is because Eliana never told her father about what happened. She'd spent the entire car ride crying, but when we pulled up to her father's villa, she wiped her eyes, fixed her makeup, and kissed me goodnight. We haven't spoken since that event. There's no doubt she's still pissed I didn't backhand Rosa for pimp slapping her, but I'm not my brother or my father. I don't believe in hitting women and I wasn't going to start just because my crazy fiancé ordered me to.

I should be worried about Eliana going to Emilio, and I had been at first, when everything had gone down. But when Rosa yelled at me for sleeping with Eliana, all the worry washed away.

Eliana can't go to Emilio. If she tells her father Rosa slapped her, he will want to know why—which means she will have to tell him it's because she spilled the beans about our sex life and got her smile wiped off her pretty little face for it. If Emilio ever learns that Eliana and I slept together outside of marriage, if he ever finds out she isn't a virgin, he will punish her for her promiscuity. And I'll likely be in hot water too. No one cares too much if I sleep around, but the daughters of high-ranking men are off limits. They're raised to respect their bodies and we are expected to respect them for that in turn.

In my defense, Eliana is the only high-ranking mafia woman I've ever been with. She's honestly the only woman I've ever been with more than once. But those are details I never got to share with Rosa before she stormed off and left me staring blankly behind her. Now, I'm not sure if I'll ever get the chance because she still hasn't come over like she said she would.

I toss the Bible onto the bedside table and go downstairs to have a cup of coffee. The annulment papers are sitting on the coffee table in my lounge, like a written omen waiting for us to bring into fruition. I don't look at it as I stir sugar into my mug and then grimace at the bitterness. It needs cream, but there isn't any out on the display. With a sigh, I start toward the kitchens but freeze in the middle of the room when I hear the bell finally chime.

Douglass enters the lounge and finds me dumbly holding my mug of coffee. I'd already told him not to bother asking permission—*if Rosa comes over, let her in without question*—had been my orders. I'm thankful he followed them.

Rosa glides into the room with all the elegance of a princess. She is exactly how I remember her; despite all the recent changes I've noticed. The Rosa I married never would have slapped another woman in the face. And she wouldn't have had the reflexes to almost break my windpipe when I'd scared her before.

She's always been called the Flower of Manhattan, and then she'd been known as the withered rose. But now she's something else—a new creature entirely. I'm just not sure what. But I'm certain I like it.

"You finally came," I say, setting down my coffee.

Rosa brushes a loose curl from her face and nods. She's wearing a long skirt and a cropped shirt to match; I hope she doesn't catch me stealing glimpses of her midsection. When she speaks, my vision snaps to meet hers.

"Sorry it took so long."

"I thought you were angry with me."

Her gaze drops for half a second. "I needed time to think."

"Think about what?"

"About whether I really want to sign those papers."

I frown. "We've gone over this before."

"No," she shakes her head, "you've gone over it. But we never made any decisions together. We never explored any other option except getting a divorce. I don't want that, Amory."

I stare at her. "I don't want to trade your virginity for help. That isn't right."

"I'm not giving it to you for help, I'm giving it to you because you're my husband and I love you."

The words hammer through me. Every single one. Rosa has never admitted to loving me. She's never even told me she has feelings for me. Not until now.

The revelation tears away every bit of self-control I have. Before I know it, I've crossed the room and taken her into my arms. She gasps and presses a hand to my chest, but only to stable herself—not to push me away.

"Rosa," I murmur, leaning closer. "Say that again."

She stands on her tiptoes and whispers it against my lips, each word is like a kiss I try to catch between us. "I love you."

There are no thoughts in my head except the desire to claim her for myself. It is instinctive. Primal. Desperate. But I can't let my carnal needs take over—not now, not like this. I can sense the hesitancy as I kiss Rosa, slowly, deeply, my hands going around her waist, slipping beneath her shirt. She lets out a noise that sets me on fire, but when she backs away, I know she's scared. Just as scared as she was on our wedding night.

There is little difference between then and now. She's still afraid, still unsure, but I'm not. I'm still her husband, I still have every right and every intention to wipe away her fears and doubts, to show her that I can be the man she needs me to be. Not the man I've become.

I step forward and kiss her cheek. She leans into me, eyes fluttering closed at the gentle contact. When I pull away, I study her a moment. So calm now. So willing. Even in her fear.

"Don't be afraid," I whisper, pulling her closer.

"I don't know—"

"I'll show you." I kiss her other cheek. "Just follow me."

Six

Follow me…

What does he mean by that? The question swirls in my head as he carries me to his bedroom—a place I had once feared as much as I'd feared him. Now, I welcome his presence. I ache for his touch.

He treats me delicately, lovingly. It sets every nerve in my body on edge. The way he places me on his bed and stares down at me. How he kisses me tenderly, as if he's afraid to touch me.

"Love me," I whisper.

And he does.

He loves me with every part of himself. His body. His hands. His eyes. His lips.

When I expect pain, he gives me pleasure. What I think is lust, he turns to passion. When I offer desire, he takes it and gives me inexplicable ecstasy.

Panting for breath. Nails digging into his back…

I feel like I'm standing on a cliff, peering over the edge.

Every part of me is alight with fire. Burning with the crackling flames of our passion.

"You still there?" His husky voice brings me back.

My eyes snap open to find his gaze locked on mine. He pulls me closer, his breath on my ear as he whispers, "Stay with me."

So I do.

Holding on for dear life, I let him take me away. I follow him into this dizzying passion. My feet peel from the edge of that cliff and I tip into ecstasy, falling headfirst. Spiraling.

Amory is there to catch me.

Muscles clenching. Eyes squeezed shut.

I cry out his name as a bolt of lightning shoots through me. And he responds, burying his face into the crook of my neck. His hands ball into fists on either side of my head as he bunches the fabric of our sheets.

His voice is strained—guttural—as he whispers my name. "Rosa…"

The sound of it nearly sends me over that cliff again. But I hold him, panting, blinking up at the ceiling. Trying to understand what just happened.

When he catches his breath, he pushes onto his elbows and rolls off me. An arm is slung over his eyes as he breathes, chest heaving.

"What was that?" his voice is low and tired.

"That was love," I say quietly.

He exhales slowly. "I guess it was."

We lay in silence for a while. I don't dare move out of

shame and a sudden, strange embarrassment.

I just had sex with my husband for the first time.

I was supposed to come here to sign divorce papers. But I ended up in his bed instead. I have no idea how to explain this or what to make of it. This was not how the evening was supposed to go.

I hadn't wanted to sign the papers, but after thinking about it—after thinking about everything I'd encountered with Eliana—I wasn't so sure that staying with Amory was worth the fight. Now, I don't think I have a choice but to stay with him. But I'm not upset about it. I'm just … uncertain.

But I don't need to be.

I love Amory and I know he loves me. Even deeper than that, we're still married. I haven't done anything wrong as a Christian or a mafia princess. In fact, I've just fulfilled our marital contract. It's finally been consummated. Now we'll have the help we need to win this war.

Yes, *we*, because I'm not letting my husband fight this battle alone. That's what it means to be married. To be as one.

Amory shifts beside me, and I turn to find him getting out of bed, but instead of leaving, he reaches over and scoops me into his arms.

"What are you doing!" I squeal, trying to wriggle away.

He laughs and starts toward the bathroom. "Taking a shower."

"Together?" I feel like I can barely breathe, but I'd be lying if I said there wasn't a little excitement at the thought of showering with him.

He laughs again and enters the bathroom. "Of course."

The water is hot. I don't know how Amory stands there, letting it spray his back. I can see steam rising from his flesh, but I suppose he's felt worse pain.

Up close, I can see all the scars he's covered with his tattoos. I'd felt them when we were together, tangled in his sheets. Deep gashes on his back, long ridges of hardened flesh going across his chest, like someone took a razor to him.

Without thinking, I reach up and touch his chest. I feel his heart flutter beneath my palm. "Did it hurt?" I ask, running my fingers along a scar over his heart.

He nods, his eyes watching me closely.

My fingers move to the next scar, near his collarbone, then the one on his right side. There's another in the middle of his chest, and a scar trailing down his abs. They flex at my touch, I don't know if it's a reflex or if Amy's suddenly shy, but he doesn't pull away. And he doesn't stop me as I explore the map of his body.

I get a sudden, wild urge to kiss him, but not on the lips. My mouth goes to the scar on his heart, and I kiss it gently. He shudders, and I move to the next one.

"Rosa," he says hoarsely, and I look up at him, blinking away droplets of water.

"Tell me how you got them."

He shakes his head.

I nod.

Not yet. But soon. It's a silent promise between us, an agreement that one day we'll both know everything about each other. We'll share the nightmares and the dreams.

Amory grabs a washcloth and soaks it with bodywash. To my complete shock, he reaches out and starts scrubbing me down. I have no idea how to react. I've never been bathed by another person before—except my mother as an infant.

"What are you doing?" I ask, taking a step back.

He kneels and washes my lower legs. "I'm cleaning you up."

"I can do that myself!" I say loudly.

He looks up at me, his hands on my thighs where there's a smear of red. "This is my mess."

I stop fighting him.

He taps my foot and I grab the bar in the wall beside me, so I don't fall as he washes my feet. Then he does the other and moves up my legs. I hold my breath as he scrubs every inch of me. This is new. This is strange. But I don't stop him. The shame I felt before is not in this bathroom. Like our time together wiped away the distrust, the worry, the doubt, and the embarrassment, too. Amory's been telling me for months, *I'm your husband, Rosa…* It isn't until now that I finally understand what that means.

"Thank you," he says when he's rinsed me off.

"For what?"

He grabs another cloth and starts washing himself now. "For letting me take care of you."

I'm glad there's too much steam for him to see me blushing. I just nod and start wetting my hair. Amory's going to be done in five minutes, but I'm half Black, it'll take another hour for me to get my curls under control. I don't expect him to know this, however, so I just tug my hair into the neatest braid I can manage and settle with that. I'll wash it properly tomorrow.

Once he turns off the water, Amory wraps me in a towel and carries me to the bed. I try to tell him that I can walk on my own, but he insists on taking care of me, so I let him place me on the bed and then I laugh when he realizes he has no clothes for me to wear.

"I can give you some of my clothes," he says sheepishly. "I'll toss your clothes in the wash so they're ready by tomorrow."

I honestly don't mind that at all. "Sounds fine," I say with a yawn. "Do you have lotion?"

He nods and runs back to the bathroom to fetch it, again insisting on doing everything himself when he returns. I begrudgingly let him apply the lotion, and I don't fight him at all when he offers a foot massage. It turns into a back massage, and then we're in the sheets again.

When we untangle ourselves, Amory is grinning. "I love you," he says, stealing a kiss.

I groan tiredly and roll onto my side. "I love sleep."

He laughs. "Are you hungry?"

I shake my head. "Only tired."

The mattress shifts as he adjusts beside me. He pulls me into his arms, just like he'd done the last time I slept in his room. It brings back memories I never thought I'd get the chance to experience again. I snuggle closer to him. I won't fight moments like this anymore. With a war going on, I don't even know how many more moments like this we'll have together.

"I love you," I say into the quiet.

Amory kisses the back of my neck, and we drift off into sleep together.

Seven

Just so you know, Rosa and I end up tangled in the sheets two more times before the sun comes up. I never knew married life could be so … active.

But when the sun does come up, it brings our doubts and worries with it. I can see the regret unfold on Rosa's face as soon as she sits up and clutches the covers to her naked breasts. She looks uncertain, like she has no idea what to do now. Like she isn't sure what to expect.

I'm not surprised by her anxiety. She's never done this before. And, technically, neither have I. I've never had a serious relationship in my entire life. Whenever I took a woman to bed, I made sure she was out as soon as it was done. No cuddling. No pillow talk. No sleeping over.

If I was too drunk or tired to get her out, I made sure she hit the door first thing in the morning. Eliana was one of the few women I let sleep over and look what happened with her. She got all up in her feelings and became my worst nightmare.

The thought of that woman brings on a heavy dose of

reality. Rosa and I slept together. We consummated our marriage. Which means I can't divorce her and marry Eliana now. The insult will run deep, maybe even deep enough to mark me as Emilio's enemy, but I don't care. I'm with my wife now—which means I'll be able to get the Willis Stronghold and the Garden of Manhattan to help me.

All I've got to do is tell the capo of the Spanish mafia that I don't want his crazy daughter anymore. That's not a conversation I'm looking forward to, but its one I've got to have.

Before that, however, I need to take care of my wife.

Rosa is sitting in bed watching me through tired, wary eyes. Her expression is cautious, like she isn't sure if I'm going to kiss her or whip out those annulment papers again. I'm not upset by the look. I'm not even sure what I'm going to do, but I know those papers are going through the shredder today. Rosa and I are married for good now. But that doesn't mean that *we're* good now. There are still questions and reservations between us, things left unspoken, things neither of us are sure we want to address.

Eliana. The war. Her grandfather and brother. Us. The list could go on.

"Let's talk, Rosie," I say, sitting up beside her.

She stares at the blankets. "About what?"

"About everything that's happened."

Her brown cheeks turn pinker than I think is possible. I look away and laugh to myself.

"What does this mean for us?" she asks.

"It means the annulment is off the table."

She looks at me with a smile ghosting her lips. I resist the urge to kiss her; I want to stay focused right now. And also, I haven't brushed my teeth yet.

"It also means we could be in big trouble," I say. "I'll have to end things with Eliana—"

Rosa shifts away from me at the sound of her name. I don't have to wonder why.

I bite my lip and then sigh. "Rosa, we need to talk about what she said to you," I mutter.

I didn't hear my ex-fiancé's comments myself, but I'll never forget the look on Rosa's face when she yelled at me. Eliana told her we'd slept together. Knowing her, she'd probably gone into all the sordid details—things I wish I could forget now. She'd been great at the time. A younger woman with an appetite I enjoyed, but there's only so many times I can do certain things before it starts to feel nasty.

I shudder at the memories and feel horrible at the realization that most of them were made in this room. In this bed.

"Was it during our marriage?" Rosa asks quietly.

The question draws my gaze back to her. She's looking off to the side, staring at her shoes on the floor, a pair of Mary Jane heels that almost make her look like a child. She's always dressed that way—very girly, very feminine. At least that part of her hasn't changed.

I swallow audibly. "No."

I should be insulted by the accusation, but it isn't an

unreasonable thought. Rosa and I never slept together before last night, despite being married for months. I'd had every opportunity to entertain myself with other women, but I never did, and I never got to tell this to my wife. By the time we finally made amends, I had our marriage annulled. Rosa's been hanging in limbo all this time, having no idea who I've been with or how many times.

And she still gave herself to me without asking any questions.

I shake my head. "Everything that happened with Eliana was before we got married." I drop my gaze to the blankets. "I haven't touched another woman since the engagement."

I can't tell if she's shocked or relieved. Maybe both. Whatever the case, it's obvious she still has questions as she looks up at me. "How many women have you been with?"

I can't stop myself from sighing. I run my hand through my messy hair in frustration and anxiety. This is not the conversation I wanted to have this morning—or ever. But Rosa deserves to know. I want her to know because I know everything about *her* past.

She doesn't have one.

Rosa entered our marriage as a virgin. That doesn't mean I have to give her a play by play of every night I ever spent with another woman, but she isn't wrong to wonder. To want to know if I have an STD, or other kids running around, or if my past is simply too much for her to handle. It's easy to understand why a man wouldn't want a woman who's worked her way through half the town. But people wrinkle their noses when a woman raises concerns about a man's history. Myself included.

It feels awkward to share these things with my wife now. For the first time, I regret doing half the things I've done. If I had known I'd be having this conversation today, I wouldn't have ever slept with Eliana. Or any other woman.

I would have waited for Rosa.

I take a deep breath and answer honestly, "I don't know how many women I've been with."

She presses her lips together tightly and nods, trying not to freak out.

Even though she didn't ask, I feel like I should explain. "I never had the same woman twice because I wasn't looking for a relationship. I picked up women from Conrad's club or I hired women."

She doesn't speak for a moment, just sits there studying me, like she isn't sure she's ready to go down this path. But it's already too late.

"Did you use protection?" she asks hesitantly.

I suddenly realize *we* didn't use protection. That makes it difficult to answer, but I slowly shake my head, determined to give her the truth. Even if it ruins us.

"I didn't always use it. But I got myself checked every month," I try to offer.

"When was the last time you were checked?"

"Before the wedding. The contract required me to get tested and give copies of my medical reports to Giovanni and Jameson, so they'd know I wasn't going to give you anything."

I can tell from the wide-eyed look on her face that she had no idea any of this happened. She was a virgin, so she didn't need to get checked or send any reports anywhere.

Just to make sure she understands what I'm saying, I add, "I'm clean, Rosa. I've never had an STD and I don't have any kids."

She exhales slowly. "I see."

"You're safe."

She nods. "Thank you for being honest."

"Thank you for caring enough to ask."

She shifts to look me in the eye. "I want you to know that I still love you. Your past bothers me, I can't deny that. But I forgive you for it."

I nod slowly.

"I didn't ask those questions to cast judgment. I asked because I was curious, and I wanted to make sure there was nothing to worry about." She sighs. "If I wanted to judge you for your past, I would have asked before … before everything that happened last night."

I can see a blush spreading on her cheeks.

"And this morning," she whispers.

"How was it?" I ask, leaning close to kiss her neck.

She giggles and tries to pull away, but I catch her and roll us so I'm on top. "How was it?" I ask again, but I cut off her reply with a deep kiss. I don't really need to hear her answer, I already know how it was. How good it felt. I'm about to make her feel everything all over again, but as soon as we get started, she sucks in a sharp gasp, and I realize she's sore.

I immediately stop and shift off of her. Questions dance in her eyes, but she doesn't speak. "Maybe we should slow down," I say softly. I could just take it slow and try to be gentle, but I don't want to risk it. I don't want to hurt her.

Rosa looks embarrassed. I think I even see tears welling in her eyes. I kiss her cheek when she sits up and grabs the blankets to cover herself. "Don't be upset," I tell her.

She nods but doesn't meet my gaze. I wish I could say something to comfort her. I wish I could convince her I'm not disappointed or dissatisfied with her. But I'm not an expert on this. I have no idea what newly flowered (or newly *de*flowered) wives expect from their husbands. Right now, I feel like anything I say will just make it worse.

I sigh.

I've been given a second chance at this marriage. I don't want to mess it up before it's even begun. I want to do things right this time around. That means some things have got to change. Rosa's got to open up and stop being so ashamed of everything. And I've got to stop expecting her to behave the way other women do. She's not Eliana. She's not another one-night stand. She's my wife. But if anything in this relationship is going to change, it's got to start with me.

I glance at the clock on my bedside table, but my attention is drawn to the Bible I left out yesterday. "Rosa," I say slowly.

She looks up at me with red eyes.

"Want to pray together?"

Her face lights up and she gives me a crooked smile. "Seriously?"

"Yes."

She reaches for my hands. "Of course I do!"

I can't help but smile. She's always been enthusiastic about her faith. "You start," I whisper as she closes her eyes. "I have no idea what to say."

Rosa nods and begins a quiet prayer. She asks God to forgive us for our sins and then starts asking Him to bless our day and to protect us as we go about our business. I drift off while she prays, not because I don't want to hear the rest, I get distracted by my own questions.

Could it really be so easy for God to forgive us?

Ask and it will be given. Just like that?

It might be easy for someone like Rosa who's never done a sinful thing in her life. But I'm nothing like my sweet wife. I've lied to people. I've tortured people. I've killed people. I don't even know how many women I've slept with.

And yet, sweet Rosa loves me regardless. If she got her kind heart from the God she serves, then maybe He could forgive me as quickly as she did.

And then what?

I toy with the thought in my head. Then I get saved, and rule the mafia with a gun in one hand and a Bible in the other?

Or maybe I leave the mafia altogether...

I feel something like electricity shoot through my chest at the thought of getting out. It's a scary idea. Leaving everything I've ever known. I was born into the mafia; this is the life for me. If I were meant to be anyone else, *God* would have made sure I was born into a normal family as a normal guy. Not as the heir to the German mafia.

I don't realize I'm frowning until I open my eyes and find Rosa staring at me. "Are you okay?" she asks.

"I'm fine," I grunt, letting go of her hands. She stares at me as I climb out of bed and go to the shower. "I've got to head to work. I'll be busy until the afternoon."

"I'm not going home," she announces.

I nod, trying to hide my smile. "You are home."

Eight

Rosa's showering in a different bathroom when I finally turn off the water and try to find some clothes. I don't feel like going out to break the bad news to Emilio, so I'm procrastinating. Eventually, I find a white shirt and some black slacks—my usual attire. I grab a suit jacket and a tie on my way out, but I never make it to the front door.

For some reason, Vater and Jameson Willis are waiting in my lounge when I descend the stairs. I can hear their voices drifting down the hall, talking peaceably for once, and when I push through the doors and find them drinking my whiskey together, I almost die of shock.

"What's going on?" I ask.

Their peaceful demeanor instantly shifts to aggressive anger when they see me. "You tell me," Uwe says darkly. "Jameson called me this morning because he couldn't find Rosa. I thought the Russians got to her, until I showed up here to ask you about it and heard you putting on a show at sunrise!" Uwe's yelling now, and even though I'm sure my guards and housekeeping heard everything last night, I feel the sudden urge to tell him to quiet down. I don't want anyone to hear him shouting about what happened between Rosa and me.

I glance at King James. He's standing with his large hands stuffed into his oversized pockets, but his face is unreadable. Uwe's anger hasn't gotten to him. He doesn't look upset or sad or even concerned. If I had to place an emotion, I'd say he looks slightly annoyed. But not at me.

His gaze shifts to my father and he sighs deeply. "Jägermeister," his voice is a rumble in his chest. "We have much to discuss."

"That's what I'm trying to do now!"

"What you're doing now is just yelling," he says patiently. "But we must decide what to *do*. The deed is done. We must move forward. All of us."

Uwe blinks at him stupidly. Then he glances over at me and curses in German. "The Morenos could hang you for this betrayal! And I wouldn't be able to retaliate!" He turns and pours himself three fingers of whiskey, then downs it in one big gulp. "*Now* you remember how to be a man? *Now* you know how to use your little pecker!"

I smirk at him. "It's not little."

Jameson laughs deeply—I swear I feel the floor shaking with each hearty chuckle. "So, what will you do now, underboss?"

I move to the whiskey for a drink, too. When I've tossed back my alcohol, I wipe my mouth and say, "I'm going to tell Emilio I've consummated my marriage."

68

"He will strike back," Uwe says.

I nod. "He might even ally with the Volkovs."

"But we will side with each other," Jameson says.

I try not to let him see how desperate I am. "You're going to be my ally?"

"Do you think I'd leave my grandson to fight a bunch of Wolves alone?"

I smile like an idiot. That's the first time King James has ever called me his grandson—not just grandson-*in-law*. I guess its official now. We're all family.

"Is this happening?" I ask, just to make sure everyone is on the same page. "We're forming an alliance for the war?"

King James shakes his large head. "We are family now. We're forming an alliance for life."

To my surprise, Uwe simply nods.

"The Willis Stronghold will send men and weapons immediately." Jameson pulls out his phone. "I've got to go make arrangements. Will you say hi to Rosa for me?" He winks at me before leaving, and I suddenly feel awkward like my innocent wife—blushing and looking away like I've been caught doing something dirty. This morning, I *was* caught doing something dirty, but I don't dwell on it. I'm just glad Rosa isn't here to be embarrassed about it. She would never live it down if she knew Uwe overheard us earlier.

We made love four times between night and morning. I don't think we were loud, but I wasn't exactly focused on keeping quiet. I make a mental note to tell my guards and house staff to keep their mouths shut about whatever they might have heard. With the string of women I used to keep, their secrecy is something I don't even have to explain to them anymore, but still. For Rosa's sake, I want to make sure they all know the drill. Say nothing—because you saw nothing, and you heard nothing.

Honestly, I've never been embarrassed about anyone hearing anything. My house has cameras in every room except my own, and there aren't any in the bathrooms. My guards have 24/hour access to the security system, they've probably seen me with women in the study or the lounge or wherever else I've had them. They probably saw Rosa and I last night before we moved to my bedroom. Of course … she doesn't know this, but I'll eventually tell her. If for no other reason than to keep her from walking around the house naked. I'd have to gouge out the eyes of whatever unfortunate security guard who happened to glance at the monitoring screens and see her prancing about in her birthday suit.

Being married suddenly seems like a lot of work.

With a longsuffering sigh, I glance at Vater, wondering how long he's been waiting to speak to me this morning. It doesn't matter, I'm just grateful he didn't decide to interrupt and burst through my bedroom doors. Rosa would have died in my sheets from the embarrassment.

Uwe takes a deep breath. "You finally did what needed to be done."

"I thought you'd be proud."

"You have just made us another enemy, there is nothing to be proud of."

70

He's right, but I won't admit that out loud.

"At least we have the aid of the Stronghold now," I say, staring at the door King James left through.

Vater pulls out a cigar and lights it. I could complain about him smoking in my house, but I wisely choose to ignore it. Stopping him isn't worth the argument it'll start.

"I don't know how you will get Giovanni to give you aid."

"We consummated the marriage. He has to honor the contract now."

"But he doesn't have the means to. You know he'll try to wiggle his way out of it, so he won't have to shed any resources."

I nod. Uwe is right again. Giovanni is a scumbag who blackmailed me and sold his sister to a rival mafia. He's a selfish brat who'll do anything to make sure he comes out on top. But now I've finally got enough dirt on him to make sure he can't squirm out of his responsibilities.

I drop my gaze to my father. He isn't much shorter than me, but he's short enough for me to look down on him. He's never admitted to hating this, but I notice the way he casually steps back, so it isn't so obvious that I'm looking down at him.

"I'll make sure Gio agrees to honor the contract."

"Do you have proof of consummation?"

I could get Vater to come with me and tell Gio he witnessed the act. He didn't see it for himself, but he heard more than enough. And the fact that King James believes his account is proof of his honesty, but Gio will want more than that. I could just go upstairs and grab the dirty sheets, show him the red stain we left behind. But that's archaic and gross.

I shake my head. "I won't need proof."

Vater raises a slightly grey eyebrow. "Why not?"

"Because I have information strong enough to blackmail him into submission."

"Information like what?"

I smile, momentarily unsure if I want to share this with my father, but he's the Jägermeister, I shouldn't keep intel like this from him.

"I know Giovanni Sr. did not commit suicide."

His mouth drops open and I know I don't have to fill in the details.

Not long ago, Mikhail Volkov came to me with information about Gio. He told me the trashy kid killed his own father and made it look like a suicide. At the time, Mikhail was only sharing this because he wanted to earn my trust. Since I'd married into the Stronghold and the De Luca alliance, I had the power to overtake him if he harmed my brother-in-law. But after Wolfgang's foolish mistake, Volkov doesn't care about Giovanni. He's solely focused on taking down the German mafia.

But I've still got the information. And I know Gio Jr. will do anything to keep anyone from finding out what he's done. It will ruin him. Might even cause the Italian mafia to stage a coup and overthrow him. At the very least, I know it'll destroy his relationship with Rosa. They aren't the closest siblings in the world, but they care enough for each other for this to tear them apart. The shame of his sister knowing the truth will hurt more than losing his position as don.

It will also impact *my* relationship with Rosa. I've known for months how her father really died and I haven't shared that with her yet. When I first learned about it, I wasn't sure she could handle the truth. Rosa was so weak and fragile. I don't know what the Stronghold's done to her, but I'm not so certain the truth will break her anymore. I'm just not sure how to tell her—rather—I'm not sure how to tell her I've known all this time. She'll hate me for keeping it to myself. But the longer I wait, the harder it is to come out and say it. I just can't.

Maybe when the war is over, and everything's calmed down. I just can't have her hating me now. I just got her back. I don't know how I'll handle her walking away, or not speaking to me all over again.

Vater blows his cigar smoke into my face to get my attention. I cough. "Stop that."

"You were drifting."

I wave at the smoke. "I've got to go now, Vater."

He nods. "Call me if that brat gives you trouble."

I can't help but smile. Vater has always hated Giovanni, almost as much as I hate him now.

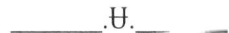

It takes almost two hours to get to Gio's penthouse. Traffic is denser with war brewing. You'd think everyone would be hiding inside, but they're all out trying to get in one last shebang before the City falls apart. It also doesn't help that Gio has three different security teams to stop and frisk me before I'm let inside.

He's waiting in his living room with a drink in his hand when his guard brings me to him. He waves off the beefy guard and smiles at me. "To what do I owe this surprise visit?"

"Rosa and I consummated the marriage. We need your aid in this war now."

Exactly three seconds of perfect silence passes between us; I swear I can hear the ice melting in his sweaty glass. With a blank expression on his face, Gio very calmly gulps down the rest of his drink and then offers me a sickly-sweet smile. "Not that I don't believe you, but how do I know you aren't just pulling my leg?"

I give him a chance to hold on to his dignity. "You'll just have to trust me."

Giovanni laughs—which lets me know I'll have to use my trump card. I really don't want to, it'll just complicate things between Rosa and me even more. Now she'll hate me for not telling her and for using the information to blackmail her brother.

I shove those thoughts away and exhale hard. Now is not the time to go soft on Giovanni—or on anyone, period. We're in a war. And even if we weren't, I'm the next Jägermeister, I can't afford to be soft. Ever.

"If you don't honor the marital contract, I'll be forced to move your hand," I say slowly.

My tone earns me a queer look, but it's my words that steal his attention.

"I know what really happened to Gio Sr. and I'm prepared to share that with the rest of the Italian mafia if you don't give me the aid you owe me."

It's always been said that Giovanni took after his father and Rosa took after her mother. She's got brown skin like Laura Willis had, and he has olive-toned skin like their Italian father had. But right now, Gio looks nothing like either of his parents. He's pale as a ghost and for a second, I wonder if the color will ever return to him.

"H—How did you find out?" he whispers, setting down his empty glass. It hits the crystal coffee table with a *clack*, and he squeezes his eyes shut at the sound, like he's got a sudden migraine. I watch him shakily fall onto the sofa and pinch the bridge of his nose. At the very least, I appreciate the fact that he doesn't think I'm bluffing. He knows I wouldn't lie about this.

"Mikhail Volkov told me. Said one of his men saw you do it through the scope of a sniper rifle."

Gio jerks his head up, a lock of his dark brown hair falls loose and sticks to his sweaty forehead. He rapidly tries to blink it away before swiping angrily at it. "A sniper rifle?" His eyes go wide. "He was going to kill me."

"Because you owed him so much money."

Gio's green eyes meet mine with reluctance, like he's embarrassed all of a sudden. I'm not judging him, but I enjoy the fretful look on his face. I let the silence linger until its uncomfortable, then I step forward and say in almost a whisper, "I know the Garden is rotting. And I know its rotting because of you. By now, most people are aware of your failures as a don. They're just too afraid to say anything. But I'm not. And I'm not afraid to let the rest of your family know of your ultimate failure—as a son."

He swallows so loudly I wonder if he's choking for a moment. His tongue slips out to wet his suddenly dry lips. "I— I had no other choice."

"There is always a choice, Gio. You didn't have to kill your own father."

He winces and glances around, like he's scared someone might have overheard. "Don't say anything. I'll get you whatever aid I can—"

"Weapons," I say.

He nods vigorously. "Not many—"

"How many? And what weapons?"

"One hundred ARs, a dozen crates of grenades, three grenade launchers. A shipment of ammo." He falls silent and just stares at me. When I blink at him, he bunches his shoulders and says weakly, "That's it."

"*That's it?*" How on earth does the Italian mafia survive on 100 assault rifles?

He takes a shaky breath. "We had to sell a few things to stay afloat. My grandfather gave me a very generous offer."

That makes sense, I grunt to myself. Of course King James took advantage of his own grandson's struggles. He bought back the guns I know he overcharged him on in the first place. Each mafia in New York has a specialty. The Morenos sell cocaine out of Queens, the Volkovs sell flesh in Staten Island,

76

the De Lucas once sold property in Manhattan before they went under, the Stronghold deals arms in the Bronx, and the Jägers sell diamonds and other precious rocks in Brooklyn.

Since the De Lucas specialized in land, I hadn't expected much from them in the war—but every gang has men and weapons. If I can't get guns out of Gio then I'll at least need extra manpower.

"How many soldiers can you spare?" I ask.

Shots have been fired twice already, both shootouts were in Brooklyn. My own territory. It won't be long before my men start looking to me for a response to the disrespect. I'm itching to retaliate, but I don't want to send them in blind or unprepared.

The Wolves live in Staten Island, they control the Verrazzano Bridge and the ferry ports. They'll see us coming miles off. Which means getting into their territory will require more manpower—manpower the Jägers simply don't have alone. There aren't enough men in our ranks to hold up security in Brooklyn, keep Wolfgang guarded at Stonehall, and infiltrate the Island. We need help.

Giovanni glances away like he's calculating in his head. "I can give you fifty men."

"*Fifty* men?"

There are 70 men at Stonehall watching Wolfgang. I've got at least 2000 men on the streets of Brooklyn at any given moment, not to mention the spies I've sent into the other boroughs to gather intel and await orders. We still have men along the city borders, contacts in Jersey, and men on security duty for high-ranking families. Plus, 300 men off-duty for rotation on schedules, and another 700 soldiers who pose as everyday people to make sure the public doesn't get out of control. And to catch spies. Spies catching spies within the ranks.

The point is, the Hunting Grounds has *at least* 3000 trained soldiers available at any given time—not to mention associates and men still in training. It might sound like a small number, but our gang specializes in diamonds, okay? I can't imagine the numbers of the Stronghold or the Morenos. You don't gain control of the entire cocaine supply of New York City without having an army to defend your snow.

King James got rich from selling weapons to the Morenos so they can arm the men who guard all their shipments. I know my grandfather can supply men and guns, but right now I'm not sure what Gio offers except a headache.

I shake my head as I stare down at him. "How do you only have fifty men to offer?"

"I cannot afford to pay all of them anymore."

Of course not.

I sigh heavily. "So, basically, you can't help me."

He shrugs sheepishly. "But I'll give you whatever I can. Just please don't tell anyone about my father."

How pathetic. The don of the Italian mafia is begging for mercy from an underboss—of a different gang, at that. Giovanni Sr. never would have fallen so low. But the son is nothing like the father. He should count his blessings he's Rosa's brother, or else I would tip off his family just to hear him scream as they killed him.

I feel guilty as soon as that thought enters my head. Rosa wouldn't want her brother to die. But not just because he's her own kin, she wouldn't want him to die because it's against her nature. Against her faith. I silently wonder if that thought about Gio's death is bad. Like, if it made God mad.

I flinch. When had I accepted His existence? Because God can't get mad at me if He isn't real … right?

I take a breath to clear my mind. Now is not the time to decide my spiritual beliefs.

"I'm a man of my word, Gio," I say calmly. "I won't tell anyone about your father's death. Even though you can't offer me anything of value."

He licks his lips again, eyes wide and bulgy. "I told you before, I can offer shelter to your women and children. The Volkovs think the Garden is worthless; they won't bother to attack us."

"Because you have nothing worth attacking for."

"Exactly," he says, almost excitedly. "Your families will be safe here. I can promise that." He smiles, like he thinks he's got the upper hand now. "And I believe the safety of your pretty wife is of the utmost importance, right?"

How dare he use Rosa against me…

I glare at him long enough to make him sink into his sofa. "I'll discuss this with Uwe and King James."

"Shouldn't I be privy to that meeting?"

"No."

I leave Junior sweating on his couch and spend the next hour sending texts and emails to Uwe and Jameson while Douglass drives me to Queens. My Uncle Oberon calls and reports that King James sent a shipment of weapons to one of our warehouses, and six-hundred soldiers arrived at Morgen's gym—he's calling in Hans to help with training while Klaus arranges the schedules. I want men on the street at all times, and I want our warehouses guarded. Jameson promised more weapons and men later, for now we don't want to overcrowd the city and we don't want the Wolves to know just how much our ranks have increased.

I put my phone away when Douglass stops outside Emilio's villa. "Stay in the car. Keep your phone on you in case things go bad," I tell him when he opens my door.

He nods and returns to the driver's seat without a word. We've been working together long enough to be able to communicate without speaking. I know Douglass will have my back if he senses even a hint of trouble. That's why he's my personal guard. I trust him with my life.

Moreno's men pat me down and confiscate my weapons when I enter his home. They also don't let me beyond the lounge on the first floor. The last time I visited, I was greeted by Emilio himself and immediately taken to his office. Now, I'm waiting in a sitting room with a pitcher of lukewarm tap water to sip until he decides to show up.

An hour passes before the doors open and Emilio strides inside. I stand to greet him, but he just walks right past me and takes a seat at the head of the long table in the middle of the room. I give him an awkward smile and take my seat in silence.

The quiet hangs between us longer than I'm comfortable with. I hate being the one getting intimidated. That's normally my job. But part of me feels bad about what I'm about to do, especially because I still respect Emilio. We had something of a friendship before all this happened—it was that friendship that led him to offer me aid in the first place. It had come at the cost of my marriage, but still… Emilio had been there when Gio and Jameson hadn't. And now I'm thanking him by dumping his daughter.

"Emilio," I begin, but he cuts me off and says loudly, "My daughter says you haven't spoken to her in almost a week."

That's right. It's been nearly five days since the wedding and the whole slapping event. Eliana hadn't bothered calling me and I was more than happy not to call her in turn. I didn't think she'd go running to daddy about it, but I'm not surprised. Emilio dotes on his family. There are pictures of them all around the lounge I'm sitting in; beautiful smiling faces that radiate happiness, despite being a mafia family. I only have three family photos, and no one is smiling in any of them. After a while, we stopped taking photos and started commissioning portraits, that way the artist could paint our smiles. Even though we never wore them.

I glance up and realize Emilio is looking at me expectantly. His raised eyebrows go up even higher. "Well?"

"Uh, yes. I haven't spoken to Eliana for a few days."

"May I ask why you haven't contacted your own fiancé?"

"Well—"

"She has been very distraught. I cannot even get her to leave her room anymore."

That's complete BS. It's true I haven't bothered calling or texting, but Eliana's just abusing her father's soft heart right now. She's angry I didn't take her side when Rosa slapped her, so she's punishing me by acting out with Emilio because she knows he will blame me for her unhappiness. No matter what she's done.

This is the only way she can get back at me for not defending her, since she'll never tell Emilio what really happened at that reception. It's childish and petty and I'm so glad I'm here to permanently end things because I don't think I could have handled a lifetime of this drama.

After the sex wore off, we would have been miserable together.

I take a very deep, heavy breath and exhale slowly. It sucks that a good man like Emilio fathered a witchy woman like Eliana. He doesn't deserve her and she doesn't deserve him. I feel bad about the situation only for his sake. Because I know she will give him an everlasting headache after today. The only joy I have in this is knowing Eliana will take the secret of our fling to her grave. She can't afford to lose daddy's trust. If he ever found out we had sex outside of marriage, he would kill her. She'll be heartbroken by this, but not heartbroken enough to try to get revenge or anything. That little fact almost brings a smile to my face.

"I haven't contacted her because I've thought things

through and decided it's best to work things out with my wife."

Emilio blinks once, clearly taken aback. "I thought we had an arrangement."

"We did, but it was contingent upon the annulment of my marriage to Rosa De Luca. When I realized the paperwork had not been finalized, I took it as a sign that I should try to work things out with her. And I did." I smile. "I've been given a second chance at this marriage. And this family. You understand the importance of family."

"I also understand the importance of contracts."

I nod solemnly. "I'm not happy about breaking the contract—"

"Neither am I." He rises and buttons his suit jacket. "We are done here, Mr. Jäger."

I squint, realizing he didn't use my first name. Emilio is the only mafioso I'm on a first name basis with. But I've just ended my engagement to his precious daughter. I guess I ended our friendship, too.

I stand and button my suit jacket as well. "Emilio, this doesn't have to—"

He holds up a hand. "Please leave my premises. Technically, you have not broken your contract since it was never finalized. So I will not retaliate and harm you. But you have insulted me, Mr. Jäger. I will not forget that."

With the promise of no retaliation, I decide it's best to just keep my mouth shut and leave. I'm thankful to make it out of Emilio's house unscathed but I'm not so optimistic as to believe he won't try something later. He didn't retaliate right then, but he'll have time to simmer and decide how to handle the slight I've dealt him later on.

There's a war brewing. Once word gets out that my alliance with the Morenos is over, I'm sure the Volkovs will come running with a new deal and a new contract to offer. Mikhail has a young son—he's too young for Eliana—but Emilio has another daughter. A nineteen-year-old girl he'd once offered to me. If their families join forces, the city will be split almost evenly. Especially since the Garden is too poor to be neither a threat nor an ally in this.

I can practically hear the Wolves howling as I slide into my car and stare out the window as Douglass peels from the driveway.

Nine

I spend an eternity in the shower. The hot water feels like a massage, and I don't want to step out, not until the steam disappears and the current starts to run cold. I shiver as I wrap myself in my towel and shuffle to the mirror. It took me longer than usual to wash my hair because I had to detangle all the curls—thanks to Amory this morning.

I blush as memories of us wrapped up together flow into my head. I can't believe we spent the night and the morning together. My first instinct is to find my phone and call Gisela, she's the closest thing I have to a best friend in the German mafia. When I first signed the annulment papers, my heart broke at the thought of never seeing her again.

Glizzy would be so proud of me. She was by my side through some of the toughest moments I had with my husband. We bonded the moment I found out she's a Christian; it was her spiritual advice that gave me the courage to acknowledge my feelings and share them with Amory. I wish I would have asked for her wisdom earlier, but I'm happy with the way things have turned out.

I missed Amory. But our time apart has been beneficial. I'm not the shy girl he fell in love with anymore, I'm stronger. Mentally, emotionally, and even physically. It's only been a month since I first signed those papers, but it feels like a lifetime.

As I sit at a vanity and begin sectioning my hair, I think about Adella and Nona and how much they've helped me cope these last few weeks. Nona showed me tough love in the gym, never holding back or going easy when we sparred. But she slipped me her phone on more than one occasion, promising she wouldn't tell if I called Amory with it. I never did, but I won't forget her kindness in those weeks.

Della was different. She was kind and warm and almost motherly, even though she's only several years older. Maybe her heart had opened to me because she's also married. Last year, her marriage hit a huge bump in the road when she had a miscarriage. It drove a wedge between her and Jared; she needed space and he needed to talk. They coped in totally different ways, and it nearly tore them apart.

Adella knows what it's like to be separated from the person you love. The distance between her and her husband might have stemmed from reasons different from my own marital separation, but it gave her perspective, nonetheless. She knew what I meant when I told her how much it hurt. She had felt the same ache when I'd clutched my chest and cried until I couldn't breathe. And she had never judged me for it. Had never shamed me for my weakness.

"When you look like us," she had said one night, wiping off her makeup and staring into her mirror. "There is an expectation to be strong. To be independent. To hold your head up high."

I rolled my eyes and thought of my mother. "*A strong Black woman.*" The phrase left a sour taste in my mouth. The idea that the color of my skin somehow made me immune to pain was ridiculous. I'd hated growing up with that stigma hanging over my head. Like I wasn't allowed to ever cry or feel vulnerable or be weak.

Adella knew how I felt.

"The truth is that we are just as gentle as everyone else," she'd told me. "We just learn how to cope faster than others. We have to learn how to cope faster."

I remember nodding and wiping at my tears, trying not to cry anymore. Adella patted my back. "When you're here, you can be weak, Rosa. You can express how you really feel. The world outside will judge you and judge everything you do, but in here it's safe."

"That won't make it hurt any less," I'd sobbed.

She had smiled. "I never said it would. In this life, the fighting never stops. You just learn to hit back."

I sniffled. "I need to get stronger."

"You already have. You're not the withered rose anymore. You're a vine of poison ivy."

I smile at the memory, working coconut oil into my curls and braiding back my hair. If there is one thing my time at the Stronghold taught me, it's that I'm only as weak as I allow myself to be. But I also learned that I don't have to be strong. I don't have to be tough. I just have to stand up for myself.

I've decided to stand up to Amory.

He hasn't done anything wrong. In fact, I think our time together has been heavenly, but I'm not a fool. Right now, we're living in a fantasy. The romance is swooning, and the sex is mind-blowing. Once all that fades away, we'll be left with reality. The gang violence, the war, the rivalry between our families, the pressure to create an heir.

We'll have to face that reality. I'm sure Amory is ready. I'm sure he already has a plan in place. And I'm sure that plan doesn't include my say or input.

The mafia is old-fashioned. They leave all the hard work to the men and tell the women to just look pretty and ignore all the madness around them. In a way, it's flattering. Like we are too precious to get mixed up in the darkness of this world. But it can also be oppressing, like we're too stupid to make any serious decisions.

I don't believe Amory thinks I'm dumb. I don't believe he looks down on me. But I won't fool myself into thinking he's so different from any other mafioso I've ever met. He's made it clear on more than one occasion that he's in charge. That his word is law. He might not boss me around the house and make me cook and clean, but I don't have complete freedom. I did not pick my personal guards myself, and they won't take me anywhere Amory doesn't approve. He has to know my location at all times, which may be for security purposes, but that same measure of safety is not in place for him. I have no idea where my husband is right now. And I won't know until he chooses to contact me. *If* he chooses to contact me.

Things weren't like that in the Stronghold. Mama Mo' stood side by side with the man everyone calls King James. He rules the Bronx with an iron fist, but it was my grandmother who forged that iron. Poured the molten metal into its mold and beat it into perfection. She placed the wrought iron crown upon his head so that others could call him the king. He pays his respects by respecting her. And he makes sure others do the same.

And because the king respects his queen, others within the gang have modeled their marriages the same way. Adella and Jared are best friends and lovers. Her parents are exactly the same. I want that connection with Amory. I want him to see me as his partner, not his property. I don't care if he's the head of this household, but this household will not be a dictatorship. It's going to be a democracy and I will have a say.

"God," I whisper, staring at my reflection. "How do I get him to understand? Give me the words to speak and the tone to speak them. In Jesus' Name, amen."

I spend the morning and afternoon directing the movers who bring over my things from Grandpa's place. I'm happy to have my own clothes to wear again, though I didn't mind walking around in Amory's large shirts and boxers. They smelled like him and each time I inhaled; my heart ached for his presence.

When we first got married, Amory had my things arranged

in a separate room down the hall from him. We weren't as close back then as we are now, so I take a huge chance and move some of my things into his bedroom.

Into our *bedroom*, I correct myself.

My dresser stands beside his and I make room in the walk-in closet for some of my things. He has a surprising amount of body washes and hygienic products in his bathroom—it takes me an hour to make room for all my hair supplies and lotions. I don't know why he has his own vanity, but I'm sure he won't mind me filling the empty drawers with my makeup, so I arrange everything as neatly as I can and shut the drawers softly—like I'm afraid he'll walk in and catch me.

Housekeeping changes the bedspread while I'm fighting for space in the shoe closet. I can't help but blush when she holds up the stained sheets, and I don't miss the shocked expression that crosses her face. When she looks over at me, she catches herself and gives me a little nod.

"I'll steam the mattress and bring new sheets, Mrs. Jäger," she mumbles.

I take that as my cue to leave and decide it's time for lunch. My heels echo through the hall while I walk to the dining room. The corridors are large and grey and stony, decorated with old statues, family portraits, and pieces of art so old I'm sure they're worth millions. The heavy curtains are drawn shut— they always are—so only slivers of light cut through the darkness of the grand hallway. It leaves the house in a constant shade of grey that reminds me of a tomb.

I make a mental note to ask Amory if he would consider

redecorating. We have two completely different styles. I don't want to turn the house into a fairytale garden, but I also don't want to live in Bruce Wayne's manor anymore. I half expect a bat or *Batman himself* to pop out one of his creepy, gothic lounges every time I walk past.

Amory is too dark for his own good. I don't know if it's the mafia's influence or if my husband is just gloomy but sometimes it's scary.

There's a display of food in the dining room when I enter. I'm honestly not very hungry, so I sip some tea and take bird bites of a slice of sweet potato bread, then I head back upstairs. The nosey cleaner is gone from my room when I return, I actually sigh in relief when I see the new sheets and blankets. A sudden urge to jump on the bed almost overwhelms me; I settle for just lying in the middle and snuggling one of the pillows.

I can't believe I spent hours in this bed, wrapped up with Amory. I want to lie here and enjoy memories of our time together, but my joy is chased away by the thought of all the women who've been in this bed. Who've slept on these blankets.

A frown tugs at my lips as I sit up and look around. I don't want to dwell on Amory's past. I've already forgiven him for it, but it's proving harder than I thought to forget about it.

Suddenly, everything in the room brings a question to the front of my mind. Did Eliana ever cuddle with this pillow? Did a random prostitute lay on this side of the bed? Did Amory ever have more than one woman in this room, at the same time?

I shiver and squeeze my eyes shut. I don't want to entertain those thoughts.

"His past doesn't matter," I whisper. It slips from my lips again and again, like a mantra I'm trying to memorize.

When I feel like I can't take it anymore, I slide off the bed and leave the room. I need to keep busy or else I'll end up thinking myself into a bad mood.

I change my clothes and hit the gym, using all of Adella's training as I take out my anger on the punching bag. When my knuckles are raw and sore, I shower and shoot a text to Gisela and both my cousins—just to let them know I'm safe and haven't been kidnapped by the Wolves.

Gisela sends a flurry of emojis and questions which I answer with blushing cheeks and burning ears. Adella sends an angry reply about missing my training, but she also tells me she's happy things have worked out with Amory. Nona sends the eggplant emoji with a winky face. I snort out a laugh as I send back a kissy face. Part of me wants to text Olivia but I know she's on a little honeymoon right now, so I just set a reminder to contact her later.

After I change into a skirt and a matching blouse, I find the library and roam the winding lines of the large room created by all the shelves. It's a two-story library with enough books to keep me busy for years. I've never seen Amory with a book in his hand, but there are some texts left open on the little round tables that dot the library, and there's a stack of books on a desk in a very impressive looking office. The books are covered in a layer of dust, so I know they've been here awhile, but still. I can't help but imagine Amy hovered over a book, fingering the old page as he mutters the words to himself.

I wonder what sort of books Amory likes to read. I wonder if he inherited this grand collection or bought most of the novels himself. My daydreams leave me roaming the library for longer than I expect to. Before I know it, I drift into the mystery section and find myself a promising book to read.

Hours pass and the sunlight pouring in from the skylight begins to pale and fade. I still don't move. My legs lose circulation and fall asleep, but I ignore the tingling and continue turning the pages. It's not until I hear a deep voice behind me that I'm startled from my book.

"I finally found you," Amory says.

I sit up with a yelp and clutch my chest. "You scared me."

"*You* scared *me*," he says firmly. "I've been looking all over the house for you."

"Sorry," I mumble.

He takes the book from my hands and then picks me up and places me on his lap. The whole thing happens so fast, I don't even have time to wonder how he's so strong.

"I'm tired," he sighs, leaning his head back against the bookshelf behind us. "Read to me."

"But I'm in the middle."

"I don't care." His eyes flutter shut as his breathing slows to a rhythmic pace.

I grab the book and start reading until I hear him begin to snore. Then I sit there and stare at him, memorizing the lines of his handsome face. I want to reach out and stroke the curve of his strong jaw, but I'm afraid of waking him.

He peels his lids back, stopping my heart. "You stopped reading."

I nod. "You fell asleep."

"I told you I was tired."

"What happened at work?"

He shakes his head and then leans forward and hugs me tightly. "Nothing important."

"I still want to know," I say, trying not to sound so pleading.

He lifts my chin. "It's nothing you need to worry about."

When he leans in for a kiss, I turn my head so he kisses my cheek instead.

"Rosa?" he says, leaning back and staring at me.

"Things have changed between us," I say, meeting his confused gaze. "I'm your wife, Amy. And I want to be treated as such."

"I do treat you as my wife."

"No." I shake my head. "You treat me like your little doll."

He sighs. "What the heck happened while I was at work? Did someone come talk to you?"

His confusion makes me laugh, which tugs a smile onto his face. *This doesn't have to be a painful conversation*, I decide. Amory was raised to be a man in charge at all times—even in charge of me. It isn't something that I like. It isn't something I expect to change overnight. But I'm patient enough to wait for him to come around. I'm strong enough to meet him halfway.

"You know I've spent a lot of time with my cousins in the Stronghold," I tell him.

His shoulders drop like he suddenly understands. "Good God, did you go there and get liberated? Are you an independent woman now?" He says this with a smirk and a gentle tug on one of my braids, so I know he's only joking. But I still tap him lightly on the shoulder.

"The point of being married is having someone to depend on. So no, I'm not an *independent* woman." I almost snort when I say that. "But I do want some things to change."

He makes a face.

"At least change a little," I say quickly.

He plays with the material of my tulle skirt. "Things like what?"

"I want to be part of the decisions you make."

"Rosa, I'm in charge of one of the deadliest gangs in the country. I make decisions that impact mafia organizations across the nation, and even the world. I've got three-thousand soldiers at my expense, twelve jewelry stores, twenty-seven dig sites, and over fifty warehouses to look after. Every day."

I nod. "So let me help you."

He doesn't speak for a moment, but he doesn't have to. I can tell what he wants to say by the way his shoulders bunch and how his chest fills with air as he takes a deep breath.

How can you help?

What use is the withered rose?

I almost let his silent criticism break me, but then I think of Adella and Nona and even Melissa, the woman who took me in when I ran away. She's an innocent Christian woman who's probably overlooked by everyone around her, but she's also the strongest woman I know. She doesn't do much, she just does what she can. And more often than not, that's more than enough.

I take a breath. "I know I don't understand as much as you do about the organization. But I'll *never* understand if you don't tell me things."

Amory presses his lips together, still fiddling with my skirt.

"I'm not asking to take over your jewelry stores and dig sites. I'm just asking to know things. Can we start with that? Tell me about your day when I ask. And don't keep things from me."

For a long time, Amory doesn't speak. He sits there looking at me, grey eyes filled with emotions I can't name. A silent storm.

When the quiet goes on for too long, I shift on his lap and try to stand, but he grabs me by the waist and holds me there. "I'll start telling you things," he says softly. "But you've got to make a change, too, Rosa."

I glance up at him, stunned by both his agreement and his new request. "Change how?"

"Stop being so shy around me."

I know the words are coming, so I say them with him—dropping my voice an octave and lowering my eyebrows to mimic his stern expression.

"I'm your *husband*, Rosa."

He blinks at me and then snorts out a laugh. "You're

goofier than I remember."

I grin at him and close my book, placing it on the cushion beside us. "I'm sorry that I'm shy. I'm just not used to …" my voice trails off, my cheeks turn pink, my ears burn red.

"Not used to what?" Amory's breath tickles my neck as he pulls me close and whispers against the sensitive skin. "Tell me, Rosa."

I suddenly feel like I can't breathe. I don't think Amy knows the effect he has on me—or he knows, and he enjoys it.

He's kissing me now, gently, tenderly. But I place a hand on his chest and push away.

He blinks at me. "What's wrong?"

I look away. "Um … I …"

"Still sore?" he says quietly.

I cannot meet his gaze, or even answer his question.

Amory chuckles as he shifts us. At first, I think he's moving me over so he can stand and leave, but then I feel his hands going up my skirt and I squeal and slap at them.

"Hey!"

My name comes out as a sigh. "Rosa, I wasn't trying to feel you up. I just want to take a look and make sure you're all right."

"*What?*" I squeak out.

"Let me see," he says very patiently as I hold my skirt down like a woman fighting off a grabby man.

"You're not a doctor, Amy!"

"No. But I am the only one between us who's had sex

before."

I stare at him, petulant and stubborn. He isn't getting under my skirt, no matter how much sense he's making.

"We had sex, not surgery," I say snappily.

A smile threatens to claim his lips. "I know that. But there are certain things you should do as aftercare. To prevent UTIs, maintain hygiene, and even help with soreness."

My anger flares uncontrollably as I think of all the times he's had this conversation before. "How many women did you go through to learn all this?" I hiss.

Amory pauses, then his face slowly shifts from open concern to controlled anger. I expect him to snap at me for my comment, but instead he just kisses my forehead and stands. I topple off his lap, but he grabs my arm to stable me.

"How about I just run you a bath?"

I nod, trying to muster the courage to apologize. "That would be nice."

"Yeah," he agrees. "I think you need some time to relax."

He turns to leave the library but stops at the end of the aisle and looks back at me. His anger is still there on his face, controlled and almost hidden behind the lines of his straight eyebrows and blank expression.

"One more thing you have to change," he says, and it sounds more like an order than a request. Like I have no choice but to agree.

I nod slowly.

"You've got to stop blaming me for my past. We went over this issue already You told me you forgave me for it."

I nod again, but he doesn't give me the chance to speak.

"I don't expect you to be happy about my past. I don't even expect you to ever fully accept it or get over it. But I also don't expect you to throw it in my face every time you get angry. That's not forgiveness, Rosa."

I stare at the floor and mumble weakly, "I'm sorry."

Amory scoffs and storms out.

Ten

Amory isn't here when I wake up this morning. Part of me fears he's still angry about our argument the day before, but I know he's just busy. With his schedule, it would be surprising if he did sleep in with me. Still, I hope breakfast is something we'll get to enjoy together more than once or twice a week.

I'm in the middle of eating my fruit and yogurt alone when one of the guards enters the dining room and interrupts me.

"Mrs. Jäger," he says hesitantly. "Dr. Köhler is here to see you."

I frown and swallow the hunk of pineapple in my mouth. "Dr. Köhler?"

He nods and then motions toward the door. "Mr. Jäger instructed me to let her into your room."

"My *bedroom*?"

The way his eyes dart away lets me know he's just as confused as I am. "Yes, ma'am. She's waiting there now."

I have no idea what's going on. I have no idea who Dr. Köhler is. I just want to finish my breakfast and think of ways to fix things with my husband, but I know that's not going to happen now.

With a frustrated sigh, I push my plate away and stand. "Thanks for telling me. I'll go see her now."

Dr. Köhler is a hefty woman with short dark hair and a gentle, warm smile. When I enter my bedroom, I find her sitting at a small table that must have been dragged inside by one of the guards. There are papers and folders and a fat leather bag on the table, I stare at them as I walk closer.

"What's going on?" I ask cautiously.

Dr. Köhler extends a hand. "You must be Rosa."

"You must be Dr. Köhler."

"I am," she nods, shaking my hand with a surprisingly gentle grip. "I came to ask you a few questions and make sure you're doing all right. To my understanding, you were just recently married." She gives me a knowing look. "Even though you're twenty-years-old, your body may still experience a few slight changes after a big event like that. Hormones, emotions, physical health—"

I stop listening, almost blinded by my sudden anger. Now I get it. Amory sent her here to check me out because of our argument yesterday. Since I wouldn't let him pretend to be a doctor and administer 'aftercare,' he decided to send this woman over to do it herself.

Like a child, I want to cross my arms, stomp my foot, and yell for her to leave. But I'm not a pampered mafia princess anymore, I have to handle this maturely.

"Dr. Köhler, I know my husband asked you to come, and

since he's the underboss, it must be difficult to refuse his requests."

Dr. Köhler swallows thickly and takes a deep breath. "Mrs. Jäger—"

"I don't need an examination," I cut her off. "I was a little sore yesterday. But I believe that's normal. Even more experienced women feel sore at times, correct?"

She nods and then drops her gaze to the table where all the papers are spread out. "Actually, Mrs. Jäger, soreness is not why I was called here." While I stand there confused, she starts digging in her leather bag and pulling out supplies. "Mr. Jäger told me he didn't wear protection. I'm here to administer a pregnancy test."

My knees buckle, but Dr. Köhler is quicker than she looks. She's by my side in an instant, gripping my arm and pulling me to one of the chairs at the table. She isn't gentle, but we make it there without me losing my footing. I mumble an apology as I adjust in the chair and blink at the paperwork in front of me.

"What is all this?" I ask quietly.

"I had your old doctor send over your medical history so I could have a look. I want to ask you a few questions to help me determine a prescription for you."

My head snaps up at the sound of her words. "Prescription?"

She nods uneasily. "Mr. Jäger told me you're not on any contraception. He requested that I provide birth control today." Like this is a normal Wednesday morning, Dr. Köhler starts putting on gloves and chatting away, oblivious to my

102

gaping stare. "We can go over our options while we wait for the results of your pregnancy test. I'll have to collect a blood sample to get a more accurate medical report, but I'm sure you'll do fine with one of the prescriptions I've brought with me." She smiles warmly, looking very much like a mother hen with her plump cheeks and red nose. "These days, you can get birth control online!"

I don't reply. I have no idea what to say.

Dr. Köhler takes my silence as cooperation and starts explaining how the pregnancy test works. We do two different kinds, one where I shamelessly hike up my skirt and pee on a stick and another that's a lot more complicated—she explains how it works but I'm not listening. I'm trying to keep myself from freaking out or passing out.

Amory and I didn't use protection. We'd had sex four different times on the first night we were together. And we've had it twice since then. I never thought about using protection because Amy's my husband and he told me he was clean the day everything went down. But condoms aren't just to prevent STDs, they also prevent pregnancy.

As a mafia princess, I'm expected to give Amory an heir as quickly as possible, but things are different now. Not only is there a war going on, but Amory and I never talked about when we wanted an heir. Or *if* we wanted an heir.

Now that I think about it, I have no idea how my own husband feels about children. I don't know how *I* feel about children. Maybe in the future. Maybe after Amory and I have learned how to be husband and wife, we'll take the next step and become Mom and Dad. But not right now. Not right away.

I've always thought it was weird when couples try for kids the instant they get married. Children are beautiful. They are gifts from God. But they're also a lifelong bill and responsibility. Being married does not automatically make you ready for parenthood. At least, it didn't for me. I'm only twenty-years-old. I'm not ready to become a mother, and even though Amory is eleven years older, he isn't ready to become a father, either.

Dr. Köhler is looking at me with an odd expression on her face. "Are you listening, Mrs. Jäger?"

I nod vacantly. "Can you repeat your last statement?"

"There are options available for you if the test results are not what you desire."

I frown, knowing exactly what she means—she just doesn't want to say it out loud. "You mean abortion."

She doesn't speak, torn between being professional and being afraid. Mr. Jäger is the underboss, but I'm still his wife. Offending me isn't any better than offending him—and suggesting that the underboss's wife aborts his heir is a great offense.

"Dr. Köhler, I'm a Christian woman," I say calmly. "I don't believe in abortion."

She lets out a breath and says weakly, "I had to let you know. It's just part of my job—I don't agree with it, either."

I smile at her, some of my anger ebbing away. As a Christian woman living in the middle of a city ruled by the mafia, I know better than anyone what it's like to be stuck in a place that stands against everything you believe in. I've felt that way almost my entire life.

"You said you have questions." I nod at the paperwork.

"Oh, yes," she says, shuffling some of the papers around. She grabs a pen and then starts reading off questions about my eating habits, my weight, my diet, my sex drive. We go over my medical history, if I've ever had an STD or if I've ever been pregnant. My answers are all more or less the same.

When she finishes, she passes me a bottle of pills and then writes out a slip for me to get a refill next month. Then I strip naked and climb onto my bed so she can give me a physical examination. I've honestly never been to a gynecologist's office before, so I have no idea what to expect, but I don't think I'd ever guess that she would start sticking tools in places I've never explored before.

The whole thing is awkward, if not humiliating. But Dr. Köhler is professional and kind. She does her best to try to keep me comfortable, asking questions, telling jokes, even making comments about how good I'm doing. I appreciate her efforts, but I'm still blushing by the time she starts packing up her stuff. She tells me I can get dressed again, but I don't want to put my clothes back on. I just want to climb into the shower and cry as the hot water sprays me down.

I shouldn't have had to do this alone.

Amory sent a doctor into our home—into our *bedroom*—to give me birth control and make sure he didn't knock me up. I feel like he used me. Had his fun and dealt with the consequences later.

I can't get pregnant alone. It shouldn't be my sole responsibility to make sure we don't bring a child into this world by accident. If he's worried about us having a kid too soon, then he should take proper precautions too. Leaving me to face this by myself was cowardly.

I had to tell Dr. Köhler how many times we had sex without protection. I had to tell her how 'active' our sex life is and how 'active' we plan to be. I had to answer for both of us when she asked if I ever wanted children and how soon.

He should have been here.

Maybe I didn't need him when I was spread eagle on the bed with Dr. Köhler staring between my legs. But I would have liked to have his support while I decided which birth control was best for my health. While I tried to figure out which one wouldn't have lasting side effects that could make it difficult for us to have children in the future. Maybe I would have liked his input on when we planned to start trying for children. Maybe I would've liked to hold his hand as I waited for Dr. Köhler to deliver the results of my pregnancy test.

My husband should have been here.

Dr. Köhler packs her things and gives me a hug. She leaves me with a copy of my test results and says she will call with a report on my bloodwork later. I crawl into bed in just my underwear, holding the test results in my hands. I stare at the words and run my finger over the paper, feeling the coolness of the dried ink.

I don't know what I will say to Amory when I see him again. I'm angry and I'm scared and I'm confused.

"Why did you leave me to deal with this alone?" I whisper as tears stream down my cheeks. "You should have been here."

Eleven

Conrad and Morgen raise their drinks as we toast one more time. It took less than 24 hours for my nosey family to find out about the consummation. Despite us being in the middle of a gang war, the boys wanted to celebrate. The entire marriage had been rushed, so we never got to have a bachelor party. When Conny pointed this out, I couldn't shoot down his offer to go out tonight.

Normally, we would have gotten on a private jet and flown to Berlin to drink real beer and enjoy German women, but that's out of the question right now, so we settled for closing down The Club and keeping all Conrad's booze and dancers for ourselves tonight. There's a gorgeous redhead on my lap and a beer in my hand, I'm a little more than tipsy, but I don't care. I haven't felt this good since before I got engaged. Uwe even let Wolfgang out of Stonehall to come have a drink with us. It took two security details and a decoy using men from the Stronghold, but he got here in one piece, and he hasn't stopped drinking since he arrived.

His drunkenness makes me a little nervous, but I swallow my worries as I gulp down the rest of my beer and then I laugh like an idiot at whatever joke the redhead just whispered into my ear. I have no idea what she said, but her breath on my neck tickles so I end up giggling and pulling her closer anyway.

"You have to tell us," Conrad says with a wolfish smile. "How was The Rose?"

I frown at him. I've got three beers and a shot of whiskey in me, but I'm not drunk enough to start handing out sexual details about my wife.

I smile back at my cousin, it's vulpine and teasing. "She was as good as Gisela."

Conrad eyes me before tipping his head and downing the rest of his drink. "Touché," he says in a drunken German drawl.

"How is Gisela?" Maximilian asks. At 6'6 and 250 pounds of muscle, he's one of the guards we have assigned to Wolfgang until everything blows over, but when he isn't babysitting my little brother, he's in charge of security at The Club. Max is quite familiar with all the women here and doesn't hide that fact from anyone. All the fifties crumpled on the dancer's platform were tossed up there by him.

His dark eyes gaze absently at the woman before he glances up at Conrad and sips his drink. "She doing okay with everything going on?"

Conrad nods. "She's been so worried about me dying every time I leave the house." He starts gyrating in his seat and gives us a lecherous grin. "Every night has been our *last goodbye*. I love it."

The guys all laugh. I laugh too—so does the hooker in my lap. I slap her butt as I chime in. "Been the same here. But that's all I'll say."

They laugh again and then raise a toast.

"The Hunter finally caught his prey," Maximilian says with a waggle of his eyebrows.

"You two make married life sound like so much fun," Morgen says with a sigh. He's engaged to a beautiful woman whose name I can't remember; there's been talk of him moving up the date, but he presented the ring less than three months ago so there's no pressure to rush into things. I'm sure he'll survive the war and make it to the altar, especially with all the new aid we've got from the Stronghold.

I glance around The Club, past the dancers on poles and into the crowd standing around our VIP booth. There's a mix of Italians, Germans, and members of the Stronghold all in one place. The last time this sort of gathering happened was at my wedding; back then, I'd been afraid all three gangs would end up tearing each other apart before we even said the vows. Now we're working together, sharing drinks, smiling like we're truly family. As far as King James is concerned, we *are* family.

I relax into my soft leather seat and nod at Douglass as I catch his eye in the crowd. He nods back and then resumes his conversation with someone from the Stronghold. I'd been worried he would feel uncomfortable working with people from his former gang, but they seem to have gotten over his Hunted status. We've all gotten over our differences lately.

Morgen's laughter draws me back to the guys, he's watching the stripper on the table take off her last piece of clothing with a stupid grin on his face. Conrad says something in German that I won't translate and then shakes up his beer and sprays her with it. Some of it hits Maximilian but he doesn't seem to mind, neither does Wolf as he lets out a howl and tosses a crumpled bill onto the platform.

I roll my eyes and distract myself with the rest of the room again. I can see Uwe chatting with Hans and Jameson; a man named Niccolò Romano is at their table, leaning in close as my father speaks. I don't know what's being discussed, but tonight I'm not going to care. This is my one night to be irresponsible and forget that I'm the underboss. Forget that we're at war. And forget that I'm married.

I glance down at the bombshell in my lap and sigh as she kisses me roughly. She's been cuddled up to me all night, dropping little hints about finding some privacy or sneaking away. It's tempting, but I've already let her give me a lap dance, this is as far as things will go. Some would say I've already gone too far, but I shove that thought away and deepen the kiss.

Guilt shoots into my gut and roars through me so violently, I gag into her mouth and jerk back from the exchange. She stares up at me, frantically wiping at her lips.

"Oh my gosh!" she says, quickly standing. "Are you okay? Are you sick?"

I glance up to find my cousins, my brother, Maximilian, and the naked dancer all staring down at me.

I stand. "I think I need some air."

My entire body feels slow and heavy as I push through the crowd of confused men. Their eyes follow me, wondering why on earth the underboss is ditching his own bachelor party. I must look like a scared virgin, scampering off as soon as things get heated with a beautiful woman. But I don't care what I look like right now; the only concern in my head is what the heck I'm going to say to my wife when I get home. If I'll even be able to look her in the eye.

I push through the doors of The Club with a sigh. The air outside is hot and sticky and offers no reprieve from the smoky sweat-soaked air indoors. I wipe at my forehead and roll my shoulders back as I take deep breaths.

How annoying... I've never had a problem with women before. Sure, I haven't been as active as I used to be since everything with Rosa, but that was by choice.

I *chose* to ignore other women during our engagement. I *chose* to ignore Eliana during our separation. But now, it's like I *can't* do anything.

"What is happening?" I mutter, running a hand through my hair.

A deep chuckle rolls over my shoulders and I turn to find King James standing behind me. He tilts his head down and presses his lips together when I nod a greeting. Silence seems to swallow any words I'd like to say. I stand there staring at him like an idiot.

"Sometimes," he says, sinking his hands into his pockets, "our body is smarter than our brain. When we're not strong enough to fight off temptation, our gut does it for us."

Literally, I think to myself, suddenly aware of the bitter taste of bile on my tongue. I can't believe I gagged into that woman's mouth.

"There's no shame in loyalty," Jameson says.

I blink at him, understanding exactly what he means.

I love my wife. I knew that before the party got started, but I wasn't strong enough to keep myself from making any mistakes. If I hadn't gagged on that hooker, I'd be tangled up with her in one of Conrad's back rooms right now.

I glance away to stare at the pavement. "I do love her."

"I can see that."

His words make me snap my vision up in surprise. Jameson chuckles deeply and then pulls out a cigar to light. I stare at the red glowing end as he puffs and then blows smoke into the air. "I've been in this game longer than you've been alive," he says calmly. "I know what it's like for men in high ranks. But it doesn't have to be that way for you." His fatherly eyes narrow on me, filled with a sternness that sends a shiver up my sweaty spine. "There is no shame in being loyal to your wife. To my granddaughter."

I shift uncomfortably. "I'm sorry—"

"Don't apologize to me," he says, blowing smoke on each word. "Apologize to Rosa."

"How?"

King James studies me a moment. "Just be honest. You made a mistake, Amory. I can tell how guilty you feel. Rosa will be able to as well. She's a good woman."

"Too good for me," I mutter.

To my surprise, he shakes his head. "She's exactly what you need."

We stand in silence until Jameson finishes his cigar. It's dark and chilly now, so I welcome the musky heat of The Club when the doors open before us. As soon as I'm inside, however, I get a prickling sense that something is wrong, and the balmy warmth of the smoke and body heat inside instantly becomes a fretful chill.

The Club is completely quiet. The lights are up, and the dancers are standing naked beside their poles, staring into the crowd of men gathered in the center of the room. Everyone has gathered around Vater, but their vision shoots toward me when I step back inside.

"What's going on?" I ask in German, then I remember there's a flood of Italians and Stronghold soldiers inside, too, so I switch back to English. "What's happened?"

Conrad steps forward and shouts, "Ladies, out! Anyone who isn't at least a General in your respective gang, out!"

The Club begins to empty. I watch as Maximilian and Morgen reluctantly head toward the exits, they take Wolfgang with them—though he is a General of the Hunting Grounds, since he's Volkov's target, his safety is far more important than his pride.

Douglass finds me and says he'll wait in the car before he leaves. Hans, Conrad, Klaus, and my Onkel Oberon all stay. Niccolò Romano (the Italian underboss), and a young, familiar-looking Italian man remain, along with King James and his twin sons, Trenton and Tyrese Willis.

Once I've made my way over to my father, he holds up his phone and says, "I've got an update from the security team in northern Brooklyn." He sighs. "They blew up two buildings."

No one speaks for a moment.

"What buildings?" Hans asks.

"A law firm and a hair salon."

I frown at the table, trying to put the pieces together.

"Who is 'they'?" Klaus asks.

Vater shoots him an annoyed look. "You know exactly who—"

"The Wolves," Oberon says with a dark expression.

I step forward. "Not the Wolves. The Morenos."

Vater stares at me. "What makes you think the Morenos played a part in this?"

"Richter Associates," I say. "They're in northern Brooklyn—the office my divorce lawyer was hired from."

Vater's eyes go wide.

"Emilio has obviously sided with the Wolves because he's insulted by the consummation." I nod as the puzzle comes together. "It's the middle of the night. The Morenos and the Volkovs could have blown up any building they wanted, any time they wanted. But they chose an empty office—"

"And a salon my wife goes to!" Conrad shouts from beside Onkel Oberon. His father glares at him for speaking out of term and rebukes him in German.

Conrad blows air through his flared nostrils. "Sorry, Underboss."

I nod. "This event is a wakeup call to what the Morenos

115

and the Wolves are capable of. They're deeper into our territory than we thought."

"That office could have easily been The Club," Vater says slowly.

"Or a warehouse," Hans adds.

"But it wasn't," I say strongly. "It was just two empty buildings. They were only trying to send a message—"

"Are you saying there won't be any retaliation?" Conrad asks.

I shake my head. "There will be a response. But it must be sent swiftly and quietly. We cannot rush into Staten Island or Queens. We must plan first."

"Plan to kill them all," Conrad hisses.

"Plan to come back alive," I hiss back. "Think of Gisela, Conny."

Her name immediately calms him, he even staggers back a step and blinks wildly like he's just come to his senses. I understand his swirl of emotions. It's a scary thought to know just how organized the Volkovs and the Morenos are. They could have blown up that salon during the day, when there were people inside. The fact that it was a salon to begin with tells us they're willing to kill civilians. The fact that they *didn't* tells us we're at their mercy.

Right now, they are in control. We're scrambling for a response while they sit back and watch. It's an infuriating fact that summons a desire for vengeance deep inside. But beneath that there is also a desire to protect the wives and civilians who survived. To keep them safe from future attacks.

Conrad stares at the ground as I speak. "Think of all of our wives," I say, an image of Rosa blooming in my head. I turn to Niccolò and the young Italian beside him, they're here in Giovanni's place since he's still locked up in his penthouse, paranoid and sweating. "Don Gio promised shelter for our women and children."

Niccolò nods. "We have more than enough space to welcome women of the Hunting Grounds and the Stronghold. Right, Aldo?"

The young Italian beside him nods and I suddenly recognize him. It's the skinny pretty boy I saw dancing with Rosa at her best friend's wedding. I instantly hate him but swallow my anger as I watch him smile and bob his head like a servant.

"That's correct, Father," he says in a silky Italian accent. It's the same accent Rosa has, except it's low and full of baritone. Whenever Rosa speaks these days, I have a hard time keeping my clothes on. But this guy's voice gives me an instant headache.

I blink away the pain swelling in my forehead as I listen to him lay out details of where our families will be sheltered and how often they'll be shuffled around to keep the Wolves from tracking them down. I'm only half listening. I can't stop thinking up plans to accidentally get Aldo killed. He had his hands on my woman. A married woman. And she had been smiling up at him like she'd enjoyed it.

The memory brings a burning anger to my gut that threatens to double me over with another gag. *Where was* her *loyalty?* I think, casting a bitter glance at Jameson. Here I am, guilty over a little lap dance, but Rosa had been melting in another man's arms mere days ago. And I'd witnessed it myself.

I don't have time for these childish emotions. I shove away my anger and grunt loudly enough to earn a quick look from my father. He raises an eyebrow at me but continues his conversation with Hans and Niccolò without missing a beat.

"When can we begin moving the women?" he asks.

"Immediately," Conrad says. "I want Gisela out of Brooklyn as quickly as possible."

I almost agree with him. I want Rosa out of harm's way, too. But I know Rosa. She's still shy and uncertain about some things, but parts of her have changed. She isn't afraid of fighting—she wants to stand side by side with me, even in a bloody war. She won't want to be sent away to hide with the other hens. And it doesn't help that I promised to include her in things now.

I take a deep breath. There are already a hundred secrets between us—whatever happened between her and Aldo, everything that happened with me tonight. I don't want to add another secret to the list. I want to talk to her about this before I make any decisions.

My deep exhale catches Vater's attention again. This time, he doesn't just quirk his eyebrow, he stops the conversation and nods at me to speak. "What is it, Amory?"

"I'm not ready to send our wives away."

He frowns. "Why not?"

"Because he's having too much *fun*," Conrad spits. He

glares at me from his stance beside his father, ignoring the angry German hissing coming from Oberon.

"I am the underboss here," I say slowly. There's a warning in my voice, but Conrad doesn't hear it.

"I don't care." He takes a step forward, teeth bared in anger. "I'm not putting my wife in danger because you aren't done screwing yours."

My hand is around his throat before he's even realized I've moved. I shove him backwards until he stumbles into the wall, choking and gagging on his own spit.

"Say that again," I tell him, pressing my thumb against his windpipe.

He sputters incoherently, eyes going wild as he realizes he truly cannot breathe—and I truly do not care. I hold him there, pinned against the wall, until his cheeks turn blue, and his eyes begin to roll to the back of his head. There is slobber sliding out the corners of his mouth, it's the only reason I let him go—I don't want his drool to touch me.

He crumples to his knees with a gasp, clutching at his throat and blinking up at me. "I'm sorry, Underboss," he wheezes.

I look down at him. "Don't ever speak to me that way again."

"I'm sorry," he repeats.

Oberon quickly comes to his aid when I step away and straighten my tie. Vater and Niccolò both give me approving nods, Jameson and Hans smirk like they're trying not to laugh. Klaus, Tyrese, Trenton, and Aldo stare with wide eyes.

Good.

I'm glad Aldo got to see me fly off. I hope it lets him know he'll be in worse condition if he ever tries to touch Rosa again. The thought of her in his arms makes me want to strangle him where he stands, but I swallow my rage and say in a dangerously calm voice, "How soon will the shelters be ready for our families?"

Niccolò answers quickly. "The shelters are already available. But you won't want to move everyone at the same time—it will draw too much attention."

I nod. "Move the lower ranking families first, just to throw them off."

Vater agrees. "The rest will follow within the week."

I turn back to Conrad; he's standing now, but his tie is loose, and his eyes are bloodshot. "You can move Gisela tomorrow morning if you want. Or you can wait like the rest of us. It's up to you."

He nods back but says nothing. I'm not surprised.

"Gentlemen, if that's all?"

Jameson pulls out another cigar. "I'll make some arrangements to help with escorting the families."

Niccolò offers him a light and says, "Our doors will be open and waiting. Just call me when you're ready to move."

"Let's end this here." My voice leaves no room for argument.

Vater nods. "Go home. Make love to your wives. And get ready for tomorrow."

Twelve

I'm in a sour mood when I get home. Two of my buildings have been blown up by a bunch of Spaniards and Russians, I've got to tell my wife that I made out with a stripper, and once her anger subsides, I have to help her pack her bags because she's about to be shipped off to a safehouse with all the other women and children.

I have no idea how I'm supposed to broach this subject. I've spent my entire adult life going from one woman to the next. I'm inexperienced when it comes to committed relationships, but I'm not stupid. I know what I did was wrong. I know Rosa will not be happy about what went down at The Club. But what makes me feel even worse about it is that I know she won't be angry—she'll be *hurt*.

Yelling, I can deal with. Tantrums, throwing things, even the huffy little fits she has when she catches an attitude with me. I find those quite adorable. But sadness—*tears*? I groan as I think of Rosa staring up at me with her freakishly big eyes, wide open and full of moisture. I love the way her cheeks and nose turn pink when she's upset, I love the way the wetness gathers on her long eyelashes. When she's had a good cry, her lips get puffy and she tends to chew them, making them look soft and plump.

She is a beautifully heartbreaking sight when she's crying, and it's at those very moments that I want her the most. But comforting my wife because she's sad over some crap with her girlfriends is one thing. Being the *reason* for those tears and puffy lips is another thing entirely.

She's going to cry forever, I tell myself with a sigh.

A thousand apologies run through my head as I make my way through the house to our bedroom. It's just after midnight; part of me desperately hopes Rosa has fallen asleep so I'll have the night to think this over. But my hopes wither as I round the corner and catch the faint glow of light spilling from beneath our bedroom door.

Great.

I gingerly open the large door and find my wife sitting at the vanity in the corner, taking bobby pins out of her hair. She freezes when she spies me in the doorway; there is no joy or happiness on her face at all.

I offer a very pathetic smile and close the door behind me. "Sorry I'm home late."

She stands. "Where have you been all day?"

"The boys wanted to have a late bachelor party."

Rosa jerks back like she's been slapped. "You've been out getting drunk while I've been home all day?"

I want to sigh, but I feel like that would make things worse.

Instead, I close the gap between us and disarm her with a hug. She tenses in my arms and when I release her, I notice some of the anger has washed away, replaced by worry.

"What's going on?" she asks softly.

"I did something terrible at the bachelor party."

Silence storms around us.

"Was there alcohol?" she asks slowly.

"Yes."

"Women?"

I pause long enough for her to squirm and push away from me. When I look down into her eyes, I expect to see tears, but there's a hard frown on her face instead. She lifts one of her hands and I notice a crumpled slip of paper clutched in her grasp. Before I can wonder what the paper is, she throws it in my face.

"I was here shedding tears over this while you were out hooking up with strippers!" she yells.

The paper smacks me right on the nose and then tumbles down my chest to the floor. I stare down at it in a dumbfounded haze. Rosa's yelling about how she had to spread her legs for a doctor while I spread mine for some unwholesome woman—exact quote.

I could correct her on how sex actually works, but I'm honestly more interested in the balled-up paper on the floor, so I keep staring at it while she whines about taking a piss test and picking out birth control. I'm vaguely aware of Rosa telling me she cried about the whole thing, but I'm not sure how picking out birth control makes anyone cry, so I'm confused.

And also not listening.

I stoop to get the paper, which feels like it takes longer than it should. Either I'm taller than I think, or drunker than I realize. The room sways as I reach for it and then tilts when I stand upright again. I unfold the paper and recognize it's the results of her pregnancy test.

My breath hitches.

Rosa *finally* goes silent.

The test is negative.

"I don't get it." I frown.

Rosa snatches the paper and shouts, "Of course you don't! You don't understand what it means to be a husband at all!"

Anger shoots through me. "You're kidding, right? I came home to lay out a plan to protect you and the other high-ranking women of the Hunting Grounds, and you say I don't know what it means to be a husband?" I step closer to her. "I could pack you up and send you off without a word or explanation. But here I am, trying to be a good husband and talk to you about it first."

"You want to talk about the hooker you slept with tonight instead?" She crosses her arms.

"I didn't sleep with anyone!" I shout at her. It's getting harder to control my temper, so I turn away and curse in German, just to put some distance between us. If I was anything like my father or brother, Rosa would be unconscious by now, knocked out by the hand I'm running through my hair.

I feel her come closer as she says behind me. "You didn't sleep with anyone?"

"No," I grunt. "But it's nice to know you jumped to conclusions so easily."

"It's not like I don't have reason to."

"There you go, bringing up the past again." I turn around and glare down at her. "But I'm glad you did, because we never addressed *your* past, princess."

Her eyebrows go up as her anger shifts to confusion.

I have one word for her. "Aldo."

Rosa laughs. "You think there was something between me and Aldo?"

"You two seemed pretty comfy at Alicia's wedding."

"*Olivia*," she snaps.

"Whatever," I snap back.

"There is nothing with Aldo. There never has been. I can't believe you would even bring that up."

"Did you forget the fact that it took you three days to meet me?" When she doesn't speak, I smirk at her. "Guess he kept you busy after the wedding."

"To even suggest I was late because I was with another man," she shakes her head, "you're despicable."

"Did you sleep with him?"

Rosa's mouth drops open. "You are the only man I've ever been with. You know that for a fact."

I laugh and then give her a dark grin. "Baby, you bled like a virgin, but you didn't moan like one."

Spit flies out of my mouth as my head whips to the side. My entire body jerks and I lose my footing, stumbling to the right. It takes me a stunned moment to realize I've been slapped. But when I regain my bearings and look at my wife, my heart stops.

Rosa's hands are balled into fists, her jaw is clenched shut tightly, and her eyes are filled with mist. *There they are*, I breathe, watching as the tears I've expected all night finally spill over and rush down her cheeks.

She sucks in a breath. "The next thing you say to me had better be an apology. Until then, we're done speaking." She turns to leave.

"An apology?" I repeat, coming to my senses. I march right behind her, following her to the bedroom door. "You think I owe you an apolo—"

The door slams in my face. It's so abrupt, I actually walk into it and whack my forehead.

My anger is volcanic.

I kick the door down. Rosa screams because she's only a few feet away in the hallway; her eyes are wide and fretful; her mouth is parted in shock. When she sees the monstrous glare on my face, she turns to run.

I chase her down.

We end up on the floor with her screaming like a mad woman. Her hands fly up and she slaps me good in my face. I grunt, using my weight to overpower her. I grab both her small wrists in my one hand and pin them above her head, then I wedge my knee between her legs to stop her from kicking. She gasps at the sudden intrusion, and everything stops. The wild anger is still there in her eyes, her hair is a mane of tight coils that makes her look somewhat crazed, her lips are puffy and

126

slightly parted. I'm so angry I could scream, but as I stare down at her, panting, I lose my train of thought.

The next moment, I lean down and kiss her. It's sloppy and wild and uncontrollable. There are no thoughts in my head except the deep-seated urge to claim her as mine. I feel insane as I kiss her. I feel like a pervert, getting off on this show of dominance. But as Rosa moans into my mouth, I realize she's just as demented as I am.

She frees one of her hands to tear at my clothes and I chuckle as I watch her pop the buttons off my shirt.

We are made for each other.

If I get off on control, then she loses herself in submission. She can fight me all she wants—argue, compromise, make up all these new rules about being equals in this marriage. I'm here for it. Honestly.

But I know my wife.

This is what she wants.

This dominance is what she desires.

And she hates herself for it.

Her kiss burns. It's almost painful. Gasping, clawing, like we're two animals fighting for control of ourselves and each other. There is a monster growing between us, and neither of us wants to acknowledge it. We just keep fighting—going through this push and pull for dominance of each other. This is how we settle our fights. This is how we love. It was an argument that ended with Rosa in my bed the first time. I'm not surprised this is happening now.

But what will happen once this is over? When our passion

burns out and the flame is extinguished?

I pull back and stare down at my wife. To my pleasure, she looks annoyed by the sudden interruption, but I need to say this. I need to make sure she understands.

"I—I'm not doing this out of anger. I don't want you to think of rough sex as punishment."

She gives me a wide-eyed look. "We're going to have rough sex?"

I was literally about to flip her over and spank her until she screamed in ecstasy. But Rosa's got this frightened looked on her face now, I feel like if I say that she'll just squeal and run away. Then I'd have to chase her down again—which I don't want to do while I'm butt naked.

Instead, I laugh like she's silly and say, "No, babe. Of course not."

She raises an eyebrow. Rosa knows me better than I thought.

"I just wanted to try something new," I confess.

She reaches up and touches my cheek. "Okay."

That's all the permission I need. But I don't want to scare her. I don't want Rosa's first experience like this to leave her with scars or reservations. Even though she's given me permission, I can tell she's still nervous. Honestly, so am I. Because I taught Rosa how to have sex, but she taught me how to make love.

Tonight, I want to show her I can do both.

I take her slowly at first, so she'll know what it means to be loved. Then I take her again, so she'll know what it means to

128

be mine.

Thirteen

I sit up in bed and hold the covers to my chest. Amory is lying beside me, snoring softly. His eyes are closed, but there's a scowl on his face—even in his sleep, he's stressed out.

It's moments like this that give me the most peace. When I can see my husband for who he really is. My eyes travel the lines of his structured face, his perfect jaw and shapely lips, down to his neck and shoulders, where his tattoos begin. I didn't realize the dark, winding patterns of his black markings covered up dozens of scars. Up close, I can see the wounds of his past, the nightmares he has never mentioned to me.

There is a bullseye on his chest, right over his heart. It's a fitting place to put the symbol of his gang. Amory loves being a Hunter of New York. He loves the mafia. I wonder if his love for me is just as strong.

I know I have put him through more drama than he wants. I know this marriage has been a challenge for him as much as it has been for me. I know I'm part of the reason he's scowling in his sleep. But each day he wakes up and smiles at me. Each day, we start over and promise to try again. To give this relationship another shot.

Today is no different.

Amory groans lightly as he shifts beneath the covers and rolls onto his side. His eyes flutter as he blinks away the sleep and looks up at me. He smiles charmingly, and I can't help but smile back.

"Good morning," he says. His voice is so low and lazy, the words come out as a dangerous purr.

I fight the instinctive urge to shy away. "Good morning," I whisper back.

He reaches up and strokes my cheek. "Last night was amazing."

It was. In ways I can't even explain. But we can't ignore the way the night began.

I take a slow breath and lay on my side, so we're facing each other. "We need to talk."

He nods slowly, grey eyes focused entirely on me.

"I'm sorry about last night."

His eyes widen. "*You're* sorry?"

"I slapped you last night. Twice."

He laughs, blasting me with his morning breath. My eyes begin to water.

"I deserved the first slap," he says honestly. "And the second one was kinky, so we're good."

I shift uncomfortably. "It still wasn't okay."

"I'm telling you it was. I'm not hurt or offended." He takes my hand, the one I'd hit him with, and kisses it. "I trust you not to do it again."

"I won't," I whisper.

"I'm sorry for the things I said. It was stupid of me to bring up Aldo."

"He's like my brother, Amy," I explain. "I love him, but only in a familial way."

Amory's eyes fill with mischief. "He can be your brother, as long as you know who's your daddy."

I stare at him with a deadpan expression until he shifts uncomfortably and sighs. "I know there was nothing between you two. I was just drunk and jealous and guilty."

"You need to go lighter on the whiskey," I say gently. It's something I've been meaning to talk to him about since we got back together, but there's been no time until now. Amory isn't a Christian—I don't even know if he believes in God—but he's always been respectful of my beliefs, and he's never done anything outside the boundaries of my faith. I don't expect him to quit drinking entirely, but I know if I ask, he'll at least cut back.

Amory studies me a moment, like he isn't sure how to respond to my suggestion. Then his sharp eyes narrow and he looks away, focused on the blankets. "I know. I've been thinking the same thing."

"Amy," I reach up and touch his cheek, "it isn't just for my faith. It's not healthy to use alcohol as a stress reliever."

He sits up, pulling away from my grasp. "I know, Rosa. Things are more complicated and dangerous than they've ever been right now." He glances at me with an accusatory look on his face. The expression startles me, but I don't say anything. I steel myself for the slight I know is coming. "Not everyone can just mutter prayers and magically feel better," he says sharply.

The comment stings, but I don't let it fester. I sit in silence, staring at my husband as he battles his inner demons. We've had fights about my faith before, especially when we were first married. I knew this battle would be long and grueling, but I've been preparing for it since Father Serrano told me of God's plans. I'm not giving up on Amory's salvation. No matter how much he fights against it.

"Do you ever think about God?" I ask slowly.

He shrugs one muscular shoulder. "Sometimes."

"Do you ever pray to Him?"

"I don't know how to pray."

"I can teach you. I can show you how to mutter prayers and magically feel better."

He glances back at me with a grin tugging at his lips. "I shouldn't have said that."

"I'm glad you're honest with me." I touch his shoulder. "I'm glad you were honest last night."

I feel his body stiffen beneath my hand. "Nothing else happened except a kiss," he says softly. "And a lap dance."

He hadn't mentioned the lap dance last night, but I exhale my anger and look at him dead on. "I forgive you."

He nods.

"But not because of the sex last night. I forgive you because I'm your wife—a Christian wife—and I can't expect God to forgive me if I don't forgive you."

Amory's face is unreadable. "I'm sorry I wasn't there with you when the doctor came. I knew I should have been. But I was honestly afraid of finding out whether you were pregnant or not."

His confession shocks me—and reminds me to reach into the bedside table and take my pill for the day. Amy watches me gulp down some water from the bottle I keep on the table, then he swallows nervously. "Why did you cry?"

"Because the test was negative. And I was happy." I stare down at my hands, clutching our blankets. "I was happy to know that we wouldn't be bringing a child into this world. I was happy that I was still free of the responsibilities and the burdens of parenthood." My eyes begin to water with guilty tears. "Children are supposed to be a blessing. But I was so happy to find out that I wasn't going to have one."

Amory's hand covers my own. "It's okay to not want children, Rosa."

"I'm a Christian, I'm supposed to want children."

He pauses. "I'm not an expert on Christianity, but I'm pretty sure the Bible never said you had to desire kids."

"It tells us to be fruitful and multiply."

"And what part of that scripture included a command to be happy about it?"

I blink at him, realizing he's right. The truth leaves me in a stunned silence. I have no idea what to say to that—but I suddenly feel the need to explain myself.

"One day I do want children. I'm just not ready yet."

"And there's nothing wrong with that," he assures me.

"When we're both ready, we'll stop using contraceptives and have a kid."

I shake my head. "We'll have an heir."

Amory grins and leans forward, but I back away, leaning into my pillows. "I still want to talk."

He frowns slightly. "What else?"

"I love you. I love being intimate with you. But we cannot use sex to solve our problems. Every time we get into an argument, it ends with us tangled up in bed."

He smirks. It's teasing and daring and sets my heart racing, but I ignore the goosebumps pebbling my flesh and try to stay focused on the conversation. "I want us to be able to talk about things with our clothes on."

Amory leans back with that dangerous grin on his face. He folds his hands behind his head as he says, "We don't have any clothes on now."

"You know what I mean."

He winks at me, but when I don't blush and shy away, he realizes I'm serious and blows out an annoyed sigh. It doesn't sound like he's irritated with me, the contemplative look on his face seems like his annoyance is directed at himself. Though I'm not sure why.

His grey eyes focus on my face. "I'm sorry," he says evenly. "I've never been married. I've never even been in a relationship before. This is just as new for me as it is for you." His grin turns sheepish. "When I promised I wouldn't be a cruel husband, I didn't realize I had no clue how to be a *good* one."

I relax beside him. "I'm sorry too. I thought that since I'm

Christian, that automatically made me a good wife. I never thought there would be things I'd need to learn and work out for myself." I laugh. "I'm sorry you married the Withered Rose."

"You aren't withered," he tells me.

I believe him. "Not anymore. Adella called me a vine of poison ivy."

He wrinkles his nose like he wants to laugh. "You aren't poison ivy. You're still a rose—still *my* rose—you've just grown thorns."

"Maybe that's what this part of our story is about," I say quietly.

Amory looks at me, silently asking for an explanation.

"Clipping thorns."

He nods slowly.

"This is us learning how to be a married couple. Learning how to love each other in a way that pleases God and us." My shoulders sag. "I haven't always done my best. I haven't been a very good wife or a very good Christian."

Amory reaches up and tugs one of my thick curls. "You are a good wife. And a good Christian. You're a good wife *because* you're a good Christian."

Silence unfolds for a long moment. Both of us stare at nothing as we think about what to say and how to say it. This is one of the few times we've been able to have a serious conversation that hasn't ended with us in bed or screaming at each other. Not yet at least.

Amory takes a breath. "It's hard to be a mafia wife. I can't imagine the inner turmoil you face as a Christian woman in this situation."

I shrug one shoulder. "God prepared me for this. He continuously renews my strength each day."

"How can I make it easier for you?" he asks genuinely.

This is my chance. This is my opportunity to sow the seeds of faith in hopes that it will lead to Amory's salvation. But I don't want to throw this at him. Or else the seeds will never take root. I learned that the hard way when we first got engaged. Just the mention of my faith caused an explosive argument between us where he declared he wasn't a Christian man and our marriage wouldn't be Christian, either.

Since then, I've done my best to follow God's prompting and use the guidance of the Holy Spirit when it comes to feeding Amory the Word. Before we separated, he'd started reading the Bible on his own, and he'd even asked questions to Father Serrano. We'd prayed together and had come to an amicable arrangement around my faith. Amory is still a mafioso, but he's not the cold man he was when we first got engaged. He has changed in small, progressive ways, and I know it's the result of my prayers and pleadings with God.

I look at him seriously and hold out my hands for him to take. "Let me show you how to pray."

He doesn't move for a moment.

"I want to share something with you that has meaning," I tell him. "We share our bed, and we share our hearts. But sex doesn't last forever, and our hearts will face challenges in this life. But when our love is rooted in Christ, it will be strong

137

enough to overcome those challenges."

He watches me thoughtfully, still unmoving.

I swallow, determined not to lose this fight. "Amory, I want us to have a spiritual connection as well as a physical and emotional one. I want our love to transcend time and space. I want it to carry into the next life. That is a connection that can only be established through God. What we have right now is amazing. But it isn't truly love."

"How can you say that?" he asks defensively.

I don't feel offended by the sudden frown on his face. Amory isn't Christian, I don't expect him to view or understand love and marriage the way I do. The Bible says the wisdom of God is foolishness to the world. In a way, Amory *can't* understand how I feel until he gets saved because it is the Spirit within that brings this understanding.

Still, I want him to hear me out. I want to sow the seeds of faith now, so they can take root in preparation for his coming salvation. "Love comes from God, Amy," I say in a gentle voice. "Only when we love God as one, can we truly love each other."

He shifts like he's thinking to himself, truly considering the things I've told him. I can only hope that I'm getting through to him.

Amory looks back up at me, then drops his gaze to my still outstretched hands. "Okay," he says in a murmur. "Teach me how to pray."

He takes my hands and we both close our eyes. "Prayer is simply talking to God. Speak to Him the same way you would speak to me. Just say whatever's on your mind, and when you're finished, always close in Jesus' Name."

He squeezes my hands. "All right."

"I'll say a prayer this time, so just listen to me and then when you're ready, you can say one of your own."

When he squeezes my hands again, I take a breath and begin.

"Dear Heavenly Father, forgive us for our sins, Lord. Thank You for giving me the chance to witness to someone I love. Thank You for this peaceful morning I've had with my husband, please give us plenty more just like this one. Bless us and protect us today. Give us the strength to honor You in everything we do. In Jesus' Name I pray, amen."

Amory waits in silence for a long time—so long, I'm not sure he's going to say anything. But then I hear him inhale deeply and his deep voice fills the room as he starts to pray. "God … Um … Please protect Rosa today. Protect her every day. In Jesus' Name, amen."

When I open my eyes, I realize he's staring at me. I don't know how long he's been watching me, but the look on his face is totally unreadable and instantly makes me nervous.

"You did great," I whisper.

He drops my hands and nods. "Thank you for teaching me."

"You prayed for my protection."

He nods again. "I don't know much about what it means to be a Christian. I haven't been to church since I was in high school. But I think I believe in God." He looks at me directly.

"I believe in the God you serve. And I believe He is the only One who can truly protect you."

"Protect me from the war," I say.

Amory sighs and shifts in the bed so we're facing each other. "The Morenos and the Volkovs have teamed up. They blew up two buildings in Brooklyn last night."

My heart begins to race. I'd been kept out of the fray in the Bronx, holed up in my grandfather's mansion. He didn't even allow us to watch the news—the less we knew, the better. But now, as Amory's wife, I'm in the thick of things. I won't be able to escape the violence or the news or maybe even the bullets themselves. I could die in this war. Amory could die in this war.

He's right. Only God can protect us now.

"It's time for the Hunters to retaliate," Amy says darkly. The look in his eyes is violent and angry. I try not to shift away from him as he speaks, I don't want him to know how afraid I am. How afraid I feel of him. I know he'll never hurt me, but the thought of Amory hurting other people makes my palms sweat.

I had forgotten that he's the underboss. I had forgotten that he didn't rise to that position through prayer and fasting. He killed and maimed and tortured his way to the top. I'm not sure what he's willing to do to stay there, especially at a time like this.

His salvation is more important than ever. If he goes around murdering Wolves and Spaniards in this war, he could be changed forever. Hardened by the violence and darkness, beyond the reach of my prayers.

I internally shake my head. I won't give up on believing in God to save my husband. No matter how dark things get. But I can do my best in trying to keep Amory from drifting too far.

I take his large hands in my own. "You don't have to fight them. We can try to compromise with them."

He presses his lips into a hard line. "They blew up a salon, Rosa. They did it at night while it was empty, but the message was clear. No one is safe."

Not even the wives and children.

I gulp as I realize the weight of his words. The mafia operates on violence and intimidation. It's what the organization is built on. But there is a code of honor in this twisted business, if you can believe it. Part of that code is to leave women, children, and civilians out of the fight. That means you don't blow up hair salons where innocent people frequently go.

Last night, the Volkovs and the Morenos dishonored the code. They made it clear they don't plan to play by the rules. That means anything can happen. Nobody is safe.

I blink at my husband, unable to hide my fear now. The angry look in his eyes should calm me, but it only sets me further on edge. Amory has every intention to retaliate. He won't let the salon incident go unpunished. He's going to step into this war.

My heart aches at that thought. I could lose him tomorrow if things go wrong. Our house could blow up right now, if the Volkovs were bold enough to do it. There's no way to tell how much time we have left together.

Amory pats my hands, and I realize I'm clutching him for dear life. "I'm sorry," I mumble, pulling away.

He reaches up and cups my face with both his hands. "I'm going to keep you safe, Rosa. No matter what."

"How?"

"Vater wants to send our families to safehouses in Manhattan. Giovanni offered shelter to us and the Stronghold."

I shake my head. "Do you really think Manhattan is safe?"

"I think it's safer than Brooklyn."

I can't argue against that, but I don't want to go away. I don't want to be apart from him.

Amory sees this in my eyes and leans in to kiss me sweetly. "I'll try to see you when I can. If I can."

"How long will it be like this?"

He leans back to look me in the eye. I do everything I can to hold my tears in. "I don't know. A few days. A few weeks."

"A few months," I say when his voice goes quiet.

He nods solemnly. "Until the war is over and it's safe."

I don't want this at all, but I know staying will only make me a target and a burden. So I close my eyes and say in a shaky voice, "Okay. I'll go to the safehouse."

I hear Amory gasp and I open my eyes to find him staring at me in shock. "I thought you would fight me on this."

"I asked you to include me in decisions. But that doesn't mean we have to fight about every decision we make."

He laughs which lightens the air a little. I suddenly feel like

I can breathe with the ache easing away at the sound of Amory's sweet chuckles. "I'm glad we're not fighting," he says.

I lean into his hands still cupping my face. "So am I."

"You'll have to start packing right away."

I nod since I can't find any words to speak right now.

Amory kisses me deeply. "It'll be okay," he says when he pulls back for air. "It'll be okay."

He keeps repeating that to me, like it's a spell he's trying to cast. I'm not sure if I believe him or not, but I certainly want to. I don't want this to be the last time we kiss, the last time he lays me on the pillows, the last time we make love.

I give him everything I can as he surrenders to our passion. My name is a whisper on his lips, my desire is a gasp in his mouth. He is the man of my dreams and I hope he can feel it in the flames I fan between us.

When he rolls off of me, chest heaving, I turn my head to stare at the side of his face. He's tired and spent, eyes closed as he pants. But I'm not done. I climb on top of him, and his eyes fly open. There's a question on his face, but I don't let him ask it. I lean down and cover his mouth with my own, tears spilling down my cheeks as I run my hands over his chest.

He breaks away. "Rosa?"

I kiss him harder

He breaks away again. "Rosa…?"

"Please," I say, finding his mouth once more. I don't get to say the rest because he finally gives in. Kissing me with more passion than the first time. Working through his exhaustion, putting my needs over his aching limbs and tense muscles.

He lies motionless as I kiss his cheeks and his jaw and his neck. "Rosa," he sighs.

For the first time, I pull away and stare at him, wondering if this is okay—if he'll let me bury my sorrows in lust. He reaches up to stroke my cheek and nods. It's a small act, a silent gesture granting me his permission.

"You need this," he murmurs.

I do. I can't explain why, but the ache of his coming absence leaves me short of breath. We only just got back together and now we'll be separated indefinitely. It's almost more than I can bear.

Without notice, I crumple into a heap of tears and choking cries. Amory lies still, staring at the ceiling as he pets the back of my head, tangling his fingers into my curls. There is nothing I can do. With our lust forgotten, all that's left is pain. I give in to it fully, heaving terrible sobs into Amory's chest as he quietly comforts me.

"I'm so sorry," he whispers.

I am too.

Fourteen

There are twenty men in our group. That feels like way too many for a covert operation, so I've split everyone into groups of five. In ten minutes, we're going to drive to Staten Island to infiltrate the Wolves' Den. The goal is to send a message—one that'll be louder than the explosion of the salon and the law firm. We aren't barbaric like our enemies, we won't try to harm civilians, but I told my men not to hold back. This is the sort of war the Volkovs want, they're about to reap what they've sown.

First, we need to get into the Island.

The Wolves control the ferries all by themselves, and with the help of the Morenos, they've been monitoring the bridge more closely than I'm comfortable with. Still, if things go wrong, I'd rather have the option to turn around and speed off in my car than try to get away in a steamboat.

We decide to chance the bridge.

I went over the plan with Hans and Trenton a hundred times. We're supposed to break into groups and travel as a caravan of multiple decoys. Decoy One will draw attention of the guards along the bridge; we're hoping they look suspicious enough to get pulled over and have their vehicle searched. Once that happens, Decoy Two will speed past to create an obvious scene—but evident or not, Moreno's men will have to take them seriously and try to stop them. This will give Decoy One the time to steal away or open fire, we've left the choice up to them.

Decoy Three and Four will only jump in if necessary. If the first two teams do their part, my teams will be free to get into the Island and plant the bombs we've packed. We plan to destroy three brothels and two warehouses. They're all in the same vicinity, so it won't be too difficult to accomplish.

With a sector of the Island in flames, we should be able to slip away in the chaos. Just in case things go totally south, we have men from the Stronghold with powerboats ready to sneak past the searchlights on the waters. I don't want to touch the water, but if the bridge is too dangerous for us to cross back over, then we won't have a choice.

It isn't the greatest plan in the world—shaky at best—but it's all we could come up with in the three days since the salon went up in flames. My men have been itching for a fight, desperate to respond to the disrespect. Now is our chance.

I glance out at the crowd of Hunters, Gardeners, and men of the Stronghold before me. It's ten in the evening and we're gathered in one of the empty warehouses my family uses for torture. King James is beside me, a reassuring partner during this dark hour. He isn't going with us on the mission, but he's provided men and weapons and has promised to have the emergency motorboats ready if needed. Uwe decided to stay back as well, he isn't even here in the garage. We got a call about suspicious activity near the west side of Brooklyn; he's tightening security in that area while we carry out this mission.

As my eyes scan the crowd, I catch glimpses of familiar faces; Douglass, who looks stern and ready for a fight, Aldo is back—I hope he dies—and both Conrad and Morgen have come out to play. These are men I trust. Men I know will get the job done.

A very confident smile stretches over my face, and I take a breath before I give my best attempt at a speech. This is the first gang war I've ever taken part in. If Vater were any younger, he'd be up here giving a pep talk instead, but I'm the underboss. I've taken the time to prove myself in almost every area of the German mafia. I have secured our finances, I have made deals with multiple rival gangs, my marriage has united three great mafias of the City—I even spent eighteen months serving in Germany where I went under and secured three sectors of territory for our Motherland gangs. But I've never been in a war. Our men have no idea what I'm capable of on the battlegrounds, or if I'm capable at all.

I've had the luxury of spending most of my adult life in the spotlight of New York, after the defunding that got rid of most of the police force. I was twenty-one years old at the time, still wet behind the ears and still more interested in hitting clubs and picking up women with Conrad than taking my job seriously. Back then, we were idiots—not much wiser than

Wolfgang today. There were days we'd both show up to our jobs high and half-drunk, wiping the Moreno's cocaine from our noses as we pretended to know what the heck was going on.

After the defunding, I didn't have to operate in secret. I didn't have to worry about getting caught and arrested. I've spent a decade helping my father run this gang, but I'm not naïve enough to think it was anything like the way he had to operate when he was in his prime.

This is my first time facing a serious challenge—and being nervous about it.

All eyes are on me. And even though he isn't here in person, I know Vater is watching. I can feel his burning gaze through the watchful eyes of Hans as he stands at the front of the crowd, his arms crossed over his broad chest, his pinched mouth frowning. I can hear his warning whispering into my mind as I lick my lips and swallow.

"They made us look like fools," he'd said before I'd left. "Fix this, Amory. And don't let me regret putting you in charge."

I feel a painful ache in my back as the scars on my flesh begin to throb. It's a sinful reminder of what my father is capable of and what he's willing to do to keep the Jäger name from falling. I am not off limits. I am not exempt when it comes to Uwe handing out punishment. I learned that the hard way.

I gingerly roll my shoulders back, hoping no one sees me trying to stretch out my back as I stand there like an idiot and

148

stare at the waiting men. When I clear my throat, the sound echoes around the warehouse, like a hundred different men just cleared their throats, too.

"I don't have to explain what tonight means."

Conrad whistles, making the other men grumble their agreement.

"They think we're at their mercy. They think we're playing *their* game."

The grumbles grow louder, turning into angry hisses.

"Tonight, we will show them they've made a mistake." I raise my hand as the men begin to cheer, immediately silencing them. "Those of you from the Garden, members of the Stronghold ... I want to thank you for joining us here on the Hunting Grounds." More grumbles instead of hisses, they actually sound somewhat cheery now.

"Tonight, you're all Hunters."

They go wild, stomping their feet and thrusting fists into the air. I have to raise my voice to speak over them. "The Wolves and the Morenos are our prey!" I shout. "Let us show them how we hunt."

Conrad runs over and slaps me hard on the back, pain shreds through me as my scars ache but I bite through it and offer a tightlipped smile. The men are still hooting and stomping, pumping themselves up. I let them make as much noise as they want—some of them may not make it home tonight, they need to leave here in good spirits.

The atmosphere even gets to Hans who gives me a clap on the shoulder as I make my way through the crowd toward our vehicles. King James moves beside me, holding my door open as I slide into the passenger seat.

He leans in so I can hear him over the shouting. "Whatever happens tonight, make sure you come home."

I nod.

"There will always be another chance to get to the Wolves. But you won't always have another chance to see my granddaughter."

I'd always believed Jameson wasn't close to Rosa, but since we consummated the marriage, he's been getting more and more protective of her—even offering me fatherly advice about our relationship. I appreciate it, but I'm not used to this sort of thing. My relationship with my own father is stressful on a good day. To have someone like King James looking out for me—*genuinely* looking out for me—is almost strange.

"If I don't make it back," I say to him, "tell her—"

He shakes his head and laughs mightily. "Just make sure you get back and tell her yourself, Jäger."

He walks off before I can say anything more. To be honest, I didn't have any last words planned. Dying in Staten Island hadn't been a thought or a worry until Jameson came over and planted the idea in my head. Now my palms are sweaty, and my back is throbbing.

I lean back into my chair as Douglass slides into the driver's seat and shuts his door with a thud. He runs through the plan with Conrad, Morgen, and a man from the Stronghold named Ja'meek, while I pull out my phone and send a text to Rosa. She's in a safehouse with the other women and children, I'm

150

not sure when she'll be able to read the message, but I just want to make sure she hears from me before everything goes down.

I love you.

I hit **send** and cram my phone into my pocket with a sigh. It takes me a moment to realize we've already pulled out of the warehouse. Buildings zip by as Douglass drives, he's following Hans with Aldo all the way in front and Trenton driving right behind us. Four cars, two decoys, one plan.

I take a deep breath and close my eyes. "Remember the plan, boys."

Conrad reaches forward and slaps my shoulder. "Let's go hunt some Wolves."

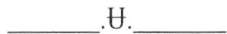

We drive the next hour in silence, only stopping to switch our plates and change drivers. Douglass and I slide into the backseats so Ja'meek and Morgen can take over. Ja'meek is a lower ranked soldier from the Stronghold and Morgen can count on one hand all the times he's been to Staten Island. If anyone glances into the driver or passenger windows, they won't recognize our men.

My nerves try to rise when the bridge comes into view, but I take a deep breath and think of Rosa. It isn't just the sight of my wife that calms me, it's the thought of what will happen to her if I don't succeed. The Volkovs will undoubtedly retaliate after this, but we plan to cause enough damage to cripple their forces.

The Wolves specialize in selling flesh—human trafficking. It's mostly for sex, but I've heard sick rumors that they have slaves of all sorts over there. The Island is insane.

Nevertheless, blowing up a few brothels is as good as blowing up a bank. All their money will go up in flames, hopefully, a few Russian mobsters will die in the fire too. Their clubs run 24/7, set up like an expensive hotel to make clients feel like they aren't icky creeps taking pleasure from an unwilling woman. My skin crawls as I think about the horrors that happen in Staten Island every day. Blowing up those brothels is honestly a good thing. They shouldn't exist in the first place.

"Guards, two o'clock," Morgen says, glancing out the passenger window.

I follow his line of sight and find the cluster of men in black fatigues walking along the bridge. Each of them wears body armor, a helmet, and carries an assault rifle on his back. They look ready for business, but there's only a few of them—five at most.

"Two more guards on horseback," Ja'meek reports, gripping the steering wheel tightly.

Traffic slows down as the men comb the lanes, walking slowly and glancing into the windows of each car. My stomach turns knots.

"Decoy One in position," Conrad whispers, glancing down at his phone. I can feel my phone vibrate with the notification too, but I don't take it out and check it. Everyone knows what to do, we went over the plan enough so that we can carry it out without needing to communicate. In fact, I gave the order to stay offline before we left the warehouse. Obviously, some of the men have trust issues and decided to text anyway.

I roll my eyes, making a mental note to break the fingers of anyone who sent a text when we get back. My orders were clear—no comms—because comms leave a trail and trails lead back to us. Not just the men on this mission, but to our wives and children waiting for us at home. If any of these idiots gets taken, the Russians wouldn't even have to interrogate them for information, they could just pull up their text messages and find everything they need to know.

I hiss through my teeth as I lean forward and pinch the bridge of my nose. My phone buzzes in my pocket again.

I'm breaking hands *instead of fingers now*, I vow to myself.

"Mission starting," Conrad whispers.

I watch as Aldo's vehicle tries to change lanes without using its signal. The sudden jump forces the driver beside him to swerve away or risk getting hit. They don't collide but there's a series of honks from the car, to which Aldo responds by rolling down his window and spewing curse words at the angry man.

That's all it takes for the guards on horseback to start making their way over to the vehicle. We're all split into different lanes now, so I have to turn in my seat to watch the commotion.

Aldo gets out of his vehicle with Jared and three German men following behind. They leave their doors open and keep the truck running, holding up traffic as they start shouting at the other car. The guards begin to yell for them to get back inside their car, but no one listens. I expect the armored men to make their way over to Aldo and his team. I expect them to start getting in their faces and issuing threats. A small part of me even expects a fight to break out before Decoy Two gets into place.

What I don't expect is the guards to surround Aldo's team and open fire.

Aldo and Jared both duck and run for cover behind the open car doors, they are joined by the three German grunts who pull their guns and begin firing back—but not fast enough. Aldo gets hit in the shoulder and goes down on one knee, screaming curses in Italian as he raises his gun and fires blindly into the crowd.

One of the German grunts tries to give him backup, but he's mowed down as soon as he steps from cover. My eyes widen and I grip my leather seat. I'm used to this. I'm used to seeing death, but the look on that grunt's face as he falls to the ground is new to me.

He looks shocked.

He truly hadn't expected to die tonight. He'd believed I would get them in and out without issue.

Before I can writhe in my guilt, Hans's truck bursts from his lane and races forward, almost ramming into another car. The guards turn toward the ruckus, but there is nothing they can do against a charging SUV. Without hesitation, Hans plows through the crowd of armored men, pinning one against the guardrail. He screams and frantically pounds his fists against the hood of the truck. Hans ignores him and gets out with his gun raised. It would have been a mercy to shoot him and end his suffering, but we didn't come here to show mercy. We came to hunt for Wolves, and we've finally found our prey.

I watch as a shootout unfolds right before me, but just as I grip the handle to open my door and help my men, I'm slammed into my seat as Ja'meek hits the gas hard.

"We're leaving them!" I shout.

Conrad punches my shoulder hard enough to slap me to my senses. "They are the *decoy* teams; we're supposed to leave them!"

I nod, trying to get rid of the image of that German grunt. His expression haunts me every time I close my eyes—every time I *blink*. Like a nightmare playing out in one-second flashes. *But Hans is there now*, I remind myself. He will get revenge.

Fifteen

We speed through Staten Island in search of our targets. I picked buildings far enough from the bridge to put some distance between us and the guards, but close enough for us to easily circle back and escape if things get bad out here. Given what happened on the bridge, I wouldn't be surprised if things go terribly wrong from this point forward.

Ja'meek pulls over outside a warehouse and glances in the rearview mirror. "Stop one," he says in his deep baritone voice.

Morgen gets out and goes around back to grab his bag of explosives. He's joined by an Italian grunt from Trenton's truck, which has managed to follow us here. With five buildings to blow up and ten men to do it, we've got to split up and plant the bombs separately. Once the explosives are in place, we'll meet at our designated point and get out of here.

The plan is to blow them altogether, but I roll down my window and call to Morgen as he leaves, "Blow them as soon as you plant them!"

He turns back and nods without question.

At this point, the Russians have shown us how ruthless they are. We aren't taking chances anymore.

Ja'meek drops me off with Conrad who carries the sack of explosives over his shoulder like it's a bag of gifts for Christmas. He whistles as we scamper over to the brothel and start planting the devices outside. Two at the entrance, and then one beneath each window on the first floor, circling the entire building. The idea is to blow out one of the floors to make the rest implode. I don't care if it actually works out that way, with this many bombs, the walls will fly off and everyone inside should be incinerated. Good enough for me.

"Ready?" Conrad asks once we've jogged a good distance and taken cover behind a small café.

I nod, staring at the building. From the outside, it looks like a luxury club; I can even hear the thumping music from our distance, but I know better. Everyone knows better. There are no *clubs* in Staten Island, not since the defunding. If there's alcohol, music, and women, then it's a brothel and they aren't just selling drinks—in fact, I'm sure the drinks are free. It's the women you pay for.

"On three," Conrad says, and then he starts counting. "*Eines, zwei, drei!*"

He presses the button and there's a split-second delay before my eardrums explode.

The sound is deafening, but it isn't worse than the bright flares of red and orange that scream toward the sky in a raging pillar. The windows shatter and the walls crumble. Shrieks erupt from what's left of the club as people crawl out the front doors. They were blown off their hinges, left to hang to the side—partially blocking the exit.

A man shoves part of the destroyed door away and stumbles down the scorched steps in a daze.

"Looks important," Conrad says.

I nod. The man is wearing an expensive suit, I can tell even from our distance. Despite the burns and debris on his clothes, he looks like he's worth something.

"He'll do well in an interrogation," I say coldly.

Conrad licks his lips. "Let's take him."

I step out from our hiding spot, gaining the man's attention. I don't know if he knows who I am or if he's just spooked because of the explosion, but he takes one look at me and then bolts down the street.

I'm in good shape. Three-mile runs every morning, weightlifting, boxing. The whole shebang. So when the man starts sprinting away, I don't panic. I don't even take off after him right away. I let him run a few blocks, scrambling and looking left and right like a scared victim in a movie. Then I roll my shoulders back and take off running.

I chase him down five blocks later. We're both panting, but he's sticky with sweat and too exhausted to put up a fight. So, when I tackle him to the ground and connect my fist with his jaw three times, he just sags and whimpers, muttering a string of incoherent Russian apologies.

I yank him to his feet and slap him hard. "Shut up!" I yell, shoving him back toward the brothel. He immediately gasps and clamps his mouth shut. "Walk," I order darkly.

158

He obeys.

Tired, it takes us fifteen minutes to walk back to the brothel. When we arrive, I realize Ja'meek and the others have made it back from their sites. In the rush of adrenaline and chaos, I hadn't heard the other explosions go off, but all the sirens wailing behind us lets me know things went well.

Douglass greets me with a nod as he takes our new prisoner to the truck without a word. Ever the hard worker, he knows exactly what my plan is and secures the man's hands with a zip-tie before loading him up. While he works, I glance around the area and take a deep breath of the blood-soaked air. The entire block is hot from residual flames, the air is grimy, thick with smoke and tears and dust. I place my hands on my hips as I scan the wreckage.

There are bodies all around the front entrance and near the windows of the club. People crawled out the door and escaped through the shattered windows only to die of their injuries on the street just outside. Most of the bodies belong to women, but there are more than enough corpses of well-dressed Russian men to ease the pangs of guilt stabbing through me.

The sound of screaming catches my attention and I turn to find Conrad wrestling with a naked woman. She shrieks as he handles her, grabbing at her waist and slinging her over his shoulder like she's a little doll. She kicks and screams, but he silences her with a swack to her bare bottom so hard I can see the red print of his hand on her butt cheek as he nears me.

"I'm taking this one home." He winks.

I grab his arm. "No, you're not."

Conrad frowns. "Why not?"

"Because we didn't come here to kidnap women."

"We just won our battle." He adjusts the woman on his shoulder, making her yelp. "This is my prize."

My voice comes out as a growl. "No, she isn't."

Beside us, Morgen spits on the ground. "I don't know why you'd want one of these hookers anyway. It was a Russian woman who got us into this mess."

No, it wasn't, I think, *it was Wolfgang.*

Conrad shrugs like it doesn't matter and slaps the woman's butt again, marking her other cheek. She starts to sob.

In one swift motion, I grab him by the shoulder and take the woman from his arms. She screams and tries to twist free of my grasp until I set her on her feet, and she realizes she's okay.

"I'm not trying to hurt you," I say as calmly as I can.

Conrad grunts. "Gisela is locked up in a safehouse. I just want one night with her."

"No," I say plainly.

"I've never had a Russian woman—"

"I don't *care*," I start to seethe, but I cut myself off as I glance down at the woman before me. It was hard to tell in the pale moonlight and the hazy air, but up close I can see her skin is light brown and even though her hair has been straightened and dyed platinum blonde, the roots are still dark and curly. Her face is youthful and appears even more innocent with the tears gathered in her eyes. She is completely naked, but she doesn't try to hide herself from me as she sniffles and wipes at her small round nose.

She looks like Rosa.

My heart climbs into my throat and I swallow hard to shove it back down. Conrad is still going on about sleeping with a Russian woman, but all I can register is this woman's similarity to my wife. It's uncanny and sends a ripple of fear up my spine.

"She's not Russian," I whisper, taking a step back.

Conrad ticks his head to the side. "What?"

I glance up at him. "She's not Russian."

My eyes flit through the crowd of survivors and corpses. There's a body a few feet to my left, her torso is charred but there's enough skin for me to make out her olive complexion and her wavy brown hair. A woman sits sobbing on the curb, naked except for her six-inch stilettos, she's got tan skin and short black hair. There's even a trio of Asian women holding hands by the entrance of the club.

"None of these women are Russian," I mutter.

Conrad and Morgen start looking around too, realizing what I've discovered. That's when it hits me. The Volkovs sell flesh—but not much of their own. They've kidnapped these women. Snatched them off the street the same way I snatched up Douglass when he was a teenager.

But this is different.

The Jägers are evil, I've never tried to deny or sugarcoat that. This is the mafia. It isn't a pretty business, but I can be honest about who I am and what I've done. The Volkovs, however, are a different story. The ladies scattered around me are not musclebound men forced to join a different gang. They are young, helpless women who spend their days pleasing men with horrifying appetites.

As I glance around, I realize something about the prostitutes. They're all wearing studded jewels latched tightly around their necks like chokers, but as I get a closer look, I realize they aren't necklaces at all. They're collars.

My stomach turns sour, and I sway on my feet. Two of the Asian women are wearing red collars, the other is wearing a white one, and the Rosa lookalike in front of me has on a pink one. I don't have to guess at what the collars mean. I've never been inside a Russian brothel before, but when Wolfgang was engaged to Sofia, I spent a lot of time in Staten Island. Enough to hear rumors and horror stories that kept me away from the clubs.

The red collars are for women aged thirty and up, they're older and more experienced, but they're also cheaper and easier to book.

The pink collars are for women eighteen to twenty-nine, relatively fresh—or at least innocent enough in appearance to charge double per hour.

The white collars …

I glance at the Asian lady and take a step in her direction. Once I'm standing right in front of her, I realize the truth. It sends a wave of nausea storming through me.

She's not a *lady* at all. Like the rest of the women, she isn't wearing clothes, save for the collar around her throat. Her skin is dirty, but I can see the smoothness to it that only comes from youth. Her tear-stained cheeks are plump, her eyes are full of innocence. And while I take no pleasure in examining her bare frame, I can tell her body is still developing.

She's a child. No older than fifteen.

I take off my jacket and move to wrap it over her shoulders, but she flinches away and holds up her hands to protect herself. My heart crumbles in my chest.

"I'm not here to hurt you," I say, but as the words leave my mouth, I feel bile rise up my throat.

There are dead men and women all over the place. No one in their right mind would believe I wasn't here to hurt these women. I just blew a hundred of them to smithereens. The realization of what I've done hits me hard.

I drop the jacket and then double over to vomit on it.

Conrad and Morgen are by my side in an instant.

"What's happened!" Conrad starts yelling at the women, but I grab his sleeve.

"Leave them!" I snarl, wiping my mouth with the back of my hand.

He stares at me in shock, but before he can question me, I grab him by the tie and yank him toward me. "You want a prize? Take these women. All of them."

"I don't understand…" his voice trails off as he eyes the underaged girl beside us. She's staring at us both through wide, unblinking eyes. The other two Asian women behind her are crying and babbling in what I think is Japanese.

Without words, Morgen removes his jacket and shocks everyone by speaking to the women in their native tongue. His

163

voice is higher, gentler, almost soothing as he carefully approaches, holding his jacket out for the young girl to take. She grabs it and clutches it to her chest and then starts to sob uncontrollably.

"Contact Gio," I grunt to Conrad. "Tell him to prepare a safehouse for these women."

"You want to house Russian women in our shelters?" Conrad challenges.

I punch him so hard I'm not sure if I've broken my hand.

"They're not Russian!" I shout, kicking him in his side as he reels back from my punch. "Look at them!" I jab a finger at the group of Asian women and then wave my hand around at all the others.

"They work for Russians." Conrad rubs his jaw. "It's the same thing. Just like the women at The Club. I don't see why you're so upset right now."

I step closer to him. "These women work against their will. They are nothing like the women of The Club."

I watch his eyes widen as understanding sets in.

The Club is just as much a whorehouse as it is a strip club and a cigar lounge. I've taken women home from there, ladies I bought for thousands of dollars for just one night. But they weren't like the women standing around me now. First of all, they were all *women*. Consenting adults who willingly accepted the money I offered and the pleasure I gave them. Nothing we did was beyond their control or desire. Yes, they sold their bodies to me and probably twenty other men that week alone. But they *worked* for Conrad, they weren't *owned* by him. They signed contracts with The Club and received pay for their time. And they could quit whenever they wanted.

My eyes lock onto the collars of one of the women in front of me. The ladies of The Club aren't dogs. They aren't sex slaves. We use their bodies. I won't deny that. But we've never abused them. Not like this.

What makes it so much worse is that these women were taken. Kidnapped from their homes or their schools—or God knows where. Any one of them could have been Rosa.

Conrad doesn't speak for a long moment. His eyes are fixed on the teenager who's sobbing at his feet. After a few moments of silence, he simply nods and says, "Okay."

"We don't have enough room in the trucks to carry all the women," Morgen says.

Douglass joins us, he isn't wearing his jacket anymore either. I glance over my shoulder to find that he's given it to the Rosa lookalike. He says, "Hans and Aldo are out of reach, sir. They made it out okay, but they had to rush to a hospital for Aldo's injuries."

"The Stronghold remains by the docks," Ja'meek reminds us. "There is plenty of room on the boats to carry everyone."

I nod at him. "Let's get these women out of here."

"We'd better hurry," Douglass says. He's standing a few feet away, staring into the distance. With the wail of sirens growing nearer, I don't have to wonder what he's looking at.

"Conrad, Morgen—get as many of the girls into the trucks as you can. The rest of us will have to make it to the docks on foot."

Both of them shake their heads. "Onkel Uwe will kill us if he finds out we let you walk while we took a ride."

"I'm also staying," Douglass announces.

Conrad grimaces. "Why? You're a Hunted grunt."

"I am the underboss's personal guard." Douglass takes a large step forward. "And I am his most trusted ally."

I smirk, proud of Douglass, but also pleased to see my cousins and my guard fighting to stay by my side. The loyalty is almost overwhelming—though I don't miss the fact that Ja'meek says nothing and offers no aid in this situation.

As the sirens grow louder, Ja'meek says, "Whoever is going or staying doesn't matter. We've got to get out of—"

Here was the next word that should have left his mouth, but he's cut off by a gurgling shriek as a bullet tears through his throat. His blood spatters everywhere, spraying me, Conrad, Morgen, and even the naked women nearby. Douglass lurches forward and grabs Ja'meek as he falls to the ground, but there is no time to comfort him. A spray of bullets flies at us from the hazy darkness. Conrad and Morgen both dive for cover, I grab the teenager and drag her to her feet as we scramble behind a hunk of twisted metal. I think it's a partially melted table flung out of the window during the explosion, but it doesn't matter now.

"We're surrounded!" I hear Morgen scream.

Conrad pulls out his handgun and starts firing over the stone steps he's hiding behind. Douglass has miraculously managed to clamber to safety behind the truck. He shouts over to us, but I can't hear over the endless assault of bullets. As I peer into the distance, I can *just* make out the inky silhouettes of the Wolves who've come to kill us.

"We have to run!" I scream. "All of us!"

Conrad turns and shoves his brother toward me. "Get out of here! I'll cover you both!"

Douglass pulls around in the truck, shielding us from the bullets, but getting sprayed down on the other side. He ducks and leans low in the driver's seat to avoid getting shot but as I open the door to let the teenage girl inside, I notice blood on his shirt.

I force myself to ignore his injury and focus on the other women, beckoning them over to the truck and helping them scramble inside as quickly as possible. Conrad and Morgen give us cover fire, but it's obvious we're losing this battle.

"To the docks, immediately!" I shout to Douglass. He glances back and gives me a firm nod before I shut the door, then I duck and run to my cousins. "Let's go before Douglass leaves! He's giving us cover!"

They both nod and start to run in the opposite direction. There are still women shrieking and running past us, one even grabs Conrad by the sleeve and starts screaming in Spanish for him to help her. He swings her up over his shoulder and keeps running like she weighs nothing. Morgen grabs a woman too, though he handles her more carefully, carrying the bleeding dancer bridal style instead of like a caveman.

I don't get to rescue my own damsel in distress. I have another person I want to save.

In the chaos, I sneak away from Conny and Morgen and

run around the back of the truck, peeking out to find Ja'meek lying on the ground. There is blood all over his shirt, but he's still alive, clutching his neck and slowly crawling away.

I drop to one knee and pull out my handgun, giving him cover fire as I shout, "Come on, Ja'meek! Just a little further!"

He sees me and a fire immediately ignites in his eyes—a will to live. I empty my gun and then reload and fire off round after round as he crawls toward me. It's a grueling process that leaves me sweating from nerves and fear and the heat of the guns blazing around us. I can hear my cousins screaming for me to leave him, but I won't. I can hear Douglass and the dancers inside the truck shouting for us to get a move on, but I refuse.

Ja'meek is on my team. He's here because King James is a good man who lent aid when I needed it. Like the German on the bridge, he's placed his life in my hands. Chosen to blindly trust me, even though I barely trust myself.

I won't leave him.

He takes a bullet to his back and his body jerks as he cries out, eyes squeezed shut, teeth snapping together in pain.

"Keep going!" I scream, reloading my gun, but I know it's already too late.

The black silhouettes in the distance have turned into blurry images of men in uniform. Black cargo pants, combat boots, and full raid gear. They march up the street in perfect formation and then scatter as they realize they're close enough for personal assault.

Two men run right at Ja'meek, but they don't kill him. They

grab him by the ankles and begin dragging him away.

There is no way I can get to him without being shot down. There is no way I can stop the men from taking him away. Even if I weren't on my last magazine, the men are in riot gear. My bullets won't do anything to them.

But they will to Ja'meek.

I had refused to leave him. I know I've failed that promise now. But I can at least make sure he doesn't die to the Russians. I can make sure they don't get to torture him all night, just as we will do to the man we've captured. I can make sure he doesn't die with a shocked look on his face, like the nameless German on the bridge.

I raise my gun before I change my mind, and I fire a single shot into his forehead.

It seems like silence rings out after the bullet penetrates his skull, sending his head whipping back like he's been struck with a bat. My cousins are further down the street, Douglass is still leaning down in the front of the truck. No one knows what I've just done. So I cry in secret, a single tear racing down my cheek.

It burns.

I wipe it away as the guards take him anyway. They're upset that I've ruined the interrogation, but they'll take his body regardless. If only to hang it outside a building and celebrate later.

When they recede into the darkness behind them, all that's left is a bloody streak on the pavement. Only when Ja'meek is gone do I turn and run to catch up with my cousins.

Sixteen

When Amy told me I'd be moving into a safehouse, I thought I'd be holed up in some underground bunker. Instead, I'm in one of the luxury hotels owned by Marco Segreto. We're in Harlem, which seems a world away from Gio's penthouse or Papa's old mansion, but I've been here enough times to still feel comfortable—especially with the double-king sized bed, the silk curtains and velvet pile carpets that feel like cushions beneath my bare feet.

I am living in luxury, but it doesn't feel like it.

There are fifty other women and children in the building with me, each of us has been given our own room, but the rooms will be changed every week and we'll switch hotels every month to make sure we aren't in one place for too long. There are five guards on each floor, and we only stay on the second and third floor, so we aren't too far from the bottom exits—or the ground. We don't want to be up high enough to kill ourselves if we're ever forced to flee from the windows.

There is still a staff assigned to the building to cook and

clean for us. Gio even made sure to bring over enough clothes to fill a mall so we can pretend to go shopping and dress up like we've actually got somewhere to go. Some of the younger girls enjoy all the new clothes, but the older ladies just wrinkle their noses and remain in their rooms all day.

I appreciate the distraction, the good food, and even the guards, but I don't feel safe. The last time I spoke to Amory was the day I said goodbye, almost a week ago. Since then, I've gotten only one text and it was a simple message saying, 'I love you.'

Believe me, I know my husband is busy. I know I'm probably not his priority right now. But I feel jittery and slightly paranoid. I need to hear something. I need an update of some sort. Anything to let me know he's still alive, at least. If I could just get that, then I can handle everything else. The anxiety, the stir-crazy, skittish nerves that make me want to climb the walls. I am itching to go out and breathe fresh air, to walk the gardens around Amory's estate and fall asleep with a book in his giant library.

Instead, I am sitting at my desk staring down at my empty journal. I had planned to write something to ease my mind, maybe even produce a letter to give to Amy, but I can't think of anything to say.

With a sigh, I close the journal and open the desk drawer to stash it away, but I freeze as I spot the leatherbound Bible in the drawer. It's my own Bible, I remember unpacking it when I first arrived. But, regrettably, I haven't read it since I put it away.

Guilt floods through me as I grab it and place it on the desk. I am immediately reminded of the scripture from I Corinthians 7, *An unmarried woman or virgin is concerned about the Lord's affairs: Her aim is to be devoted to the Lord in both body and spirit. But a married woman is concerned about the affairs of this world—how she can please her husband.*

My prayer life has been lacking since Amy and I were reunited. When we aren't fighting, we're rolling around in bed making up for fighting. It's a cycle of love, hate, and making love. I'm overjoyed that we're finally getting along—at least somewhat—but I can't deny that our peace has become a distraction.

In a twisted way, this war and our separation is a blessing. I'm worried for my husband, but I can see the benefits of our time apart now. We needed this break. We needed to reset and get our heads straight. I can't lead my husband to the Lord if our time together is only ever spent in bed. One day we'll have to throw the covers back—that's when our marriage will truly begin. That's when our conversations will really matter.

I need to be prepared for that.

"I'm sorry, God," I whisper, opening the Bible and reaching for my study notebook and pen. "I'm sorry You had to completely separate us just to get me to focus on You again."

My fingers brush over the pages and I smile down at the words. It's open to Psalms 37:23-24. *The Lord makes firm the steps of the one who delights in him; though he may stumble, he will not fall, for the Lord upholds him with his hand.*

"Lord, I have neglected You. I have stumbled. But You kept me anyway, You made sure I didn't fall. And You even made a way for me to slow down and shift my focus back to You. Thank You, Jesus. I won't waste this opportunity."

I dance between reading and praying until my eyes go blurry and my throat feels dry, but even then, I still want to keep studying. It's only when I hear a knock at my door that I stand and stretch and give myself a break.

The guard at the door is Italian, but I don't recognize him. He likely works in Harlem, exclusively for Marco. He gives me a smile that makes the scar on his chin stretch, I try not to stare at it as I smile back and say, "Is something wrong?"

"Mistress Jäger has summoned all the women to the lobby."

I almost tell him *I'm* Mrs. Jäger, but I stop myself when I replay his words in my head.

Mistress Jäger.

It's the title given to the wife of a mafia boss. Just as Uwe is the master of the German gang, Christina is the mistress. I might be married to the future master, but I'm not the mistress yet.

I nod at the guard and grab a cardigan from the closet beside the door, then I follow him in silence to the stairs. We don't use the elevators in case something ever malfunctions, we don't want to get stuck. There's a trail of other women following behind me, along with the rest of the guards stationed on our floor. The kids have all been left in their rooms, which means this meeting is important.

As I enter the lobby, I scan the crowd of worried-looking women for familiar faces. With the Stronghold, the Garden, and the Hunters all working together, we've been clumped into random groups as diverse as the multicultural festival that parades through Harlem every summer. Still, there is *some* order to our assigned hideouts.

Christina is the Mistress here because she's the highest-ranking woman among us. Monique, the Queen of the Stronghold, is in another building, and since Olivia is married to Marco, a General of the Garden, and daughter of Niccolò, the Italian underboss, she's in another building—undoubtedly acting as the Mistress over there. If Christina weren't here, I would be the Mistress, but I don't let her presence burn me. I wouldn't even know what to do if I were in charge. Maybe this is my chance to sit back and learn, to get a peek at what my responsibilities will be once Amory becomes the Jägermeister.

I freeze as the thought runs through me. Amory doesn't *have* to become the Jägermeister. He could refuse the position. Once the war is over, he could leave the mafia entirely. It's not like being in it has served either of us any good, and if God has His way, there won't be a mafia for much longer.

Maybe they'll all tear themselves apart fighting each other.

Adella is waving at me from her perch on a sofa across the room. I smile as I spot her and make a beeline in her direction.

"Do you know what's going on?" I ask, sitting beside her.

She shakes her head. "I was going to ask you the same thing."

"Have you spoken to Nona?" The sisters were separated

to keep them from being in the same place in case one of the safehouses was located by the enemy. I can tell the distance has gotten to Della; she's been pulled out of the Bronx and separated from her mother, her husband, her grandmother, and her sister. It's a miracle she doesn't hate me for any of this. Her husband, Jared, is out there fighting because of an alliance I sealed in blood just weeks ago. If it weren't for me, the Stronghold wouldn't be involved in this at all, but I see no judgment in my cousin's eyes as she smiles and shakes her head.

"I haven't gotten any messages through today. I think they're scrambling the phone signals again."

The guards randomly do that to keep our comms from being hacked and traced. I appreciate it, but I hate it.

"I'm sure we'll find out something today," I say, turning to watch as Petra and Christina enter the room.

Christina takes a seat on a chair and motions for us all to quiet down. We immediately hush, not wanting to delay this any longer. I'm practically sweating from my nerves.

She clears her throat and I notice the envelope she's clutching in her hands. "I have received information from the leaders of our respective organizations," Christina says. Her voice is heavy with emotion. "A few days ago, our men carried out a mission in Staten Island which was a great success."

Both sighs and gasps erupt throughout the room, but Christina holds up her hand and we all fall silent right away.

"But with great success in this business, there is always loss following close behind." She sighs and lifts the paper. "This is a list of all the men who did not make it."

The room is so quiet I feel like I can hear my own sweat pricking through my pores.

Christina opens the envelope and begins to read. My heart pounds with each name she announces, men from the Stronghold, men from the Garden, a few German soldiers too. Adella squeezes my hand, and the pressure is comforting yet stressful at the same time. She's a married woman, just like me, I know she's nervous too.

"Ja'meek Williams," Christina finishes the list and passes the envelope to Petra.

Someone in the back of the room shrieks and begins to cry hysterically. There is movement in the crowd as women rush to comfort the crying lady. She could be anyone. His widow, his mother, his daughter, his sister. I have no idea, but my understanding of their relationship doesn't matter. She is hurt. And right now, there is nothing anyone can do to offer her comfort.

I shift on the sofa to watch as a familiar figure works his way through the women toward the crying lady. It's Father Serrano. I'm not exactly surprised, but I can't say I was expecting to see him here. My guess is, he's making rounds to all the safehouses to offer spiritual guidance and support. I wouldn't put it past him, he's truly a man of God. Probably the only one in the city.

"I know some of you have just heard terrible news," Christina goes on, "but there is more I have to tell you." She stands and motions to Petra who is standing by the door now.

With a nod, the young woman opens the door and in files a line of women I've never seen before.

Christina explains, "As you know, the Wolves sell flesh in their clubs and bars. These women are some of the victims who were rescued by our brave husbands, fathers, brothers, and sons. Please welcome them, ladies. They will only be here until it is safe to reunite them with their families." She sighs. "I know some of you must feel the urge to hate or blame these women because they are from the Island, but they are victims, I assure you. Our men died defending them. The least we can do is honor their memory by welcoming these women."

Women is an overstatement for most of the ladies who enter the lobby. Half of them look younger than me, with downturned eyes and nervous frowns on their faces. I know exactly what they've been through, and I feel horrible because I know who played a part in their capture and enslavement.

Arthur Hart.

The man I once thought I loved helped set up these women to be kidnapped by the Wolves. He knew what was happening to them, but the money he was getting from my brother and Volkov was enough for him to turn a blind eye.

I refuse to dwell on Arthur's betrayal. These women are proof that good can come of this war. That even gangsters can do the right thing, given the chance. I can't stop myself from smiling, knowing that Amory played a role in their rescue. *Thank You God for keeping Amy safe*, I pray internally, *and thank You for blessing him to right some of Arthur's wrongs.*

I stand to go introduce myself to some of the rescued

177

women, but on my way across the room, someone grabs my arm and pulls me aside. I glance up to find Petra smiling at me. "Amory and Eike are okay," she says quietly. "My aunt doesn't get much information, but she says she's sure the men will be able to visit soon."

Excitement shoots through me and I hug her. "I'm so happy!" I whisper.

"Me too."

"I wonder if Gio will come visit." I haven't seen my brother in what seems like forever. I definitely don't miss him the way I miss my husband, but I wonder how he's managing in this war.

Petra's nose wrinkles as she frowns and tilts her head to the side. "Why would you want to see him?"

"He's my brother," I say, unsure if she was aware.

Her frown deepens. "You still consider him family after what he did?"

Now I'm frowning, totally confused. "You mean selling me to Amory?"

Her face slowly changes from wrinkled confusion to total shock. "Oh no," Petra says quietly. "You don't know."

"Don't know what?"

Petra presses her lips together and shakes her head.

I reach for her hand as panic starts to bubble inside me. "Petra, what are you saying? What has my brother done?"

She glances around at the women, just to keep from meeting my eye. When my grip on her clammy hand tightens, she winces and then sighs. "When the men come to visit, ask

Amory how your father died."

When Petra's eyes finally meet mine, I cannot make out the expression on her face because of the tears that blur my eyes. I can't even speak for fear of the words coming out in a wobble. Her words make no sense, yet they explain so much.

As far as I know, Papa killed himself because of all the damage I caused to the business after running away from home. But it sounds like that might have been a lie—and that Amory knows the truth.

Why would my husband—my *Amy*—keep the truth from me?

I start to shake my head and close my eyes to stop the tears from flowing. I'm overthinking things. I'm jumping to conclusions. I could be totally wrong about all this, but the way Petra squeezes my hand and then pulls me in for a hug lets me know I'm right about everything. Even my worst fears.

That my husband is a liar.

Seventeen

Rosa is in my arms, but I don't feel any warmth from our position in bed. She is stiff and cold, instead of relaxed and joyous like she usually is after we make love. I love the first few moments after we finish, she's always left with a warm blush on her cheeks and a lazy, satisfied look in her half-lidded eyes.

Tonight, she's different. Even though this is the first time we've seen each other in over a week. Even though neither of us is sure when we'll get to see each other again once I leave. She is quiet and detached. She isn't taking advantage of our time together.

Maybe she's tired, I tell myself, gazing down at her. I gave her everything I had today. From the moment I walked through the doors of the safehouse this afternoon until now—late in the evening—all I've done is show her how much I've missed her. She didn't protest when I pinned her against the wall instead of saying hello. She didn't complain when I finished and took her again, like I couldn't get enough of her. And she certainly had no qualms about the last hour we spent in the bed.

Like a man deprived, I wouldn't let Rosa go until I'd had my fill. But I thought that was what she wanted. I thought it was a turn-on for her. Maybe I was wrong. Maybe I should have said 'hi' and had a conversation instead of tearing her clothes off and devouring her body.

It's hard to tell what she wants sometimes because she's always so compliant until it becomes too much. And then she just randomly explodes.

I can't fix something if I don't know its broken. I feel like tonight is one of those moments with Rosa. When something is clearly wrong, but she isn't going to say anything until she can't take it anymore.

"Rosa," my voice is a husky whisper.

She stirs beneath the covers but doesn't turn to look at me. I stare at the side of her face, contemplating if I should reach out and brush the dark coil from her cheek.

"Something's wrong," I say calmly.

She nods.

"Talk to me."

Suddenly, there are tears in her eyes. The sight of it sets my heart to racing, but I don't speak. My wife is eleven years younger than me. She was a virgin when I met her. And she's been sheltered all her life—not to mention her fairytale faith that's got her believing in all things bright and beautiful. She might be physically tougher now, thanks to the war and her kickboxing lessons with her cousins, but I've learned she's still emotionally fragile. If I push too hard, she'll just run away, and

181

I'll never find out what's wrong.

So I sit in silence as her tears wet the pillow, and I try to dig through my mind—try to go over all the details of our afternoon and evening together to see if I said or did something wrong.

I take a slow breath and stroke her cheek, folding that loose curl behind her small ear. "Was I too rough with you?" I murmur.

She stiffens and then cranes her neck to look at me. "This has nothing to do with sex."

Oh.

Rosa sits up, clutching the blankets against her body. "I'm going to ask you a question, Amory, and I want you to give me an honest answer."

I nod.

"How did my father die?"

The question leaves me sitting in stunned silence. This is not the conversation I thought I'd be having tonight. I was supposed to visit the safehouse with all the other men, make love to my wife, and then fall asleep with her in my arms until I regrettably have to leave in the morning.

Instead, Rosa is looking at me with tears running down her puffy cheeks as she starts to sob quietly. One of her small hands goes to her mouth, muffling her cries as she lowers her head and groans in despair. I still haven't answered her question, but I get the feeling that I don't need to.

She already knows the truth. The question is, how?

The only person I have ever told about Gio's betrayal is

Vater. From there, it's easy to pick up the breadcrumbs. Uwe told Christina, who likely told Petra—her favorite niece. And, of course, Petra couldn't keep herself from saying something to Rosa.

This is my fault, in more than one way. I should have told Rosa the truth from the start, and I shouldn't have told Uwe. She doesn't deserve to find out this way. She doesn't deserve to feel this sorrow and betrayal because of my cowardice.

I had no idea what to do with the information when I first received it. I was afraid of Rosa hating me or breaking entirely. But now that exact thing is happening right before my eyes. I can see the bitterness building in her hazel orbs, I can see the moment she recedes into the chambers of her mind, leaving me hanging somewhere in limbo.

She doesn't trust me anymore. I wouldn't even be surprised if she wasn't sure she loved me anymore, either. She's that broken. And it's because of me.

I shift in the bed and take her into my arms, to my surprise, she lets me. Her breaths come out in choppy little pants as she gasps and sobs into my chest, soaking my front with her tears.

I rub circles on her back as I whisper into her hair, "I thought I was doing the right thing by keeping it from you. I wasn't sure you could handle the truth."

She pulls from me, like she just remembered she should be angry with me. Her face is alive with rage. "And what is the truth, Amory? What did you keep from me?"

My shoulders drop, but I hold her gaze. I won't allow myself to look away from her. *I will accept her pain*—even though it kills me—*I will take her tears.* Every last one.

"Giovanni killed your father."

She crumples into a heap of shrieking tears, small hands fisting the blankets, her body trembling from the force of her sobs.

"I'm sorry," I say softly.

"You lied."

"I did."

"You let me believe he killed himself all this time." She sits up and slaps a hand to her chest. "You let me believe he killed himself because of *me!*"

I don't speak as she doubles over and cries again. I'm not even sure what she's weeping over—the fact that I kept the truth from her, or the fact that the truth is her brother is her father's real murderer.

There is no light in this darkness. There is only Rosa and her tears and me and my deception. I still love her, and I think she still loves me. But I'm certain I've committed the unforgiveable sin now. I'm positive we will not recover from this. And how could we? How could I expect my loving wife to forgive me when I know I wouldn't forgive myself for this?

But Rosa isn't like most women. She's kind and good and Christian down to her bones—to her *marrow.* Forgiveness is a huge part of her faith, probably the most important part. But am I asking for too much this time? Has Rosa reached her limit with me?

I clench my jaw as I watch her pour her heart into the blankets through her bitter tears. *God,* I say inside…

My thoughts trail off. Other than when Rosa prompted me to try, this is the first time I've ever prayed. I'm not exactly sure what else to say except how I feel. If Rosa is right about God knowing everything, then He's already aware of how I feel, so there's no point in hiding.

I take a slow breath.

God, please help Rosa. Please let her forgive me. In Jesus' Name.

I know He heard, but I have no right to believe God *listened* to my prayer. I have done nothing but sin since the day I was born. And I'm not even sorry. Guilty, yes, but sorry? Not in the least. I've always done what I needed to do. Even those prostitutes were just collateral damage. Their burned bodies gave me nightmares for days, but what happened wasn't my fault. None of this is.

It isn't my fault I was born into this sick family in this twisted city. It isn't my fault I've had to kill and lie and cheat just to stay alive most days. This is the mafia, if God wanted me to be anything else but the monster I've become, He would've given me an out. An escape from this dark world.

You have never asked for one.

The Voice that whispers into my thoughts sends a tingle over my skin. I stop breathing as I glance around, sneaking a look down at Rosa to see if she heard the words, too. She's still crying like I'm not even here.

Who was that? I ask myself. But in my heart, I already know the answer.

Rosa cries herself to sleep. When she wakes with tear-stained cheeks, she doesn't speak to me, but she's too exhausted and sore to put up a fuss when I carry her to the bathroom and give her a bath. I'm aware it's a patronizing act, but I don't do it to treat her as a child. I do it because I love her and I want to take care of her, even when she wants nothing to do with me. She's in pain because of me, if humbling myself and washing her feet will somehow make it better, then I'll scrub her down every day.

After I pat her dry and apply lotion, Rosa finally speaks. "I don't need help picking out clothes," she says when I head to the suitcase she has open on the floor. Since the rooms will be shuffled every week and the safehouse changed every month, she decided not to unpack anything. I don't blame her.

I nod as I turn toward the bathroom. "I'll go clean myself up."

"Don't," she says. "I'd like it if you just leave, actually."

I stare at her. "You'll let me give you a bath, but you won't let me bathe myself?"

Her brows flatten. "There's a bathroom down the hall. There are plenty of empty rooms down the hall."

I could fly off the rails and turn this tense but calm conversation into a screaming match. I could start throwing things. I could remind Rosa that I'm the underboss of the German mafia and I don't have to care what she would like, prefer, or want. But I'm not my father or my brother. I won't let my mafia ego ruin my marriage.

I don't like it. I feel used. But I do understand.

Rosa needed my help in the bathroom. She was tired and weak from last night—both the crying and the lovemaking. I'm the reason for her exhaustion no matter how you look at it. So I'll accept this as my punishment.

She needs her space. Fine.

But there is one niggling concern that I can't let go of. So I turn to my wife and spear her with a serious gaze. "How long will it be this way?"

She looks at me, her gaze just as even. "I don't know."

As badly as I want to set my anger loose, I decide it's best to just give Rosa what she wants this time. Some battles aren't worth what it'll take to win them. So, with a huff, I gather my clothes, kiss my wife on the forehead, and leave without another word. I don't know when I'll get to see her again, but I hold on to the hope that maybe my little prayer worked and whenever I do see her again, she will have forgiven me and gotten over my transgressions.

Until that happens, I'll distract myself with work. There's a war going on, after all. I shouldn't let the worries of a woman get to me in the middle of all this. If my head isn't on straight, I could end up getting shot in it. Though it sounds heartless, I need to forget about Rosa right now. And prayer too.

It was cute when I was desperately trying to get my wife to feel better, but I don't want to do that again. Or, more accurately, I don't want to hear that *Voice* again. I don't want to be faced with the truth.

That God is real.

Because if He is, then He's right. About everything.

I've never asked for a way out.

I've never liked being in the mafia, but I can't name a single time where I set myself up to get out. Even Rosa, with all her tears and trembling and hysterics, was brave enough to run at some point. But all I've done is complain and blame God for something so simple.

It's not like I don't have the means to get away. It's not like I don't have the connections. The Jägers are known for mining diamonds and precious stones overseas at illegally operated mines, but we have several sites that are completely legal. I even personally own one of our jewelry stores—LLC approved and everything. If I run, I wouldn't have to shack up at a women's ministry like Rosa. I could live a very comfortable life as the owner of a lucrative diamond store.

My wife and I could settle down, away from the city, away from the violence and danger. I could live an honest life, buy her a beautiful home, put a beautiful kid in her, and adopt a beautiful dog.

Maybe. Someday.

For now, I've got to finish this war. Until that happens, all those fancy thoughts are just hopeful dreams. Prayers I refuse to utter.

I bet you were thinking I was on my way to salvation, right?

Sorry to disappoint.

Have you forgotten that I'm a selfish monster? When will you learn.

Eighteen

I want to go straight to my office after I finish my shower. There is no time for breakfast. Even though my stomach protests against this decision, I don't feel agitated by the hunger. As I walk through the lobby of the hotel/safehouse, I notice other men tiredly sneaking out of bedrooms, wiping sleep from their eyes and buttoning their clothes. I guess I'm not the only one who had a busy night.

I smile as I see Eike leaving Petra's room, but he doesn't smile back. His eyes are wild with fear and worry which immediately makes my pulse race.

"What is it?" I snap.

He wets his lips. "The Jägermeister called a meeting. He says its urgent."

I frown and pull out my phone. Seven missed calls. They all must have happened while I was in the bathroom with Rosa.

"Round up the rest of the men," I order. "Tell them to get to HQ immediately."

I don't wait for Eike to respond before I turn and jog down

the hall. He didn't go with us on our last mission, he doesn't know how serious Vater's summoning truly is.

After we got back from Staten Island, I made the executive decision to send men right back in. Uwe and Onkel Oberon had been opposed, as had most of the men, but I was adamant. The idea was to hit the Wolves when they least expected it. Going right back into Staten Island after barely escaping was certainly not smart, but it *was* bold enough to catch them off guard. At least that's what I'd hoped. Right now, it seems my gamble was too risky—that I've bitten off more than I can chew.

When Douglass pulls up to The Club—yes, The Club is our HQ, at least for this week, we've been moving around a lot to stay safe—we jump out together and walk side by side toward the entrance. His nearness only momentarily surprises me, I'd almost forgotten how big of a role he's played in the business recently. He isn't just my guard or my driver anymore; Douglass shed blood for me, he fought beside me, he experienced loss with me. He's my brother now, as much as Wolfgang is.

I stare at his shoulder where he was shot while I'd tried to save Ja'meek. The doctors said it was just a flesh wound, but it's left him with a wince as he reaches for the door, and probably a wicked scar once it's all healed up.

He catches me staring as I pass into The Club and says in German, "My scars are for you, brother."

I nod. "And mine for you."

Vater is standing at a tall table with a bottle of whiskey when I approach. Onkel, Klaus, King James, Giovanni, Niccolò—almost every head of each respective gang is present. Conrad is sitting in a booth, staring at a sweaty shot he hasn't touched, Trenton and Tyrese are by his side, muttering to one another. Aldo is missing, but I heard his injuries were worse than we thought so he's still in the hospital. Hans and Jared volunteered to be on his security team until he's well enough to be discharged.

"What's going on?" I say as I approach.

Vater glances up from his conversation with Jameson and slides the bottle of whiskey over to me. It's a gesture that makes my heart pound. If I'm going to need a drink before hearing the news, then things are worse than I thought.

"I have two things to say," Vater says, looking up to glare at me. "First, your little covert mission was a total—" he cuts himself off as the doors open to let Eike and Marco Segreto inside. They mutter apologies as they rush over to join the crowd.

Uwe clears his throat. "Your mission was a failure, Amory."

I nod.

With all the suspense, I had expected as much. The mission was to sneak back into the Island and use the intel we got from the Russian we tortured to destroy another warehouse. Failing was not the outcome we wanted, but it's nothing to be torn up about. Even if we lost everyone, I'd only sent in a small team

191

of six men to minimize possible losses.

"I'll contact the families of the men who were killed."

"That's not all," Vater says, and then his tone darkens as he slides his phone across the table. "I got a message."

I glance down at the phone and gasp. It's a text from Morgen's number. But the message is signed by Mikhail Volkov.

Six men. Five dead.

I scroll down to see five bodies, each with a bullet in their head. I know those men—some of them were grunts, one was an Italian I'd only met last week, but they were good men. Loyal men who'd volunteered for a mission they knew would likely go up in flames. They had trusted my judgment and I got them killed.

I look up at my father.

"Keep reading," he instructs.

You can take the last man home. But you must come get him yourself. Amory Jäger.

My heart stops when I see my name. Volkov wants to lure me out, and he's using a hostage to do it. But not just any hostage.

I scroll down once more to see the picture of the last man and my eyes immediately blur with rage. My head starts to throb, my breath hitches in my throat.

I want to respond to Volkov's summons, if only to look him in the eye as I shoot him dead.

"Morgen…" I mutter, clutching the phone so hard, my hand starts to ache. "Volkov has Morgen."

In the photo, he's on his knees with his hands tied behind his back. Blood mats his whitish blonde hair and trickles down his forehead into his left eye. His right eye is swollen shut; his top lip is busted. I think his nose might be broken, but it's always been crooked so it's hard to tell. He looks a mess, but he's definitely alive. I can see the fear in his one good eye.

This is my fault.

I sent those men out there, against Vater's wishes—against Onkel's wishes.

I glance up at Oberon and exhale an apology, "Onkel, I'm sorry."

He closes his eyes and shakes his head solemnly, but when he finally looks up at me, I see an odd mix of anger and sorrow swirling in his orbs. No judgment. No blame. Just a desire to see his son and get vengeance on his kidnapper.

"Don't blame yourself," Onkel says slowly. "Nobody here blames you."

"I do." Conrad shoves away from his table and storms across the floor. He throws a punch as soon as he nears me, but Eike grabs him from behind, pinning his arms at his sides.

"Let me go!" my cousin shouts, spit flying. "You got my brother killed!"

"He *isn't* dead," Vater says harshly, then he turns and slaps the taste out of Conrad's mouth. His head jerks to the side, neck cracking with the harsh blow. The room falls quiet, even Conny calms down for a second. He sags in Eike's arms, leaning into his hold and breathing heavily. Blood runs from a cut on his cheek. When I look at Uwe's hand, I see blood on his signet ring.

Vater leans into his face to hiss, "If you ever raise your hand at my son again, I will cut it off."

Conrad nods. "*Jawohl, Jägermeister.*"

Uwe turns to the crowd of shocked men. "I understand this is a difficult time, but you must all remember this is war. Death will happen. Even to the best of us."

"*Bruder,*" Oberon says in his rumbling timbre, "you are right, my son is not dead. But he will be soon if we don't do something."

There is only one thing we *can* do.

I clear my throat. "I'm going to see Volkov."

"No, you're not," Vater says firmly.

"If I don't, Morgen will die. I won't let that happen."

"I'll go with him," Conrad volunteers, wiping the blood from his face. He walks over and takes the entire bottle of whiskey, chugs down more than he should, and then glares at me. "I'm going to get my brother back."

"No one is going anywhere," Vater grinds out.

I shake my head. "We can't ignore Volkov. Not this time."

"I won't let him kill you!" Uwe shouts.

I don't allow myself to believe that statement is coming from the bottom of my father's heart. More than anything, he doesn't want to lose his underboss, and he doesn't want to suffer the insult and shame of losing his son to the Alpha of the Staten Island Wolves. But his hysterics send a ripple of silence shooting through the room, which calms everyone long enough for me to say, "Volkov isn't going to kill me."

Vater stares at me. "Why not?"

"Because I'm not the one he wants."

Wolfgang is.

But as long as my little brother is locked up in Stonehall, he will be perfectly safe. Out of Volkov's reach. That's what this meeting is going to be about.

"Volkov likely wants to offer me some sort of deal to get to Wolf," I explain.

"And what do you think will happen when you refuse?" Klaus asks.

"He will kill you," Uwe says.

I shake my head. "This meeting was requested by Volkov himself. If he wanted to kill me, he would have just sent the picture of Morgen and his location. Then he would have ambushed us when we went out to retrieve him. Volkov wants to talk. Nothing more."

"Why do you trust him so much?" Onkel asks.

"Because I've been alone with him before. More than once. He could have killed me twice now if he'd really wanted to." My gaze narrows on the whiskey in Conrad's hand. I suddenly want a drink more than anything. "When Mikhail Volkov is truly ready to make a move, he won't send a text message to get started. He'll flatten Brooklyn." I glance at all of them, holding their gazes for a few moments so they know I'm serious. "Why do you think he hasn't retaliated yet? We blew up five buildings in Staten Island almost a week ago and his only response is to send a text message and ask for a meeting?" I shake my head. "He just wants to talk. If he wanted anything else, he would have done it by now."

I can see my words are sinking in, though Vater doesn't look entirely convinced, but his indecision doesn't matter to me. I've already made up my mind.

"I'm going," I say, turning away.

"Right now?" Klaus asks.

I stop and nod. "This needs to be dealt with immediately."

"I'm going with you." Conrad appears by my side, eyes wild with anger and vengeance.

I slowly turn to face him. "No, Conny, stay here."

"He's my brother."

"That's why you need to stay. If things go wrong—"

"How could they go wrong?"

I swallow. I can't believe he's going to make me say this.

"Volkov is going to ask me to give him Wolfgang in exchange for Morgen."

Everyone in this room knows that's not going to happen.

As much as I love my little cousin, I simply cannot give up my brother for him. Not just because Wolf is more closely related to me, but because he's also a higher rank than Morgen. That's the dark reality here. Just as I wouldn't trade Conrad for Maximilian, I won't be forced into giving up Wolfgang for Morgen. It isn't a trade worth making.

I glance around at the other men as understanding dawns

on everyone. Uwe looks grim, Oberon simply stares at the near-empty whiskey bottle, Niccolò and Gio say nothing, but King James looks at me with a hard face. His brows are knit firmly together, his chin is wrinkled as he frowns, but I can just make out the hint of agreement in his dark eyes. He knows better than anyone what it's like to be in this position. *I* put him in this same position six years ago when my men Hunted Douglass and he was forced to choose between starting a war with us or letting go of one of his distant relatives.

Though Douglass was the son of a General in the Willis Stronghold, he wasn't high-ranking enough for Jameson to justify a full-blown retaliation. He wasn't worth the bloodshed. He wasn't worth the sacrifice.

The same goes for Morgen.

If this were any other case, I would storm Staten Island for my little cousin, but if the choice is him or Wolfgang then I've got to let him go. For my brother and for my reputation. I will not trade a lower ranked man for the son of the Jägermeister.

Conrad sways as he takes a step back, sputtering his words in a wobbly voice. "B—But he's my brother."

"I know…" I say quietly. "That's why it's best you stay here."

"So I don't have to watch Volkov kill him!" he shouts. "Why are you even going if his life has already been decided?"

I take a breath. "To retrieve his body."

Nineteen

For the first time in years, I sit in the driver's seat and take the steering wheel for myself. I don't remember the last time I drove anywhere, but I refused to let Douglass or Conrad drive me. Conny is too emotional right now and even though I told everyone Volkov wouldn't hurt me, the truth is that I'm not so sure. He could kill me. And if it comes to that, I'd rather it happens alone so no one else is caught in the crossfire.

This whole thing is my failure. I should have listened to Vater and Onkel. I should have double checked to make sure no one else joined the mission at the last minute without my consent. Now I may have to take my own cousin's body back home—if Volkov even allows me to return home.

Again, I find myself grasping desperate strands of hope as I mutter a prayer under my breath. "God ... help me."

I won't allow myself to believe anyone is listening—even though I've been faced with undeniable proof that there is, that *He* is. It's too much to think about right now, so I whisper the words in a shaky voice and then I punch the radio on, so I won't be left in silence to hear that strange Voice again.

When I pull onto Volkov's property, I'm not surprised to find no guards or security or gates. He's so confident I won't show up guns blazing, it pisses me off, but not any more than the fact that he's right. I've shown up with my tail tucked and my balls clipped.

I reach into the glovebox and grab my gun, and just to show Volkov he's not entirely in control here, I don't bother hiding the weapon as I storm up to the front doors. With a shove, they part to let me in. My footsteps echo through the hall as I walk through the mansion like I own the place, gun gripped so tightly, my knuckles are raw and red.

There is a set of double doors at the end of the main corridor, they're left wide open, and I can hear voices coming from inside. As I approach, I make out Volkov's familiar tenor. The sound of it gives me the anger I need to march right inside without hesitation.

Volkov is sitting behind a large desk, a laptop in front of him, with three men crowded around him. They're dressed in all black suits, but there is nothing gentlemanly about them. Ugly scars mar their faces, intricately designed tattoos mark their hands, arms, and even their necks. The massive creature standing right beside Volkov is totally bald, but his head and face is covered in a coat of ink. Black lines decorate his skin to make him look like a walking skeleton. The sight of it almost throws me off, but I keep my resolve and walk right up to Volkov's desk, gun in hand.

He glances up. "You came." He nods at the weapon in my

hand and then looks at the bald skeleton man. "Yuri, you owe me a thousand dollars."

I squint as the big man chuckles. As if to explain, Volkov says, "We made a bet—two, actually—if you would come alone and if you would come armed."

"This is not a game," I growl, leaning over his desk.

His smile withers as he stands. Mikhail is a tall man, but he's thin and willowy and older than Vater. I'm not afraid of him physically, but it's his unassuming nature that makes him so dangerous. What he lacks in his form, he more than makes up for in his mentality. They call the Volkovs 'Wolves' but 'Vipers' is a more fitting term, in my opinion. Like a snake, he attacks at random. The bite itself is never too painful—it's the venom that takes you down. Because you never feel it right away. Not until it's too late.

"No, Jäger, this is not a game," Volkov says darkly. His Russian accent is so thick, I have to concentrate when he speaks, but I understand him perfectly when he turns to Yuri and orders, "Bring in the boy."

Boy. Morgen is twenty-four years old. Engaged. And on his way to becoming a General in the German mafia. He isn't a *boy* at all. But as Yuri steps away and returns with the whittled frame that is my cousin, I can't see him as anything but a child.

He is bloody and bruised, but it isn't his injuries that reduce him to that of a boy. It's the wild look of fear in his eyes. It's the way his face is creased with worry that turns to relief when he sees me standing there. I am his rescuer right now. He knows I've come to help him … that's why it tears my very soul apart when I see Volkov take out his gun and aim it at him.

I immediately point my gun at Yuri which makes the other two Russians in the room lift their guns toward me. Volkov just smirks.

"Calm down, Jäger," he orders.

"No."

"You knew this would happen when you first saw the message."

He's right, but I don't have to admit that.

"You haven't made an offer," I say hoarsely. "Let's talk, Volkov."

"What is the point? We both know you will refuse my offer."

Morgen squirms and cries against the fabric stuffed into his mouth. Yuri responds by yanking his head back by his hair and kicking in the back of his knee. He buckles and drops to the floor with a groan, glaring over his shoulder at the massive Russian.

"Call off your men," I order gruffly.

"No."

"*Volkov!*" His name comes out like a curse, my voice filled with rage. I cock my gun to show him I'm serious—so do the other two Russians.

Volkov's lupine grin flattens into a more serious expression. To my surprise, he lowers his gun—even sets it on the desk as he walks around to the front and rests his butt on the edge.

"All right, Jäger," he says smugly, "let us talk. Like gentlemen."

"Call them off," I repeat.

He lazily waves his hand, and they follow the order right away. Morgen heaves a sigh behind his gag as Yuri takes a small step back. He isn't safe yet, not by a longshot, but he's still alive. That's something.

"What's your offer?" I ask, lowering my gun.

"You already know what it is."

The same offer it's always been.

"Wolfgang," I mutter.

He nods slowly, then crosses his ankles and stuffs his hands into his pockets. In the dim lighting of his office, his silvery hair is dark grey, it makes him look more ghostly than normal—especially when he grins and lets out a low chuckle that seems to fill the room. His voice is haunting as it swells around me, a deep timbre sharpened by his Russian accent.

"Because I am merciful, I will make this offer even better than the last one."

My eyes narrow on him.

"The last time we spoke, I wanted your little brother. In exchange for his life, I promised to leave Giovanni alone and spare your gang the struggles of war." Volkov pauses, letting his words hang in the air. "Now, I will offer you the same thing. We can end this war right here and now. You can have your little cousin back. And you can rest assured that Giovanni will be spared. All you must do is give me your brother."

"That offer isn't much better than your last," I tell him.

He nods at Morgen, still on his knees in front of Yuri's threatening figure. "Is your cousin's life not important to you?"

Morgen says something behind his gag that I can't make out, but from the way he's shaking his head, I know he's trying to tell me not to give in. Not to trade his life for Wolf's. I'll remember to tell Onkel and Conrad of his bravery when I get back, with or without him. It's strange that he's so easily accepted his fate, but Conrad tried to assault me over it. I don't blame either one of them. It's a horrible situation to be in.

Too bad no one spares any empathy for me. I'm stuck in this too. I'm just as screwed as Conny. But no matter what happens here today, I will be the villain. I'll be the man who let his cousin die, or the man who traded his brother's life for a deal with the Russians. I will not win here. I can't choose who to save, I can only choose who gets to hate me more.

"You know I can't take this deal," I say in a dark voice.

Volkov tilts his head to the side, the movement almost makes him look like a cat. Or a wolf. I'm not sure.

"What if I make it even better?"

"There is nothing else you can offer me. I will not give you my little brother."

Morgen gasps into his gag but straightens his back and keeps his gaze forward. When I look at him, I see no judgment in his eyes, only the hardened stare of a man who's made up his mind. A man who has realized this is his last day alive— and decided to die with his chin up.

"How do you think I so easily captured your little covert team, Jäger?" Volkov asks me.

It never dawned on me how it happened, just that it *did* happen and now I've got to fix it. I don't let Volkov see the questions swirling in my head. I won't give him the satisfaction of knowing just how much I've begun to sweat. I sharpen my gaze and harden my features, refusing to give him a verbal response.

He smiles like he's looking at a child. "I allowed your men to sneak back into my Island. I even allowed them to reach the warehouse they intended to blow up. It wasn't until they moved in to plant the explosives that I had them taken in." He uncrosses his ankles and folds his arms across his chest. "I killed five of the six men you sent in. How do you think I knew which man was your cousin?"

I glance down at Morgen. With all his cuts and bruises, I assumed they tortured the information out of him, but that doesn't make sense now. Not after seeing Morgen so willingly accept his impending death sentence. That's not the decisiveness of a man who would start singing after one night of torture.

Morgen has more grit than that. More backbone.

"How?" I spit out the word, hating the look of Volkov's wolfish grin and pale grey eyes.

"You have a mole in your midst."

The words almost knock the wind out of me. A mole. A snitch. A traitor. Someone who spilled our plans to Volkov and got my own cousin taken in by the Russians. Someone who set us up to fail.

But who?

"I will tell you who," Volkov says, reading my mind. "It must be hard to tell who is a friend and who is a foe with so many mobsters in one alliance." He chuckles at the jab he's just thrown at my contract with Jameson and Gio. I thought having three mafias united as one would give me a leg up in this war, but I've just provided Volkov with more men to bribe.

If this war were one on one, there would be no mole. My men are loyal to me. They would never turn against each other, especially not if it meant weighing Morgen's life against Wolfgang's. But what about the members of the Stronghold? What about the Garden? Are there rogue soldiers in their ranks? Men who just want to go home and love their wives and protect their children? Men who were spooked by the salon blowing up and the unexpected turns of our first mission?

I squeeze my eyes shut to silence all the questions screaming through my head. In the silence, I hear Volkov say, "I will tell you who the mole is."

My eyes fly open. That's the meat of his new deal. He will spare Giovanni, he will give me my cousin back, he will end this war right here, and he will give up the rat who's been feeding him information. In exchange for my brother's life.

The scars on my back begin to ache as my stress rises. This isn't fair. This isn't right. How can I possibly make a choice?

"How much is your brother's life worth?" Volkov asks.

I lift my chin. "How do I know you aren't just bluffing?"

Without a word, he walks behind his desk and turns the laptop to face me. "Watch," he says, clicking a button.

The screen lights up and I see myself. And Rosa.

It's footage from last night in our safehouse … We're in bed, making love.

I grip my gun as rage crackles through me. "How dare you!"

"You asked for proof," Volkov says with a nonchalant shrug. "Here it is."

It isn't that he's gotten access to our security systems. It isn't that he's got a mole working for him in my alliance. It's that he could have used any sort of footage as proof that he wanted, but he chose to disrespect me with this.

My wife is naked on the screen in front of my cousin and four Russian men. She is the wife of the German underboss. This video—playing it like this in front of everyone—is a dishonor to her name. And an insult to mine.

Volkov knows this. He chose this recording on purpose. To humiliate me. Because he blames Wolfgang for the dishonor that happened with his own daughter. The murder of Sofia Volkov. He has no proof it was murder, but Mikhail is a smart man. He doesn't need any proof. Deep down, he's always known the truth. He just never had the evidence he needed to justify starting a war with us over it. Not until now.

This is his vengeance. This is his way of redeeming his daughter and the shame he endured in seeing her battered, bloody body.

I get it. I really do.

I have never tried to justify Wolfgang's behavior. I've only tried to protect him from a death sentence. But no matter how I feel about my brother and his cruel actions, nothing justifies what Volkov has done to Rosa. She is innocent here. She doesn't deserve to have her privacy invaded like this. She doesn't deserve to suffer the shame of having a bunch of men stand around and watch while we tangle in the sheets.

I lift my gun. "Turn it off."

One of the men steps toward the laptop, but Volkov stops him. "Let it play."

I can hear myself in the video, whispering to my wife, telling her things only she should hear. Rosa screams my name, which makes Yuri glance at the screen and smile—then he makes the mistake of reaching down to grope himself.

I put a bullet between his eyes.

Then I shoot the laptop.

And because I know it's inevitable now, I look down and shoot Morgen too. His body hits the floor with an audible *thud!* right next to Yuri's.

The silence that follows almost deafens me. It is a storm of unspoken threats, promises of danger and violence and death.

I welcome them.

"No deal," I say finally. My voice is hoarse and low, it matches my blackened mood.

Volkov doesn't even look at Yuri. His vision remains focused on me. "You just made a grave mistake."

"No. I didn't." I lift my gun again, pointing it right at him. "I don't care about Giovanni's life. I can find the mole on my own. And I've just killed my cousin. You don't have anything to offer me anymore." I step forward and press the gun to his forehead. "No deal."

"Would you shoot a man in his own home?" Volkov asks, though there is no fear in his voice, only a hint of boldness I recognize as a challenge. He *wants* me to shoot him, so he can die knowing his men will immediately shoot me in response. I suppose one dead Jäger is just as good as the other.

I lower the gun. "There's been enough death today."

"I agree. Especially since there is so much more to come." Volkov walks around his desk, not even flinching when he steps over Yuri's big body. "I offered you peace. You spat in my face for it. Now I will not hold back. I will not spare any member of your family." He smirks. "Not even your pretty wife."

I *pray* he dares to say more than that so I can shoot someone else, but he leaves his threat at that and jerks his head toward Morgen's body. "Take your cousin. We will not attack for two days so you can have a proper burial, as we will have to bury Yuri now."

I nod and tuck my gun into my waistband. "Two days."

Twenty

The drive home is long and quiet. If I didn't hold on to the steering wheel for dear life, I would swerve off the road from my shaking hands. I'm trembling harder than Rosa on the night I stole her innocence. It's embarrassing.

This isn't the first time I've killed someone. I don't even know how many times I've pulled the trigger. I don't want to know. But I do want to know why it's affecting me this way right now. Even when I killed Ja'meek, I'd surprised myself by shedding a single tear. It was just one, but still. I've never cried over a death before. Not when I was the killer.

Maybe it's because what happened in Volkov's home wasn't just about Morgen or Yuri. It's about all of New York City now. Volkov promised he wouldn't hold back anymore. He won't keep our wives or children or anyone else out of it. He wants to devour the entire Apple. Even if it means Staten Island will burn too. And it's all my fault.

My temper got the best of me. I let him bait me into shooting one of his men, giving him the excuse he needed to declare no holds barred. I should have taken Douglass with me to keep my head clear. Showing up alone was a mistake. Volkov knew that. He'd betted on it.

I grit my teeth as I realize I'd fallen right into his plans. It makes me want to turn the car around and do what I should have done in his office. But I never would have walked out of there if I had pulled the trigger again. The only reason he let me get away with killing Yuri is because he knows he'll have his vengeance soon enough.

He's got a mole in our ranks. And I have no idea who it is. Someone who's been at all of our meetings, someone who knows the layout of the safehouses and our visiting/rotation schedule. But that could be anyone. Whenever we've handled business, there has been at least ten men present—not to mention the security details on the safehouses and the women we rescued from Staten Island.

Maybe one of them is sneaking out intel on the safehouses. Maybe someone from the Italian mafia is trying to protect what's left of the withering Garden. Maybe one of the Stronghold soldiers wants to get revenge on Rosa for getting her mother killed months ago. They were bitter about the Willis princess's death to the point of disowning Rosa. Our marriage was her reinstatement into the family again.

There's just no way to tell.

Giovanni De Luca Jr.
Niccolò Romano
Aldo Romano

Marco Segreto
Jameson Willis
Trenton Willis
Tyrese Willis
Jared Washington
Oberon Jäger
Conrad Jäger
Klaus Brandt
Eike Brandt
Hans Vogt

So many Generals... Each with their own connections. Each with their own secrets. Their own motives. That leaves a lot of room for potential leaks, spies, traitors, and liars.

When I get to The Club, I pull around back and enter the small garage Conrad keeps for VIP parking. By the time I get out and walk around to the trunk of the car, my cousin, uncle, and father have entered the lot. I'm glad it's just them. No one else needs to see or hear this right now.

Onkel's eyes are hard and focused, but his face is soft and dewy like he's been crying. Conrad just looks angry, staring at the trunk of the car in silent anticipation.

Uwe steps forward and pats my shoulder. "I know you did your best."

I nod. "Is there anyone else in The Club?"

"A couple men are inside. We asked them to stay back so

Oberon and Conrad can do this in private."

"Good."

I turn and open the trunk to reveal Morgen. He's still bound and gagged and bloody, his suit disheveled and his head resting on the red-stained carpet of the car. A stiff silence engulfs the entire garage as we all stare at him. Judging from the solemn looks on everyone's face, I can tell they all expected this outcome. Which is why I'm not surprised that Conrad screams when Morgen coughs and lets out a tired groan.

"Brother!" he shouts, rushing over to the trunk of the car. He reaches inside and grips Morgen's shoulders to help him sit up. His hands roam his brother's frame, checking for the bullet hole he doesn't have. Then he looks back at me. His face is wet with tears and his eyes are filled with wonder. "How?"

"I shot him," I admit. "Just not in the head."

I knew the only way to save Morgen would be to shoot him myself. That's why I made sure I shot Yuri first, to distract everyone from the slightly inaccurate shot I delivered to my cousin. The bullet just grazed the skin, tearing across his eye and temple with enough force to whip his head back and knock him out—making Volkov think he was dead.

Looking back, that disgraceful video was the perfect excuse to lose my temper and shoot everyone in the room. In a way, Volkov helped me save Morgen's life.

My little cousin blinks at me weakly as Conrad gingerly unties his hands and removes his gag. Up close, I can see the blood dried around his ear, matting the hair on the side of his head. He will lose his left eye and probably part of his hearing in the left ear, but he'll be alive.

Onkel turns me around and crushes me in a hug. "You saved my son. I can't believe it."

"He needs a doctor, one we can trust," I say once he releases me. "The Volkovs think he's dead and we need it to stay that way."

"We'll announce the death and hold a funeral," Vater says with a thoughtful nod. "It must look real."

"Which means no one besides us and Morgen's doctor will know the truth." I look at Onkel with hard eyes, hoping he can see how serious this is. "You cannot tell *Tante* about this."

He drops his gaze for a moment. Viktoria Jäger—my sweet German aunt—is the love of Oberon's life. He dotes on her, going through painstaking efforts to keep her as far away from the mafia as possible. She knows who he is and what he does, but Tante Vikky has always been distant—out of the loop. She isn't even staying in one of our safehouses because she doesn't live in the city. Oberon keeps her in a house just outside NYC, a two hour drive every day, but he makes it without complaint because it helps him sleep at night knowing she's safe.

But her sons aren't safe. They're right in the thick of things, and now we've got to convince her that one of them is dead because of the very business Oberon worked so hard to keep her out of. It will break her, probably as badly as it would break my little rose. So I sympathize with Onkel on a deeper level than the rest of the guys when he sighs and claps my shoulder.

"I understand," he mutters. "I'll tell her tonight."

"The funeral must be immediately," I say, glancing up at

213

Vater. "Volkov said he would give me two days before resuming the war."

"And you believe him?"

"I shot one of his men while I was there. But no, I don't entirely believe him."

Conrad's eyes go wide. "You shot someone?"

I nod. "That's why Volkov wants two days, to bury one of his own. But it's also why I don't believe him, because now he's hungry for revenge." I look at each of them with the most serious expression I can muster. "Morgen wasn't the only reason I shot one of Volkov's men."

Uwe raises his eyebrows. They go up even higher when Morgen lets out a hoarse chuckle. I should punch him for laughing at what I'm about to say, but he's been through enough.

"What I have to say cannot leave this garage." My jaw tics when I clench it, trying to erase the memory of the lewd video on the laptop. "Volkov told me there is a rat among us."

Both shock and rage fills Vater's eyes. "A rat." He spits on the ground. "He would dare suggest one of our men is a traitor!"

"He had proof," I tell him calmly. "A video of me and Rosa in the safehouse last night." I don't need to say the rest for them to figure out what I mean.

Conrad whips his head at Morgen to look into his one swollen eye. "Is it true?"

He nods slowly. "I saw it."

"And you won't speak of it again," I say darkly.

He nods.

"Someone is feeding Volkov intel. They have access to our security network. They know the layout of our missions. And they're aware of the setup of our safehouses."

"It's someone high-ranking," Onkel says slowly.

"And someone who isn't German," I say.

"What makes you sure of that?" Conrad asks.

"Because we are the only ones who lose from this. Despite our contracts, the truth is that the Stronghold and the Garden could both abandon us the moment they think we aren't worth the struggle anymore."

It sucks, but it's the truth. Jameson Willis already disowned Rosa once, and Giovanni killed his own father. We're not allied with very loyal people.

"Until we pinpoint the spy, everyone outside this garage is on a need-to-know basis from now on." I watch each of them nod. "That means Morgen is dead to us. We'll patch him up and send him off, make the announcement, and hold the funeral."

"You two need to be in mourning," Vater tells Onkel and Conrad.

"I will be mourning for my wife's broken heart," Oberon says. Conrad just stares at the ground. He loves his mother as much as his father does.

"And we need to move our families from the safehouses," I say.

"Won't that let everyone know there's a spy?" Conny asks.

"We're rotating them around anyway. Doing it after

Morgen's 'death' won't surprise anyone."

"With a mole, it won't matter if we change location," Onkel says. "They'll just tell Volkov the new addresses."

"Not if we keep everything close," I say confidently.

"How can we move our families around Manhattan without at least Gio and the rest of the Italians and the Stronghold guards serving as their security finding out?" Conrad crosses his arms.

When I pause to think, Vater fills the silence. "We can't." He looks at me. "There are some things we simply won't be able to keep a secret."

He's right. I just hate it. Because it means Rosa will always be in danger.

"Maybe we should let the men take their families back home," I suggest. "No one is safe anyway with a rat on the streets."

"But that will let the rat know that we're on to him," Conrad points out.

"Not if I blame the decision on Morgen's 'death' and Volkov's threat to come for everyone."

Morgen nods agreement. "That might work," he says, then he leans over and starts to wheeze out ragged coughs.

Conrad rubs his back. "He needs a doctor."

I pass him my keys. "You and Onkel take care of him. Vater and I will go inside to make the announcement."

Every eye is glued to me when I enter The Club. I don't have to try very hard to put on a solemn face. I'm happy Morgen is alive, but that's just one small blessing in a sea of curses. Against the coming war, the mole, and the very real threat to the lives of every woman and child in Brooklyn—it feels like I got my cousin back only to lose everyone else I love in exchange.

This weighs on me as I stand before the crowd of Hunters, Gardeners, and soldiers of the Stronghold. Douglass is by my side in a heartbeat, patting my shoulder as I take a deep breath and share the terrible news about my cousin's death. I tell the men that Volkov is responsible and that we must be ready for what may come next. I tell them that no one is safe—but not because of the mole—I blame it on my recklessness in killing one of Volkov's men. I blame it on Mikhail's thirst for blood and desire for vengeance on behalf of Yuri's untimely death. I tell them we're prepared to do whatever it takes to protect ourselves and the ones we love.

"If you want to take your wives and children back home, you are welcome to," I say loudly. "Or you can leave them in our safehouses. The choice is yours." The men murmur to themselves. "For now, let us drink to Morgen's memory and get ourselves prepared for his burial."

Vater makes a toast and then breaks a beer bottle over the counter in his honor. The men cheer mournfully and then pass a bottle around until we're all swaying where we stand. I don't drink much. I'm not in the mood, and I want to keep my wits about me.

As I glance through the crowd, I wonder if I'm looking

into the eyes of the traitor. I wonder which man is pretending to care about Morgen's supposed death. When my eyes grow weary from staring and my mind starts to fuzz with paranoia, I grab a bottle and head to one of the private rooms. I realize it's a wise move when the back doors open and some of Conny's best women file in, ready to serve alcohol—and whatever else the men want.

The door to the VIP room shuts softly behind me, the leather couch groans as I lay down, setting the half-empty bottle on the table before me. I dig out my phone and call Rosa, not surprised when the call is diverted to voicemail. There is no way she wants to speak to me right now. I don't know if or when she will ever speak to me again. But I need her. I need to hear her voice.

I listen to the recording of her voicemail, just to hear her speak in a tone that isn't filled with rage or sorrow. Then I hang up and call again, pressing the phone to my ear when her recorded voice starts up again. It's a plain message—one of those that just tells me to leave a message at the tone—but right now, with death hanging over our heads, it's as beautiful as a song. I could lay here and call her phone all night, but that'll just make me feel pathetic in the morning, so I call once more and then set my phone on the table just to get it out of my hand.

The door opens behind me, and I roll my eyes. "I came back here for privacy—"

"Just refilling drinks." The voice is feminine, which immediately makes me sit up and glance over my shoulder.

There's a dancer standing in the doorway, undoubtedly one of Conrad's girls, but she looks familiar. Her hair is poorly straightened and dyed a cheap blonde color, leaving her dark curly roots exposed. Her bare shoulders are light brown, shimmering from the gold dust she painted all over her body, the rest of which is covered in a fishnet leotard that hides almost nothing from my view.

When my eyes trail up her frame to her face, I realize she's smiling at me. "It's you," I say quietly. The Rosa lookalike.

She steps inside and closes the door behind her. "Conrad took me in." Her smile turns sheepish. "And a few other girls from the Island. He said it would be better than working for Volkov."

"Yeah…"

"So far, it is."

I stare at her, noticing the bruise on her neck from where her pink collar used to be. She's tried to cover it with a gold choker, but I can still see the slightly discolored skin underneath. There's even an imprint on her throat. She must not have ever taken the thing off. Not until we came along.

"I thought you ladies wouldn't ever want to step foot into a club again."

She looks guilty. "I didn't want to be holed up in a safehouse."

"You didn't have to work in another club to get out."

"This is the only thing I know to do."

I squint at her, watching in silence as she glances away and shifts uncomfortably. She even holds the round platter in her hands against her body, shielding herself from my view. I wasn't trying to ogle her. But I can see why she'd get that idea. She's probably never had a normal conversation with a man before. At least not one that didn't lead to her sleeping with him afterward.

"How long did you work for Volkov?" I ask in a quiet voice.

She doesn't look at me as she says, "Four years."

I swallow. "You don't have to do it anymore."

"Well, it's not like anyone has offered me some other job."

I can't blame her on that one. I had no idea Conrad had approached any of the women we'd rescued. I make a note to confront him about it later. Having the prostitutes from the Island running around in our club adds even more suspects to the list of people who could possibly be the mole.

What better way to gain info than by milking it out of drunken gangsters, anyway? Aside from sex, that's what these women are trained for. It was a stripper from this very club who ratted me out to the Morenos when I discussed my marital issues with Conrad before.

An idea suddenly hits me.

I stand from the couch and walk up to the woman. She cowers, backing herself into the door. "What's your name?" I ask.

She brushes a trashy blonde lock behind her ear. "Amana."

"How old are you, Amana?"

"Eighteen."

I cup her chin. "Are you lying to me?" She looks like she

could pass as sixteen, maybe even younger. But she had been wearing a pink collar when we picked her up. Volkov wouldn't label her as an older girl if she weren't—especially not with the money he could make for passing her off as a child.

She shakes her head. "I turned eighteen last month."

Jesus.

With a deep breath, I place a hand on the wall beside her head. Caging her in. She tries to back away even more, practically flush against the wall now.

Still cupping her chin, I tilt her head up to make her look me in the eye. "Listen to me, Amana. I'm going to take you home with me tonight."

Her eyes widen, but the shock quickly settles into quiet understanding. She knows she doesn't have a choice.

"Do you trust me?" I ask softly.

She doesn't speak for a moment, but when I lean down and kiss her cheek, she nods stiffly. "Yes. I do."

"Good girl."

I turn away and grab the whiskey from the table, then I march to the window and pour half of it out. I run a hand through my hair, untuck my shirt, and then loosen my tie. When I walk back over to Amana, I place an arm over her shoulders and reach around her to open the door.

"Just follow me," I say as we exit together.

The men inside barely glance at us as we walk through. Half of them are drunk and passed out in chairs, the rest are seeking comfort from Conny's women, huddled together in booths while a dancer swings on a pole in front of them. I nod at

Douglass who catches my eye, and he gets up to grab the door for me.

"I'm heading home," I say, lazily waving my almost empty bottle of booze at him.

He looks at Amana. "Alone?"

"No. She's coming with me."

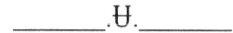

Amana doesn't speak during the entire ride. I don't blame her. She has no idea what's about to happen and, to be honest, I'm not sure she can handle it. I made a split-second decision that I can't really back out of right now. I'm hoping she's as capable as she looks.

When we get inside, I take her to my bedroom and tell Douglass to find her something to eat while I go to my bathroom and take an aspirin from the medicine cabinet. I feel a headache coming on and I don't know if it's from the stress, the hunger, or the fact that I've barely slept in two days.

It doesn't matter.

I toss the aspirin back, gulp a mouthful of water from the faucet, and then emerge to find Amana stripped naked and lying in my bed. She gives me a sultry smile when I walk out the bathroom and then rolls onto her side to give me a full view of her body. I've already seen her naked once, and her fishnet leotard didn't leave much to the imagination before, but I'm not impressed with her show right now.

Calmly, I remove my jacket and walk over to the bed. She

responds by opening her legs and lying spread-eagle with absolutely no shame.

I drape my jacket over her body like a blanket.

"Put this on," I say, sitting on the edge of the bed.

She stares at me, her legs still open beneath the makeshift covering. I can see the points of her knees jutting up through the fabric like the peaks of mountains.

"I thought—"

"That I brought you here to sleep with you?" I shake my head. "That's what I wanted my men to think. But that's not what I want to happen here tonight."

Embarrassed, she sits up and holds my jacket against her chest. "What am I here for?"

"Another job."

Douglass enters with a robe in one hand and a tray of food in the other.

I nod at the tray as he sets it on the bedside table. It's just a ham sandwich and a handful of potato chips, but Amana looks at it greedily.

"Eat," I tell her.

She obeys without question, first slipping on the robe Douglass brought her.

"I asked you if you trusted me back at The Club," I say.

She nods.

"Can I trust you?"

Amana freezes. The sandwich is clutched in her hand, her cheeks are full of food, but her eyes are sharp and focused on me. When Douglass shifts his weight from one foot to the other, she glances at him and I see the first hint of worry in her eyes, but she quickly blinks it away and refocuses on me.

"Yes. You can trust me."

I lean toward her. "Don't lie to me, Amana. That will be the worst mistake you ever make. Understand?"

She nods and wipes at her mouth. "What am I here for?"

"There's a rat in my ranks. He's likely Italian or he's someone from the Stronghold. I need you to find him."

Her eyes bulge. "How?"

"Don't tell me Volkov's men only paid you in *money*." I laugh. "In this business, information is more valuable than gold."

Her gaze darkens. "You want me to get info from my clients."

"I do."

"I can do that," she admits. "But Volkov's men *did* pay me in money. Not just in words."

I nod at Douglass who produces an envelope. He's been my closest companion for six years now. Unfortunately, he remembers all the women I used to take home from The Club. He knows exactly how much I pay them.

Amana eagerly digs into the envelope, fingers brushing over the bills. Then she looks up at me in wonder. "This is at least ten thousand dollars."

I've always paid my girls well.

"Conrad is a much better boss than Volkov," I say with a smirk. "But he does expect half of that when you get back tonight."

"Tonight?"

I nod. "I never let women stay over. It would look suspicious if you didn't return."

She presses her lips together, looking almost upset. As flattered as I am by her disappointment, I have to admit I had no intentions of doing anything but talking tonight. And every other night I'll see her. Not only am I a married man, but Amana is only eighteen. Yes, she's legal—and willing—but at thirty-one, there are certain lines I just won't cross. *Rosa* is barely old enough for me, and she's twenty. If our marriage wasn't part of a contract deal, I wouldn't have touched her.

"Douglass will take you back to The Club," I say, rising from the bed. "When you get back, act as if you've been with any other client. I don't want to stir suspicion."

She nods.

"I will call on you in the future—for updates. Everyone will think we're sleeping together. Let them. I need them to believe that or else our meetings will draw attention. Understand?"

She nods again and then makes a face. "Will I get paid for each meeting?"

I smile. "Yes. We have to make it look real, right?"

Her eyes light up at the prospect of getting 10k just to sit down and talk for an hour. "Thank you," she breathes.

"You're welcome. Now, get dressed."

Amana shrinks into the robe. "Can I keep this on?"

I'm happy she's uncomfortable exposing herself to me now, that means she likely won't try anything in the future. But

225

I can't let her keep the robe.

"I don't let women take anything from my home," I say plainly. "I need the men at The Club to believe we slept together. That means I can't treat you any differently from any other escort I would have taken home."

She seems to understand, though I can see the shame in her suddenly reddened cheeks. "Can you turn around?" she asks in a whisper.

I nod and face the other way. Douglass does the same.

When she's dressed, she clears her throat. "Done."

I keep my eyes focused on her face when I look back at her. That leotard is horrible. "Remember to give Conrad his pay."

She nods.

My cousin takes half of whatever his girls make, whether in tips from the strippers or in payment from his escorts. He never tells them how much he charges clients as a test of their trust. Amana thinks there's 10,000 dollars in her envelope, but once she counts it out—which I know she'll do in the car—she'll realize I included an extra 1500. If she gives Conrad the right amount he's owed, then I'll know I can trust her. If she doesn't, I'll have her killed by the morning. She knows too much about the rat to stay alive if she's deceitful.

"Amana," I say. She's standing in my doorway, clutching the envelope to her small breasts.

"Yes?"

"Take as many clients as you can. But don't do anything you don't have to do."

A long moment of silence stretches between us. Finally, she nods. "Okay."

When she walks out, Douglass pats my shoulder. "I'll look after her whenever I'm there."

"Thank you, Douglass."

"You're welcome, sir."

When the door closes behind them both, the weight of the last two days hits me full on. I almost feel sluggish as I crawl into bed fully clothed. I lost five men on a failed mission. I'd lost men not long before—I shot Ja'meek with my own gun. I killed a Russian. I shot my own cousin. I made this war far worse than it needs to be. And I lost Rosa's trust. All in less than a week.

Losing my wife's trust is the worst offense. Now that I'm no longer riding the adrenaline high of killing men and scheming to catch rats, the fracture of our marriage nearly shatters me. My chest heaves as I suck for breath, staring at the ceiling in the inky blackness of my dark room. I gulp down bitter tears and dial Rosa's number, leaving it on speakerphone so her sweet voice can fill up the room.

Her words echo throughout my chambers, and I welcome the sound. It gives me a few more seconds with her voice. A few more seconds of her sweet laugh as she tells strangers to leave a message. When it's over, I send her a simple text and hope that she answers. Hope that she will one day laugh again. That she will one day love me again.

How could she, after what I've done? After the grief I've brought her?

I don't even love myself.

I love you.

The Voice is but a whisper, but it seems louder and clearer than any I've ever heard. I roll onto my side and clamp my hands over my ears. How could God Almighty love me? After everything I've done? And *if* God loves me then why is all this happening? Why am I in the middle of a gang war right now? Why'd I have to shoot my own cousin today? Why was *I* the one who saved him instead of the God who supposedly loves me and him and everyone else in the world?

"Where were You!?" I shout into the darkness.

No one answers.

Twenty-One

I stare into the darkness around me, listening to the whir of the air conditioning. I am not crying; I'm done shedding tears. I'm done feeling sorry for myself. It's not as if it'll make any difference anyway.

With as much courage I could muster, I had looked Amory in the eye and confronted him about the secret he's been keeping from me. The conversation ended with me breaking down into sobs and him offering muted comfort that had no effect. If anything, Amy's strong arms wrapped around me only served to remind me of just how alone I truly am.

I've lost my parents, and now I've lost my relationship with my brother, and part of my connection with my husband too. I was already taken away from my friends and what little family I had; thanks to the war, I'm barely in contact with the new friends I've made now. If the ones in charge hadn't assigned Adella and Petra to my safehouse, I'd be alone here, too.

Amory is all I have.

I am totally dependent on him in every area of my life. My

safety, my provision, my peace of mind, my comfort—emotionally and physically—for companionship, and for information on what's happening outside the four walls of my luxury prison. Without Amory, I have nothing.

So this betrayal cuts deep. Because he took advantage of my trust, of my submission to his reign in my life, and treated it as if it meant nothing. I gave him everything I had to offer—my body, my mind, my heart. I was a submissive wife. Trusting that with Amory in charge, things would turn out fine. With Amory as the head of my household, nothing could go wrong.

But I was wrong.

Amory took all I had and did what he wanted in return. That happens all too often in the mafia and, sadly, in the Church as well.

"Submission."

The word leaves a foul stench in the air as I whisper it aloud. *What does it mean to submit to my husband?* Do I have to submit to someone if he isn't saved? What happens if I submit and he leads me astray? What happens if he abuses my submission?

I roll onto my side and stare at the thick Bible on my bedside table. If I squint, I can just make out the gold lettering going up the spine. The swirl of each cursive letter is like a strike through my heart.

Wives, submit yourselves to your own husbands as you do to the Lord. For the husband is the head of the wife as Christ is the head of the church...

Father Serrano had read that scripture to me when I'd gone

to him to help me write my wedding vows. I remember sucking in a gasp and squeezing my pen, unsure how to respond to the Word.

"How do I submit to someone in the *mafia*?" I had asked in a shaky voice.

Father Serrano took a deep breath. "You know, I have read that scripture to many young women over the years. None of them are ever surprised to hear it."

"We hear it all our lives," I had said, almost bitterly.

Father Serrano patted my hand. "People love to quote that scripture to young, vulnerable women." He ran his aged finger along the pages of the open Bible, stopping at Ephesians 5:21. "But they forget the scripture that comes right before it; Submit to *one another* out of reverence for Christ." He looked up at me with a smile. "God doesn't ask women to do anything He hasn't already asked of men."

"But the Bible says the husband is the head of the wife—"

He cut me off with a nod. "As Christ is the head of the church. But do you know how Christ leads the church?"

I shook my head and then took a guess. "He rules the church, right?"

Father Serrano laughed. "When Jesus was on earth, He washed the feet of His disciples. He offered comfort to the weak. He fed the hungry." He leaned over and patted my hand again. "In other words, Jesus *served* the church."

I gasped, which made him smile like a proud grandfather.

"Most people have that reaction to such a revelation."

"I don't understand."

"Most people don't." He laughed. "The Bible was first written in Hebrew and Greek, did you know that?"

I nodded. I had learned that in school, though I'd never taken the time to study the Bible in its native languages.

"The word used in that scripture for *head* is a Greek word that doesn't mean what most people think." Father Serrano leaned back in the pew. "*Kephale*. It means 'the source' or 'the fountain' for something. It can even be translated as 'the origin.'" He'd smiled at my wrinkled brows. "We are raised to believe that being the *head* of the wife is the same as being in charge—or being the boss. But that's not true. Yes, Christ is the head of the church, but His leadership is one of *servitude* not dominance.

"He *served* the Body while He was here on earth—even giving Himself up on the Cross for us. That servitude is what God wants husbands to imitate here on earth. He wants them to do for their brides all that He did for His bride."

"The Bride of Christ," I said breathily, trying to understand.

Father Serrano had nodded.

"So, Amory is supposed to be my servant?" I'd asked.

He snorted. Even I knew I was stretching the truth with that one.

"A husband's position of servitude is not one of inferiority. He serves his wife because he is capable of taking care of her. Think of chivalry. Holding the door for his wife, paying for dinner, making sure she is taken care of before anyone else. We

232

call that being polite, but the Bible calls it servitude—being a *man.*"

I'd nodded, thinking of how kind Amory had been. How patient. Even though I'd broken my promises to him and had tried to run away. Even though I had rejected him, insulted him, and had even lied to him. Amory had forgiven me without hesitation and had still tried his best to keep me safe and treat me well. He had done his part as a husband before we'd even gotten married.

Father Serrano closed the Bible, gaining my attention. "So, when the Bible asks wives to submit to their husbands, it isn't asking for them to submit to his dominance or his control in their lives. It's asking wives to submit to their *source* or *fountain.* Submit to their husband's protection, provision, and love." He'd sighed. "The mafia, and honestly the rest of the world, has a very skewed understanding of this scripture. So you might have to endure some hard times during your first few years of marriage with Amory. But I think you're strong enough to get through this, Rosa. I think you're strong enough to lead Amory to the truth."

Lead by example…

"Can you do that?" Father Serrano had asked me.

At the time, I'd just nodded and agreed without a second thought. I was still high and giddy off the revelation of the Word and the knowledge that God had even wanted to use me in His plans. But now I see what Father Serrano had meant. Now I understand the struggles he was referring to.

What happens when a husband abuses his wife's submission?

I slide off the bed and get down on my knees. Like any good daughter, she takes that offense to her Father. And like any good Father, God comforts and defends His precious little girl.

I'm so angry at Amory for keeping this secret from me. I'm angry that he didn't love me enough to tell me the truth. And I'm hurt because I've been reduced to nothing but a trophy wife. A pretty doll for him to dress up and use whenever he's ready.

This revelation is just another reminder of my role as a mafia wife. I am at Amory's mercy. I am nothing without him. But I knew that before I married him. I knew how marriage worked for mafia women long before I said, 'I do.' But I'd convinced myself that things would be different with Amory. Because Amory is different.

He had promised not to lie to me. Had promised to let me in. To see me as his equal. All while keeping secrets behind my back.

"God," I say quietly. I don't realize I'm crying until the tears fall from my chin and plop onto my clasped hands as I mutter my prayers. "I'm so hurt. I'm so angry. I don't even know what to say or what to do." I reach up and swipe at my tears. "I need Your wisdom, Jesus. I need Your guidance, Holy Spirit. What do I do?"

In the silence, I hear a Still Voice as clear and resounding as my own.

Tend my lamb.

My breath hitches in my chest.

Tend Your lamb?

Why do I have to tend to Amory when *I'm* the one who's hurting? *I'm* the one who's been betrayed! This isn't fair! Who's going to help me through this pain? Who will tend to *me?*

I AM.

My hot anger instantly cools. All at once, I feel like a petulant child instead of the Christian woman I'm supposed to be. Embarrassment unfurls somewhere deep inside, and I whisper an apology to my Father.

"I'm sorry, God. I thought this would be easy. I thought I'd be strong enough to face these problems. But I'm nothing without You." I gasp and wipe at my snotty nose. "Help me, Lord. Give me the strength to forgive Amory and Gio and show me how to tend to Your lamb."

I sit there for a long time, kneeling with my hands clasped in front of me, chin resting on my fist. I don't expect the Lord to crack the sky and rain down His wisdom like a sudden storm—I don't know what I expect, to be honest. But I remain beside my bed, whispering prayers, quoting scriptures, and asking for the Lord's strength and the Holy Spirit's wisdom until I feel a sense of calm wash over me.

My tears dry and my anxiety ebbs away. I still feel angry at Amory. I still feel betrayed. But I know these feelings will pass. I know God is here to help me through this. I don't feel so alone anymore.

There's a knock at my door that I almost don't hear. When I stand, both my knees pop and I groan as I limp to open it. Adella greets me with a somber smile and my heart leaps into my throat.

"Mistress Jäger summoned us," she says calmly.

I glance into the hall, searching for the guards.

"They came to get you earlier, but you were praying. Mistress says she can't wait any longer, so I came to get you myself."

I nod, wondering how long I've been in my room crying and praying—my train of thought is disrupted as I reach into my closet for a sweater and catch a glimpse of the time. It's just after midnight. Which means this meeting is dire, once again.

"Has something happened?" I ask my older cousin as we walk towards the stairwell.

"She got another list."

I swallow, flinching in surprise when Della grabs my hand. She doesn't say anything, just squeezes my fingers as she pushes through the doors of the lobby. I squeeze back, and the gesture is worth more than a thousand words.

"While you were praying," Adella whispers as we find a seat in the back of the room. "Did you say anything for Jared?"

Her husband. He's been working with Amory and the rest of the men to fight in this war. I'll bet Adella is twice as nervous about Christina's list as I am. Even though Amory is out there fighting too, he's the underboss. He takes the best men with him; his life is valued above all others except his father's. If things go wrong, his life will be the priority. Not Jared's.

Adella's father, Trenton Willis, is the underboss of the Willis Stronghold, which means Jared will become the underboss one day and eventually the King of the Stronghold after Trenton passes on. But right now, he's just third in line to the throne. He isn't as important as some of the others in the business. He's no better than Aldo right now—who's been hospitalized for a gunshot wound.

I feel bad for the reality of the situation. Adella has to go to sleep every night knowing her husband won't be granted the same protection as mine. I can't imagine how she manages to keep so calm every day.

I squeeze her hand again as I adjust on the lounge sofa. "I pray for all the men."

She lets go of a breath. "Maybe I'll start praying too."

"I can teach you."

"I'd like that."

The room was filled with chatter when Adella and I first entered, but as I espy Christina in the center of the room, the area falls quiet. She's sitting in a grand chair with Petra standing beside her. At the flick of her wrist, everything stills. I even hold my breath as I wait for her to tear open the envelope.

"I know it is late. But this information just came in. I won't wait until morning." She shakes her white-grey head. "I *cannot* wait."

Everyone swallows at the same time. I can feel the anxiety rising in the room, it's so thick, I could reach out and take a handful of nerves. Bundle them up and toss them away. If only.

Christina begins her death tally. "Kevin Harrison, of the Stronghold."

Someone wails in the background, but she keeps going like she doesn't hear it.

"Dominic Rossi of the Garden."

I recognize the name—a man who had once been my mother's security guard when I was a young girl. He'd moved to Harlem to work for Marco long before her death. I heard the pay was better, but I'd never asked questions. It wasn't my place.

Christina keeps going down the list, ignoring the shrieks and cries of the women around us. Someone actually collapses when the name of a man from the Hunting Grounds is announced. I don't know the name, but I do recognize that something is wrong when Christina gets to the next name.

She sucks in a gasp and pauses as she clutches the paper in her hands, tears welling in her eyes. The paper begins to quiver from her shaky grip, and I realize whoever it is, they're someone important to her—which means they're important to me.

I don't realize I'm standing until I feel Adella's hand on my arm, gently pulling me back. I glance down at her, wanting to shove her away, but then Christina's voice fills the room and my knees buckle.

"Morgen Jäger."

He's one of Amory's cousins—a younger cousin, I remember. He had a boyish charm with a sweet smile and kind, dangerous eyes. He looked like a happier, blonder version of Amory. If he ever laughed or joked or had fun. I remember Conrad very well, I'm close friends with his wife Gisela. But I've never spent any time with Morgen. I've only ever seen him in passing. But I know enough about the Jäger family to understand the horrible pain his sudden death has caused.

Christina is weeping now, leaning over in her chair, and crying like a child. Petra rubs circles on her back as she offers comfort, but it seems to have no effect. When it becomes obvious that Christina won't be able to regain her composure, Petra peers into the crowd and looks right at me.

At first, I have no idea why she's looking at me, and then it hits me.

I'm the next highest-ranking woman in the room. With Christina indisposed, the responsibility of being Mistress falls on me.

My heart begins to pound as I glance around and realize everyone is looking at me now, wondering what happens next. I'm wondering the same thing, but I don't get to voice my confusion. If I show any weakness now, they will never accept me as Mistress. Not in the safehouse, and not if Amory ever becomes Jägermeister. I have to take command. I have to be brave.

I take a deep breath and march over to Christina, hand extended. "Let me finish the list."

She passes it to me without argument. My hands tremble as I raise the paper and scan the words. They're just names. Just ink on parchment. But as I peer into the crowd of onlooking women, they suddenly become brothers, fathers, and husbands.

I'm not sure I can do this. I'm not sure how Christina has handled this stress all this time. But she did it without hesitation and managed to keep her head held high until the pain hit home. Morgen was her nephew. I can't imagine what she's feeling right now, but I don't get to indulge in those wonderings. I've got a job to do. I've got women looking at me, wanting to know if their loved ones are on the list.

I'm happy I can ease their fears. "Morgen's name is the last on the list."

A collective sigh of relief rushes through the room.

"Because Morgen was a high-ranking Hunter, the Bosses of New York will honor the burial tradition with two days of peace." The room shifts, I'm not sure if this is good news or bad news. "During those forty-eight hours, Morgen will be laid to rest at a small ceremony and families will be allowed to visit one another." I feel nervous at the thought of seeing Amory again. Even though I'm angry at him, I still feel horrible for the pain he's enduring right now.

"Due to the sudden increase in the brutality of the war," I go on, reading the last few paragraphs typed at the bottom of the page, "the Jägermeister, King James, and don Giovanni have decided to rotate the safehouses earlier than expected. More details will be shared after Morgen's funeral."

The women all blink at me as I fold up the paper and tuck it into the pocket of my oversized sweater. With a shudder, I realize they're waiting to be dismissed. Even Christina is looking at me, respecting the authority she just handed over.

I take a breath.

God wants me to feed the Word to Amory. To tend His lamb—who is my husband. But nothing says I can't take advantage of an opportunity to feed these lambs too.

"I'd like to end this meeting with a prayer." I hold my hand out to Christina who takes it with a bit of hesitancy. The gesture seems small, but to the rest of the women, it's bold and sends a loud message. She is in agreement with my suggestion.

The rest of the ladies slowly take hands and bow their heads as they wait for me to begin. To my surprise, Petra reaches out and takes my other hand—even though I hadn't offered it to her. The last time I'd asked to pray with her, she'd gotten an attitude and pretty much said prayer was worthless. I'm used to hearing comments like that, so it didn't bother me, but I'm glad to see she's changed her mind. At least somewhat.

I look at her with a question in my eyes and she shrugs sheepishly. "I'm still not sure if I believe in your God. My cousin died. And so did many others. But it's clear that no one is safe. I'll take all the help I can get."

I nod and squeeze her hand. "God is a rewarder of our faith. Trust in Him, Petra."

She gives me a brittle smile. "I will try."

I bow my head and lead them all in prayer, asking God to protect our husbands, brothers, fathers, and friends. I ask God to forgive us our sins and to forgive the men who are fighting. I ask Him to look after them and to do all He can to end this war with as little death as possible. Then I ask for Him to comfort the women who have lost people and to strengthen the women who haven't. I ask Him to touch the hearts of everyone in our three gangs. To change New York for the better. And to bless His children to accept the gift of salvation that He's set before us.

When I open my eyes, I see tears running down Petra's cheeks. She pulls me into a hug and trembles in the embrace. I wait for her to ask me about getting saved and accepting salvation, but she doesn't.

I'm disappointed, but I'm not discouraged. One day she'll give her life to Christ. This was the first step.

When I get back to my room, I collapse in my bed and almost fall asleep right away. But I roll over and grab my Bible first, determined to have a moment alone with God before I drift away. I'll need His strength to make it through this funeral. I'll need His strength to be strong for Amory.

I can give my pain to God Who comforts me, but Amy has no one. The thought is sobering. He's the one who's alone. Not me. It was never me.

Feeling guilty, I reach for my phone and my heart flutters at all the missed calls. Some of them I had ignored on purpose, others came in while I'd been praying and spending time in the lobby. It's too late to call Amory back, but it isn't too late to reply to the text he sent.

Do you pray for me?

I stare at the message, almost overwhelmed with joy and grief and sadness and shock all at once. My emotions are everywhere. But I get myself together enough to type out a reply and hit **Send**. Then I lay down and fall into a peaceful slumber.

Twenty-Two

We have the casket closed at Morgen's funeral. Tante Viktoria sobs as she sits on the front pew. Her cries are soft and ladylike, she gently pats her cheeks with a handkerchief as pale as her skin. My aunt has always been a delicate woman, despite her sturdy build. She is hefty with full breasts, thick thighs, and enough hips to spare, but that's only made her more loveable.

I remember warm hugs and sweet kisses from my Tante as a kid. She was my mother when Christina couldn't be. Because Vater had her locked away or had taken the belt to her for too long, leaving her too weak to leave her quarters.

Viktoria is a good woman. Beautiful with plump cheeks that dimple when she smiles, which used to be all the time. But as I gaze at her across the church and take in her silent tears and her fragile resolve, I wonder if I will ever see her smile again.

When this is over, she will smile, I tell myself. Morgen is alive. This funeral is just a ruse. Someday soon, Tante will learn the truth and her pain will be forgotten. But for now...

The Priest finishes his prayer, and the organ starts, we're free to go view the closed casket or give our condolences to Viktoria. There aren't many people here, Vater insisted the ceremony be small and private—I agreed with him, for once. Only Morgen's immediate family, my family, and a few Generals are here. King James sent flowers but told us ahead of time that he wouldn't attend in case the Wolves don't honor the grace period allotted for this event. We'd said two days, but I won't make the mistake of underestimating Mikhail Volkov.

I killed one of his men right in front of him. I'd like to think I'm nothing like the Wolf, but I'm not sure if I would honor the grace period if our roles were switched.

Something tugs my sleeve and I glance down to see Rosa looking up at me. She hasn't spoken more than six words to me since I picked her up from the safehouse this morning, but I'm not surprised. The last time we spoke, she'd basically put me out and said she wasn't sure when she wanted me back. Her anger proved a stronger flame than I'd initially assumed when she'd ignored all my calls and then waited hours before texting me back. The exchange is still fresh in my head.

Do you pray for me?

Every day.

"Are we going?" she asks in a whisper. Her small hand is still gripping my sleeve, slender fingers curled into the fabric. I look down at my arm as she speaks, startled that she'd even want to be around me right now—let alone touch me—but she takes the gesture as an act of annoyance and slowly peels away from me.

244

I grab her hand before I lose her completely. I kiss her fingers. "Let's go," I say, gently pulling her away.

We shuffle in line toward the casket, sniffles and coughs echo throughout the cathedral. "I'm sorry about Morgen," Rosa says quietly. She's looped her hand through my arm to hold on to me. I feel her squeeze my elbow. "I didn't know him, but I am sorry."

I nod. "He was a good kid."

"How old?"

"Twenty-four."

She's silent a moment. "How is his fiancé taking it?"

I scan the crowd for Silke, an eighteen-year-old German girl who stole my cousin's heart. They've been together since she was sixteen, which nearly gave Viktoria a heart attack and earned Morgen a black eye from Conrad. But Silke's parents were heavily involved and forbid them from being alone together or from seeing each other on weekends, except at church. Morgen even attended her baptism last summer. It was a cute little event.

I remember Silke's eighteenth birthday party. I'd gone as a show of respect and approval of their relationship on behalf of my father. Their age gap was a concern, but I trusted Morgen and I needed the connections Silke's family offered us. The Biekers are well established back in Germany, running four districts which happen to overlap with two mines I wanted to explore for diamonds.

German cut stones are a hot commodity here in the States. I'd already slept with Silke's older sister to get into one of the mines—having Morgen marry into the family would've eliminated the need for me to bed her a second time. Turns out, I ended up rolling around with the other sister, Edeltraud, to get into the other mine, but still... I look forward to Morgen's wedding once he rises from the dead.

I spot all three sisters standing near Viktoria when Rosa and I finally make it to the casket. "You didn't answer the question," Rosa murmurs, placing her hand on the coffin. She closes her eyes and says a prayer, then turns and looks up at me. "How's his fiancé taking it?"

"Let's go find out," I say, guiding her toward Silke and her sisters.

Silke's eyes are red, I can see that as we get closer. But she still looks elegant in her slim black dress and modest stockings. Her attire makes her seem younger than her eighteen years and I suddenly feel heartbroken for her. I have to remind myself that my cousin is all right as I glance at the other crying women.

Edeltraud, the oldest—and prettiest—stands beside Viktoria, holding her hand and whispering something in German. She doesn't look at me right away when I walk over, she was the most torn up about our one-night stand compared to her sister, Aloisia, who'd apparently had a fling with Conrad before I'd gotten to her.

Aloisia shakes my hand and then dips her head like she's supposed to when greeting the underboss. Then she looks at Rosa and actually bends her knee in a quick little curtsy. "Underboss, Lady Rosa."

Rosa inclines her head. "I am sorry for your loss," she says

246

with an air of regality. For a moment, I'd forgotten Rosa was raised in the mafia. And not just as some grunt's daughter— she's a princess, even without marrying me. This is her territory, this is where she shines, exchanging small talk with the women, accepting their gestures of admiration and respect. Even though we're at a funeral, she never allows the other women to forget her rank. To forget that she's my wife.

I'm proud of her. And I can't stop myself from smiling as I watch Silke incline her head and curtsy. Even Viktoria does it. And Rosa accepts their reverence with her head held high, though she doesn't look down on them. She grasps Viktoria's hands and tells her she will pray for her strength, she even hugs Silke and tells her she looks beautiful—and that when the pain passes, she will still be beautiful. Meaning, she's expected to find another man to marry.

That's what happens in this business.

When the women are done paying respects to their future Mistress, their attention shifts to me. I lean down and kiss both of Viktoria's cheeks, speaking softly in German, "You'll be all right, Tante."

She nods and sniffles. "Thank you, Underboss."

I shake my head. "Just Amory for you."

"Make sure you see your mother before you go back out there. Don't leave without telling her you love her."

Her words go straight to my heart. I wish I could tell Viktoria that Morgen is alive, that she doesn't have to worry about my mother never seeing her son again, like she thinks she'll never see hers. But that's too dangerous. Too risky. I

247

won't let my heart ruin the plans we've put together.

I clear my throat and kiss my aunt's forehead. "I'll make sure I see Mutti."

She nods and hugs me once more. "Do that, Amory. Do that."

When I finally get away from the women, I find Conrad by the exit. He's standing with Gisela, looking as exhausted as I feel. This whole thing is probably harder for him than me. But at least he got to play the part of grieving brother and hide out in the back the entire time.

He smells like whiskey when I walk over. That annoys me, so I ignore him and kiss Gisela on the lips when I greet her— just to piss him off. Glizzy barely bats an eye, she's a touchy sort of woman, but I notice the way Conny's face turns red as he straightens beside me.

"How are you holding up?" I say to Gisela.

She licks her lips and shakes her head. "I'm scared, Amory."

Before I can answer, Conrad steps between us, his face pinched in anger. "There's something urgent, Underboss," he says in German.

I roll my eyes and then nod at Gisela. "I'll be back. Take care of Rosa while I'm gone."

When I'm outside, Conrad shoves me down the front steps. There are only three, so I don't get angry and shoot him over it, but I do turn around and slap him in the head.

"Chill out," I say calmly.

"You kissed my wife on the lips." He spits on the ground.

"You noticed? I thought you might be too drunk."

Conrad glowers and then sighs. "It's my brother's funeral."

"Really?" I say sarcastically—because we both know the funeral is a sham.

"Look, I can't deal with all the gloom, okay? I just needed a little drink to get me through."

I slap his head again. "There is nothing keeping Volkov from breaking the grace period. I need you on your toes, Conny. Especially today."

"I'm sorry, Ay."

It's a nickname I rarely hear, which lets me know Conny is serious.

I slap his shoulder. "Don't worry about it. Just head home, I'll go get Gisela for you."

"I'm supposed to be on Wolf's escort," he says sadly.

Uwe and I decided to let Wolfgang attend the funeral, if only to convince any spies that Morgen is truly dead. Wolf doesn't know the truth, so he's been torn up since he found out the news. He was quite close to Morgen, as close as I am to Conrad.

Conny, Vater, and Oberon are supposed to escort Wolf back to Stonehall instead of going to the gravesite. They plan to share the news with him on the drive so he doesn't try to kill himself out of grief—he's doing that bad—but with Conny half-drunk, I feel like it might be better for him to go to the gravesite and for me to go with Wolf instead.

Or maybe Conrad should just go home. I don't want him to accidentally tell anyone the truth.

249

"Take Gisela and get out of here," I tell him. "You should rest for the day."

He makes a face. "You're sending me off."

"You need the time off. And Glizzy said she's scared. She needs you."

Conrad laughs, it's loud and grating. "I think Rosa needs you."

I roll my eyes.

"She saw you kiss my wife."

"I'll make it up to her."

With that, I turn and march back into the church. Rosa and Gisela are holding hands when I walk over, it's not until I'm close enough to hear their whispers that I realize they're praying. The sight makes me pause—thinking of the text I'd sent to Rosa the night before.

I'm glad she responded, but I don't really want to think about prayer right now. There's a small part of me that feels paranoid about it. Like, if I think about prayer and God and the Bible for too long, then I'll hear that Voice again.

It isn't a scary Voice, in fact, each time I've heard it I've felt a sense of calm or order … or peace. And each time I hear it, the tug in my heart gets stronger. But it's almost overwhelming. Like having a light suddenly switched on in the darkness. I know the light is good, I'm just not sure I'm ready to leave the dark just yet.

I'm comfortable here.

Rosa finishes her prayer and opens her eyes to find me waiting by the door. The look on her face doesn't surprise me.

She's angry.

Of course she is.

I'd kissed Gisela on the lips right in front of her—it was just a little German greeting, but still. I would have dragged her out by her hair if she'd kissed Conrad on the lips.

"Conny is waiting for you," I tell Gisela as I step over.

She nods and then turns to Rosa. "It was nice seeing you again."

Rosa smiles. "I'll be praying for you."

Once Glizzy is gone, we're left in silence.

I clear my throat. "You two seem close."

"I could say the same about you."

Ouch.

"Rosa, the kiss didn't mean anything."

"To you."

I smirk—which is rude, but I can't help myself. Rosa isn't angry, she's *jealous.*

It's the first time I've seen her behave like this and I don't know how to respond. Like a cat with its claws drawn and its fangs out, she stalks over to me with a glare on her face and a hiss in her voice, though I can only interpret it as a seductive purr.

"You're despicable."

I am.

This is supposed to be a funeral and here I am getting turned on by my wife's attitude. Oh well … it's not like Morgen is *actually* dead.

I grab her by the wrist as she walks by. She turns and tries to yank her arm away, but I pull her close, and before she can catch her bearings, I kiss her.

It's an angry kiss, one I have to steal from her lips as I force my tongue into her mouth, but once she realizes she's lost this battle, Rosa melts into me. Her body sags against me until I have to hold her up, hands going to her waist, which makes her let go of a shameful little moan. I swallow the sound as I deepen the kiss. It burns between us, her lips tasting like fire—extinguished by tears.

She gasps when I pull away, mist gathered in her eyes. She can't even look me in the eye now, staring at my tie, counting the buttons on my shirt. She's looking at every other part of me except my face.

I lift her chin and brush away the tear slipping down her cheek. "Don't ever be embarrassed to want me," I whisper.

"Why do you do this to me?" she asks. "It's cruel."

The monster inside me answers before I can stop the words from spilling out. "You love it."

Now, she meets my gaze—but she isn't angry, she isn't even embarrassed anymore. She's shocked. Like she's just realized this herself.

I've said it before. I get off on control. I love dominating Rosa. I love overpowering her, overwhelming her, reminding her that she is mine. But I can admit that. I can acknowledge the dark parts of myself.

Rosa can't.

She can't accept that she enjoys this little game between us. Enjoys submitting to me. Enjoys letting me take over—inside and outside the bedroom. It's her denial that makes it harder for us to get along. We both know what we want, but she's fighting against it. As adamantly as she fought her attraction to me in the beginning of our marriage.

I want to sigh, but the truth is that I'm excited by the challenge. If Rosa won't accept her desires on her own, then I'll teach her to. It's just one more wall for me to break down. One more gift to give to my cute little wife.

Freedom.

I kiss her again. "It's okay, Rosa. I want you just as badly."

She pulls away. "We can't do this. Not here."

Right. I forgot it's a funeral.

I straighten my tie and glance at my watch. "You should get going. Douglass will take you home." I decided to pull her out of the safehouse for a little while, at least until we figure out what to do about the mole.

She nods, blinking up at me with her big, hazel eyes.

"This conversation isn't over," I tell her.

The look on her face is so innocent, I almost feel like the devil standing beside her. "Okay," she says softly, then she turns and walks back into the church.

Oberon and Uwe share a cigar, passing it back and forth like it's a blunt. I'm sitting on the curb with Maximilian and Wolfgang, waiting for them to finish so we can go. Wolf insisted on having one last drink with Onkel before getting locked up again. Like a sucker, Vater let him have his way.

"So, he's alive?" Wolfgang says in German. He's only been speaking German lately, I guess being locked up in Stonehall, surrounded by our ancestry and culture, has reminded him of his roots. It's made Vater smile, so I won't complain.

Onkel nods. "Morgen yet lives. We're thinking of moving him to Stonehall with you when suspicions die down."

I glance at Vater. I hadn't heard of these plans.

Maximilian throws down his cigarette and steps on it. "Whatever we do, we can decide on the road. If this is my only day off, I don't want to spend it babysitting Wolf."

My little brother glowers at him. "I thought we'd gotten close, Max."

"Closer than I'd like," he grumbles.

Max is funny. He's four years older than me, has six different girlfriends from The Club, and is as ruthless as Hans when it comes to handling business. I have no idea why Vater decided to put him in charge of Wolf's security detail, but my brother isn't dead yet, so I guess he's doing something right.

"I want to see Morgen," Wolf says.

"No," I say sternly. "That's too risky."

"Vater?" Wolf asks, completely ignoring me.

I stand and walk over to him, but Max stands too and gets between us. "Calm down, Underboss."

"Step aside, Max."

"Let him," Wolf orders.

Max just shakes his head and mutters, "Stupid kid," then he steps aside and doesn't flinch when I grab Wolf by his collar and yank him into my fist.

He takes the punch like a man, but I don't miss the look he shoots over my shoulder at Vater. He expects him to come to his rescue, but Uwe just keeps smoking his cigar like he isn't even listening to us right now.

"You're not seeing Morgen until I say so. Understand?"

Holding his bloody nose, Wolfgang nods slowly.

I shove him away and shake out my hand. "Let's go. I'm done waiting around."

Wolfgang yanks open his car door and slides into the back, when Maximilian moves to get into the car, he shouts in German, "Ride with Amory! I don't want to see you!"

Max and I both laugh as he switches cars. We end up riding together, with Onkel, Vater, and Wolf driving in front of us. I don't care to ride with my brother, I love him, but I'm not going to put up with his drama king attitude right now. I know he's antsy from being locked up in Stonehall, but I'm not sympathetic. This entire war is his fault. Morgen could *actually* be dead because of him—thank God I was able to save him.

As we peel away from the curb, I hear that Voice again. It makes me freeze in my seat, slamming on the brakes so hard, Max jerks forward.

Don't go to Stonehall.

Max grabs my shoulder. "Underboss? What's wrong?" his voice is slightly panicked, and I realize that's not the first time he's asked me the question.

I blink at him. "Nothing's wrong." Except the fact that I just got a divine message not to go to the safest place in the city.

What's wrong with Stonehall? I wonder, hitting the gas again. The Voice doesn't answer me. I'm left in a stifling silence as I drive through Brooklyn. I have two choices … I can listen to the Voice, or I can go forward with my plans.

Stonehall is our ancestral home. It is the most heavily guarded place in the borough. If the Volkovs think they can get away with attacking it, they're sorely mistaken. If they even think they *can* attack it, they're idiots. The place is a fortress, gated off and guarded by two acres of flatland. We'd see them coming miles away.

Still… I can't stop the worry from building inside me. I can't stop the anxiety from rising. I feel like I'm making a mistake.

As the front gates come into view, I slow down and glance over at Maximilian. "I don't think we should go to Stonehall."

He raises an eyebrow. "Why not?"

"I…" I can't tell him because a Voice in my head told me not to. He'll think I'm insane.

I think I'm insane.

Who says this Voice is right? Who says it's actually God?

Where was God when I had to shoot Morgen? Or when Ja'meek died? Or when those women from Volkov's clubs were kidnapped and forced into sex trafficking?

I grip the steering wheel and let out an angry grunt. It shouldn't be this complicated. It shouldn't be this hard to believe in God.

Or maybe I already believe. I'm just fighting against it.

Max is speaking again. "My team swept the place already. It's clean. But we can sweep it again."

I shake my head. "I don't know."

"Well, it's too late anyway." He nods toward the looming gates. "We're here now."

I look at him. "I guess—"

BOOM!

Everything tilts, like gravity folded over. I don't realize I'm flying backwards until I hear the *crunch* of the car and my head whips back, smacking against the leather seat. Everything goes black for a second, and when I blink, I realize I'm upside down.

Smoke is everywhere, debris falling from the sky. It takes another moment for things to make sense. I shove at my car door and fall out onto the gravel. The front gates of Stonehall have been blown off—taking the first car with them.

Wolf's car.

I suck in a gasp of smoky air and begin to choke. His car is nothing but a pile of burning metal. But there are parts all over the front lawn. I even see a body a few feet away, but I can tell from the size that it's Maximilian. I don't know if he's dead or alive, but he's not my main concern right now.

I need to find my brother.

I limp through the area, vaguely aware of a sticky wetness on my arm, and an ache in my head. I have no idea how bad my own injuries are, but I know the moment I pay attention to them, I'll start to feel the full measure of pain. I don't think anything is broken, but I don't stop to find out. I just keep walking through the burning car parts as guards rush out from the mansion and join me in the wreckage.

Some of them scream my name and try to get me to go inside, but I refuse. "Where's my brother!" I shout, falling to my knees.

I suddenly feel weak, my injuries catching up to me as the adrenaline wears off. The pain in my head turns to a burning throb, so intense my vision blurs. The wetness in my arm has soaked through my sleeve. I'm dizzy. I'm exhausted. But I need to see Wolfgang. I need to know whoever did this didn't accomplish their goal.

Wolfgang has to be alive.

One of the guards catches me as I topple over. He drags me to the side, away from the debris and the flames and out of the smoke. "You're going to be okay!" he shouts, tearing off my suit jacket and administering first aid.

I nod vacantly. "Wolfgang…" I whisper.

He nods. "We're looking for him. And the Jägermeister, and Oberon too."

My father, uncle, and brother were in that car. *I* should have been in that car, but my spat with Wolfy separated us. Even so, the Voice tried to warn me. It had tried to keep us all safe. But I hadn't listened.

I'd been given two choices—trust the Voice or continue with my plans.

I made the wrong choice.

Twenty-Three

The hospital room is dark. I blink to adjust my eyes as I stand beside Amory. It's late—almost midnight—but I would have gotten up for this no matter the time. I can still remember the look on Douglass's face when he came to my bedroom, knocking politely, but speaking in a harried, trembling voice.

"There's been trouble. I'm taking you to the hospital," he'd said.

I had frowned, my mind immediately going to the worst possible scenario. It was late and Amory still hadn't come home. I hadn't been too surprised by his absence; we'd spent the last week or so apart because of the war, I'd suspected he would be busy with his work. But I hadn't ever guessed that he'd be in trouble. Trouble that required me to go to the hospital.

"Where's my husband?" I'd asked, panic arrowing through me.

Douglass had swallowed and exhaled slowly. "At the hospital."

I remember running down the hall in my nightdress, angry at Douglass, shouting at him like this was all his fault. "Why weren't you with him!?" I had yelled, as if his presence would have somehow made a difference.

Douglass had taken my insults in stride, keeping pace with me as he passed me a black piece of fabric. It took me a moment to recognize it as a dress—that's when I stopped and realized I was leaving the house in my lingerie.

After changing into something more appropriate, Douglass escorted me out and drove me to the hospital. We arrived with a full security detail. When my car door opened, I saw Hans and three men from the Stronghold waiting for me at the hospital entrance.

"Take me to him," I'd ordered.

To my shock, they had obeyed without question. Hans even inclined his head and said quietly, "This way, Mistress."

His words stunned me.

Mistress...

If he's calling me Mistress, that could only mean one thing.

"Explain it again," Amory's voice brings me back from my thoughts.

I glance up at him, trying to gauge his emotions, but his face is unreadable. It's like he's not even there anymore. Vacant eyes, a dead look on his face. My husband has always been a distant man, but this is something else entirely. He doesn't seem faraway, he seems gone. Hollow.

I can't blame him. The attack on Stonehall was brutal— Douglass and Hans filled me in when I arrived. The front gates had been rigged with explosives, blowing up the first car and sending Amory's flying fifty meters away.

There were three men in the first vehicle. Uwe, Oberon, and Wolfgang.

Only two survived.

I know it was the grace of God that my husband wasn't in the first car. Though, he didn't walk away unscathed. His left arm is in a sling, there's a bandage on the side of his head— soaked red and sagging—but he won't let anyone touch it, and he suffered burns to his chest.

Add them to the dozens of scars peppering his skin. But what about the scars he has inside?

I can see the weight of the ordeal pressing down on him as he listens to the doctor explain the injuries again. We've heard them three times now, but Amory insists. It's like he's convinced himself that hearing the report again will somehow change things.

He's in shock, I tell myself. But the look on his face doesn't seem shocked or in denial. In fact, Amy looks like he's already accepted the doctor's report. Like he wants to hear it again, so he won't forget it.

Wolfgang was thrown from the vehicle—they found him unconscious and burned some feet away. He's alive, but in a coma getting his burns treated. Oberon was trapped in the vehicle. They found him still belted to his seat, his flesh charred beyond recognition. Uwe was found somewhere near the front of the property. Other than burns, he wasn't hurt too badly ... except when he was thrown from the car, he hit his head on impact.

Amory's right hand curls into a fist as the doctor finishes the report on his father. "He's alive. But unresponsive."

"Brain-dead," Amy says through clenched teeth.

I want to reach for his hand, but I'm afraid he'll flinch away. That's how different he seems. How unrecognizable.

Or maybe he's always been this way. Maybe this cold man is who he really is—and the man I knew at home was different.

I shake my head which earns a queer look from Gisela, but I don't pay her any attention. I'm thankful for the tears in my eyes, everyone thinks I'm crying because of the brain-dead man before me. But I'm not. My tears are for the dead man standing next to me.

Christina is here. She's shed enough tears for Uwe to make up for the rest of the dry eyes in the room. I'm shocked by how upset she is, considering how ruthless Uwe was. Then again, he was still her husband, and he didn't deserve to be blown up—at least not by the Russians and the Morenos.

Gisela and Conrad are beside Christina, along with Klaus. I don't have to wonder why they're here. With Uwe in this condition, it doesn't matter if Amory decides to pull the plug or not. He's not going to get better. That means Amory is now the Jägermeister. And since Conrad and Klaus are the only men he allowed in the room, I can assume one of them will be named as the next underboss.

Glizzy dabs at her eyes as she sniffles quietly, her dainty hands are trembling from her emotions. The tips of her slender fingers are stained black from rubbing at the streaks of black tears that wet her cheeks. Her mascara is running down her face, but as she swipes her dark bangs aside, I can see that she's still as beautiful as ever.

I can't believe she's so upset, but I shouldn't be surprised. Gisela lost her father-in-law, and now she might have to watch her Jägermeister die. She is the perfect mafia wife. Much better than me, in her four-inch heels and simple dress. Even in an emergency, Glizzy made sure she arrived in appropriate attire and she's trying her best to keep herself in control.

I feel like an idiot, blinking around the room and waiting for my husband to say something or do something. My dress is fine, it's black and stops just below the knee—but I can't pretend it was my idea to wear it. Douglass picked out my clothes and even passed me the low heels I'm wearing. If it weren't for my security guard, I would have arrived in the negligée I'd been wearing as I waited for Amy to get home.

Amory drags his gaze from his father to look at the doctor. "Thank you for—"

A sob cuts him off. It comes from Gisela.

Conrad hisses, "*Quiet*, woman." His voice is low and throaty, a menacing threat if I've ever heard one. "You come in here dressed like a *whore* and now you can't keep yourself together?"

I frown.

Gisela is wearing a black dress—it's strapless and formfitting, but she doesn't look like a whore. And even if she did, she doesn't deserve to be insulted like this. She's still Conrad's wife. But that makes no difference to him.

He lifts his hand as she continues crying. My heart begins to race, especially when Glizzy leans away, anticipating the blow.

Amory stops him.

"Enough, Conrad." His eyes are grey storms in his face, but his voice is deadly and calm. He glances at Gisela. "Let her cry."

"Now is not the time," Conrad snaps.

Amory nods. "Klaus, take the women out of here."

Klaus follows orders, shuffling us out single file like we're children being dismissed. "Come on, ladies. I'll take care of you," he says. His voice is warm and comforting, completely opposite of Amory and Conrad. The kindness in his tone is so disarming, I don't even feel upset about being put out of the room. If I'm being honest, I'm happy to get away.

I reach for Gisela once we're in the hall. "Are you okay?"

She sniffles and nods, blubbering only a single word. "Christina."

Oh, right. I had almost forgotten about my mother-in-law. It's her husband lying in the hospital bed, but Gisela is the one who can't keep it together. I'm sure it's just nerves. I'm anxious and jittery too. I have no idea what's going to happen from here. But Christina has decades of experience under her Gucci belt. She knows her husband is lost and she knows Amory will be taking charge from here. Her role is done. Her service to the German mafia is over.

Like a retired grandmother, Christina holds her head high as I turn to her and offer a packet of tissue from my purse. She shakes her head, regaining some of the dignity she'd lost through the tears running down her cheeks. Now that her crying is over, she looks different. There is an air of regality and elegance to Christina that seems to transcend age and stature. No matter who runs the mafia, she will always be the Huntress of New York.

Her silvery white hair is meticulously curled, like she's just removed a fresh set of rollers, her lashes are painted in clear mascara, so she doesn't bleed black tears like Glizzy, and her lipstick is still perfectly intact. A deep shade of red that looks like velvet on her lips.

In this moment, as she takes my hands and pulls me close enough to smell her Chanel No. 5, I don't see the former German Mistress, I don't see a retired Huntress, I see a mother and a wife. A tired woman who has finally removed her crown and is about to place it on my head.

"Remember what I told you on the night you first visited the estate?"

I nod, trying to hold her powerful gaze.

Christina's diamond earrings wink in the fluorescent lights as she shakes her head and squeezes my hand. "No, child. Do you *remember?*"

"I do," I tell her.

"What did I say?"

"Diamonds are just pretty shackles."

She sighs and her grip on my hands loosens somewhat. I understand her anxiety—so far, Christina has been right about everything. I love my husband dearly, but I am shackled to this life because of him. I am shackled to him because of this life.

"What else did I tell you?" she asks, giving me a stern shake. "What else?"

"To be the wife he needs me to be."

She nods. "Rosa, you are no longer a De Luca—"

"I know that." I accepted my place in the German mafia the moment I said, 'I do.' But Christina doesn't seem to believe me.

"No. You are not an Italian in the German mafia. You *are* German now."

Without thinking, I glance up at Douglass. A man who was Hunted, branded, and forced into a rival mafia. He drinks German beer, sleeps with German women, and even speaks the German tongue now. I have to be like him. Amory will have it no other way.

I'm no longer a captive bride, here against my will—hiding behind a contract I didn't want and a marriage I had no say in. I am the Huntress of New York.

I think of what that means as I stare into Christina's wide eyes. I think of how it felt when I walked with Amory through Morgen's funeral and had every man and woman in the room incline their heads in respect as I walked by. And I think of what it was like to stand beside my husband in that hospital room.

I was the closest person to him. On his right side. Even closer than Conrad and Klaus. Christina had cried and was ignored. Gisela had cried and was threatened. But I had stood strong. I had kept my composure. Better than Conrad who had insulted his wife and threatened to hit her. Even better than Amory who had clenched his jaw and curled his fists.

Amory needs me now more than ever. Maybe more than I need him. Because if there is someone who must keep a cool head at all times, it shouldn't be the man in charge. It should be the woman who has that man's ear.

Christina's death grip goes slack as she takes my hands in hers and cups them like she would a child's hands on a cold wintery day. She raises my hands and kisses the back of each one. Her next words come out in German. I don't understand a single one, but I nod and look her in the eye, letting her know how much this moment means to me.

"You are ready," she says with a tremble in her voice. "It is not an easy job. And you will receive no rewards and no credit. But you will have the admiration of every woman in New York. Because we know what it's like."

I bite my lip, thinking of my mother and all that she endured as the Mistress of the Italian mafia. It'd been even worse for her because she wasn't Italian. She'd been a Black American bride taking command of the Italian gangs of Manhattan. The older families had nearly declared a civil war until my father put his foot down.

Born and raised in Italy, Giovanni Sr. was not one to be challenged. When he demanded respect for his American wife, the others fell in line. Not as quickly as my mother would have liked, but by the time I was born, whispers of 'darkies' had ceased. Those insults died on the slit throats of the unfortunate souls who'd been caught muttering them.

When Christina steps away, Gisela appears by my side. The older woman smiles at both of us, reaching up to pinch each of our cheeks. "Such beautiful women." Her face grows serious now. "My husband is lost—"

"There is still a chance—"

She shakes her head. "He is lost. That means I am now retired. You are the wife of the Jägermeister." She looks at Gisela. "And the wife of the underboss."

I gape at my friend. She's just as shocked as I am, but our surprise only lasts a moment. As I glance over my shoulder, I realize Klaus is still outside in the hall with us. If Amory were considering him for underboss, he would be in that room right now. But he was only Uwe's best friend. Not Amy's.

"Two amazing women," Christina says. "Two friends."

"Two Christians," I say without thinking.

Christina smiles and gives me a nod with so much reverence, I wonder if she might have an idea of what my purpose is in this city.

"You're both in a position to make a difference now. To change the men who can change the city."

Gisela and I nod in unison.

"Do it," Christina says sternly. "In this business, we are taught to stand behind our men. In the Church you are taught to stand beside them." She smiles. "I'm going to tell you it doesn't matter where you stand, as long as you're close enough to whisper in his ear. Tell him what he wants to hear so he will listen when you say what he needs to know."

Christina steps back and gazes at us, but her face shifts into concern when Klaus walks over. "Sorry to interrupt, but I've been instructed to escort you to the estate, Mrs. Jäger." He's looking at Christina, which lets me know the statement isn't for me. It's somewhat confusing when there are three Mrs. Jägers standing in the hall. But I suppose if he were speaking to Gisela, he would say 'Lady Gisela,' and if he were speaking to me, he would have said 'Mistress.'

The realization hits me hard. Christina is truly retired. And even though there hasn't been an official announcement yet, we all know the unspoken truth.

Amory is the new Jägermeister.

"Why is she going to the estate?" Gisela asks.

Christina smiles at her. "To pack my bags." She turns to me. "The home is yours now. I'll be moving out as quickly as possible."

I don't respond because I have no idea what to say, but Christina isn't offended by my silence. She simply nods and pats my shoulder as she walks away with Klaus following behind.

Gisela and I watch her go, only stirring when Douglass appears behind us. "May I have a word, Mistress?" he asks.

Glizzy inclines her head and steps away without me asking her to. I look up at Amory's guard. "Yes?"

"Do you know what she said to you in German? When she took your hands."

I remember Christina speaking German as she'd kissed my hands and then told me I was ready. "I have no idea," I say honestly.

Douglass nods. "She said … There's a girl inside you. A twenty-year-old virgin who sees the world as black or white."

I swallow, trying not to be embarrassed.

"Kill that girl," Douglass says. His dark eyes are glued to my face, making his words seem more haunting than they really are. "Kill the girl inside, Mistress. Because you aren't a child anymore."

I nod in silence.

"But you don't have to grow up so quickly. I'm right here. And so is Gisela. There are people in this organization who care about you. Genuinely."

"God cares about me," I whisper. When I look up, I see Douglass smiling. He's only two years older than me, but the years he's spent beside Amory—protecting him, fighting for him, killing for him—makes him look so much older now.

"He does care," Douglass says. "I believe that."

"Christina said I'm ready for this. But I don't know if that's true."

"It *must* be true. You have to make it true." Douglass steps back and takes up position by the door again. His eyes linger on me for a second longer before he glances away and stares ahead. Back to business as usual.

Twenty-Four

There is only silence. The Priest beside me is whispering a prayer as he performs Vater's last rites, but I don't hear any of it. It's as if my ears have been shut off, my eyes switched to the pitch darkness of the void. I cannot see. I cannot hear. All that I register is my screaming thoughts. The same beating questions that have been haunting me since I accepted my place in this organization.

Will you accept this position?

I remember when my father first posed the question, the day I was initiated into the gang. I was naked and bloody, sobbing uncontrollably on the floor of one of our warehouses. I'd been beaten within an inch of my life by a team of six German men. Klaus had been there. Oberon had been there. They'd watched as I was reduced to a sniveling child. Had watched as a razor had carved into my flesh, as a bat had cracked my ribs, as a grown man had held me down and violated me.

I killed that man two years later. Vater had saved him for

me. Had said it was justice to have him as my first hunt. My first execution.

I'd pulled the trigger with a smile on my face.

Sometimes, when I'm alone, I can feel his hands on me. I can feel the razor cutting my skin open. I can feel the jolt of my ribs cracking. And I can hear Vater's voice in the background—over my own screams.

Will you accept this position?

Did I really have a choice? What would have happened to me if I had said no?

I never thought about it. Just as I don't think about it when the Father beside me closes his Bible and looks me in the eye.

"The rites are done," he says calmly. "Before he passes, I must ask for his sake. Uwe has named you as his successor. Will you accept this position?"

Vater had asked that question again when I was named as the underboss. There was another beating. Ten men that time—I'd gotten stronger. And smarter. I knew what was going on, had been waiting for it to happen. So, when I was snatched out of my bed and dragged to one of our warehouses for the second time, I made it my business to fight back.

I sent three men to their graves before they managed to strip me naked. I broke the arm of another man before they disarmed me. And when one of the men tried to touch me the way the first guy had when I was just a boy, I strangled him with my bare hands.

I didn't fight them because I wanted to become the underboss. I did it because I wanted to live. They would have killed me in that room. That had been their assignment. Kill or be killed.

It was a bloody night. But that was what Vater had wanted. To show everyone that he'd made the right choice in naming me as his successor. That he'd found someone just as ruthless as him.

The memories of my initiation send a shiver down my scarred back as I stand in the hospital room staring down at Uwe's body.

Will I become the Jägermeister?

There's still time for me to say no. To walk away from all this. But I won't leave this life behind. Not when the men who murdered my father and uncle still draw breath.

Mikhail Volkov killed my family. And he had help from a traitorous rat.

He will pay for this.

For whatever reason, the Voice saved me that day. It tried to warn me, and I made the mistake of ignoring it—of ignoring *Him*. The Voice of God. If I had chosen to believe even a second earlier, Vater would be up and walking around. Oberon would be alive. And Wolfgang wouldn't be in a coma—not to mention Maximilian who's been hospitalized the last three days.

My injuries were mostly superficial. My bandages are gone, leaving a scar going through my right eyebrow, six stitches in my left arm, and fresh burns on my chest. I'm fine. I wear these new bruises like badges of honor, but revenge will be my real reward. I will not let the Russians get away with this.

273

I had once entertained the thought of salvation. I had heard the Voice of God. Had felt His welcoming presence. And I saw the repercussions of rebellion. I learned firsthand what happens when you ignore a divine warning. But I'm not angry at God. I'm angry at myself.

"Father," I say quietly, staring at the Bible in his hands.

He raises an eyebrow, undoubtedly annoyed that I still haven't answered his question. "Yes?"

"What do I have to do to become a Christian?"

He eyes me a long moment, and when he crosses his hands one over the over, the sleeve of his cassock slides up and I see the bullseye tattooed onto the back of his right hand.

I almost laugh.

"Never mind." If I were to get saved, I doubt this guy would be the one to help me. He's the same Priest who blessed me before my initiation. The same man who stood by and watched a fifteen-year-old kid get beaten and raped and didn't say a word to intervene.

"You didn't answer my question, sir," the Priest says.

I look at him, enjoying the way he shrinks beneath my glare. "You asked if I'll accept this position."

He nods.

I can still get away… I can still pack up and take Rosa and leave. The thought is tempting. I think it's what I truly want to do, if I'm being honest. But every time the thought of escape works its way into my head, I see Onkel's burned body and Uwe's brain-dead figure lying in the bed before me.

The machinery beeps as it keeps him alive. He is nothing

but an empty vessel. His soul gone to hell long ago.

"Will you accept this position?" the Priest asks once more. He's stepped closer to me now, irritated by my silence. If he weren't a member of the clergy, I'd gut him where he stands. But there's a rule in the mafia that even people like Volkov must follow.

We don't kill members of the Church. Because, whether we believe or not, they are Children of God. And not even a fool would risk the wrath of God just to gain petty vengeance. So I let the Father step into my personal space and disrespect the boundaries of the future Jägermeister. Just this once.

He's a smart man, because he backs up as soon as he sees the look on my face. "Sorry," he mumbles. "But it is imperative that you answer while he still breathes."

I've got to accept the role while Uwe is still alive, otherwise those in opposition of my rule can say I stole the title, or even accuse me of having Uwe killed just to get it.

I don't want to be the Jägermeister. I don't want to be in the mafia anymore. I'm so tired…

But I do want revenge. I want to keep Rosa safe. And I want the Jäger name to stay afloat. This is the only way I know how to do that.

When this is over, I'll take my wife and get out of here. I'll escape. I'll even do right by the God who saved me. But first, I have to end this war.

I walk over to Uwe's bed and grab his hand, but not to hold it. I pry the signet ring from his swollen finger and slide it onto my own. As I adjust his hand, I see the bullseye tattooed onto the inside of his wrist. He was a true Hunter. The Master of Hunters. And now his hunt is over.

I turn to the Priest and nod my head. "I accept this position."

Twenty-Five

I knew Amory would change. No one would remain the same after what he's been through. I'm not even sure *I'm* the same anymore. I can't be if I want to carry out God's will. I can't be the same if I want to stand side by side with the most powerful man in New York City.

Uwe died two days ago.

I remember when Amory first came home with the ring on his finger. All he said was that he needed to make funeral arrangements. I'd asked if he was afraid of another attack, but he'd shaken his head.

"Uwe was a boss. There will be a ten-day grace period out of respect for his position."

Since then, he's been busy with the arrangements. We've barely had time to speak. So I wasn't surprised by the cold look in his eyes when he entered our bedroom this morning. I wasn't surprised by the distant sound in his deep voice as he told me he'd missed me. But I was surprised by how different he was in his passion.

I had expected Amory to change. In more ways than one. In his behavior, his attitude, his goals. But I hadn't expected him to love me differently.

With a shiver, I realize how different he is as he lets out a long groan. His entire body tenses when he's finished, and as he rolls off me, I notice the blank expression on his face. He doesn't look at me. Doesn't speak to me. Doesn't even seem to realize I'm still lying there. He just gets up and walks to the bathroom.

As the door closes behind him, I feel tears prick the backs of my eyes, but I blink them away. I cannot cry. Not right now.

Kill the girl inside.

The words play on repeat in the back of my head. I have to grow up. I have to be stronger. If not for myself then for Amory. No one else can bring him back from the cliff he's staring over right now. No one else can remind him of who he used to be, because they all love who he's become.

When Amory opens the bathroom door, he takes one look at me and then sighs. "Get cleaned up."

"That's all you have to say?" I ask quietly, scooting to the edge of the bed. I let out a whimper as I move. There was no pleasure in our lovemaking. Only a dull ache as Amory took what I hadn't offered. Claimed my body for his own.

I had let him. Had even welcomed him—because I thought it was what he needed. But as I gaze at the vacant look on my husband's face, I realize I was wrong.

Amory glances down at me, his eyes lingering between my legs. "Sorry it was rough."

278

Something crackles through my chest. Not anger, just red-hot emotion. "You can't do this, Amy. You can't treat me like I'm here for you to use."

He folds his arms over his scarred chest. There are more of them than before. "Things are different now, Rosa."

"But you don't have to be different."

"Yes, I do." He glances away, and I think I see a flicker of remorse pass over his features before he blinks it away and meets my stare again. His eyes are cold. Like that moment of warmth never happened. "I'm the Jägermeister. And you're my wife. Things are different."

I start shaking my head. "It's the day of your father's funeral, and this is how you start it."

"You need to learn your place. As a mafia wife."

"Was that your way of teaching me?" I snap. "Bend me over to remind me that I belong to you."

He steps forward, making me shrink into the blankets.

"First of all, I didn't bend you over. But I can certainly do that if you keep dropping hints."

I swallow thickly.

"Second of all, this isn't just for me. You aren't the wife of an underboss anymore. The German mafia has a standard to uphold. You are part of that standard now. You've got to change."

"You mean I've got to start doing whatever you say." I wrinkle my nose.

"Wives, submit to your husbands." He laughs. "Isn't that what your Bible says?"

Your Bible. Amory says that like he doesn't believe. Like he has no connection to Christianity, even though he's read God's Word, even though we've prayed together, even though he's confessed to believing in God.

He's changed.

"Do not try to weaponize the Word of God against me," I say hotly. "You have no idea what you're talking about."

He narrows his eyes.

"But since you want to quote scriptures at me, here's one you ought to remember." I stand up and walk right over to him, unashamed of my nudity and too angry to care about the lecherous look on his face. "Husbands, treat your wives with respect so that nothing will hinder your prayers."

Amory looks at me dumbly.

"That's First Peter chapter three, verse seven." I lift my chin. "Remember it."

I can tell from the look in his eye that he's never heard that scripture before. I'm not surprised. Many men haven't. But it's there and the meaning is clear. Respect your wife, or your prayers—the very line of communication between you and God—could be crippled.

Amory doesn't understand this. He wasn't raised Christian, so he has no idea what it even means to be a Christian husband. But if he thinks he can spout misinterpreted scriptures to me, and use them to control me, then he's got another thing coming.

I watched my mother get beaten by my father. I watched her sob in the pews of a church. And I watched as a Priest patted her on the shoulder and told her to go back home to the man who'd beaten her and be a good, *submissive* wife. I watched Christina get dragged away by Hans as her husband laughed. I watched Conrad raise his hand to Gisela—and the only person in the room who seemed disturbed by it was me.

I will not allow Amory to treat me the same way.

He doesn't speak for a long moment, just stands there studying my face and my body. The lust in his eyes is still there, as if he hadn't had enough the first time around. But he doesn't make any moves toward me. I'm glad. Because I don't know if I have the strength to push him away. If Amory really wanted to, he could overpower me. Though I don't believe he's sank to that level just yet.

Still. This is not the man I first made love to. This is not the man who carried me to the shower and got down on his knees to wash my feet—to clean up what he described as 'his mess.' He *is* a mess now. And I don't know how to clean him up.

"This isn't you," I whisper, hugging myself.

He seems to soften, sucking in a little gasp and leaning back against the bathroom door. "This is who I need to be."

"No, it isn't."

"It won't be this way forever."

"It shouldn't be this way right now."

"I can't…" his voice trails off. He's staring at the floor now, like he can't meet my gaze. I step closer and take his hand, but he still doesn't look at me. I lean in and kiss his chest, the center of the bullseye where his heart is at.

"Don't…" he says quietly.

I stare up at him and he slowly wraps his strong arms around me. "I need you to love me for who I am right now. Not for the man I used to be. Or the man I can become. This is how it is."

Be the wife he needs you to be…

I remember Christina's advice—and I also remember the fact that she's never been wrong. But I don't know if she's right about this.

Amory wants me to love him for who he is right now. The Jägermeister. The cold man who took me roughly, like a stranger. Like a hired woman from The Club.

I step back from his embrace. "I can only love you like this if you answer my question."

He nods, grey eyes sharpened on me.

"Do you love yourself?"

Amory doesn't speak.

Is this what it means to tend Your lamb? I pray inside, staring at my husband like I barely know him. I'm truly not sure I know him anymore. But I can get to know him again, as this strange creature who seemingly stole into my home overnight.

Love him unconditionally. Forgive him endlessly. Welcome him gracefully. *Is that what it means to tend Your lamb, God?* To show Amory that I won't give up. That I will wrestle him down with love, until it overwhelms him. Just as You do for us.

I touch his hand. "You know God loves you…"

He flinches away. "Not now, Rosa."

"Amy—"

"My father and uncle are dead!" He's yelling now, hands balled into fists.

I should drop the issue, but I can't. I won't let this go—not when the battle is over his eternal soul.

"Death happens in war," I say shakily. "Even to the best of us."

"What's the point in serving your God if we're still going to lose the people we love?"

"Because God will be there to comfort us in our pain. But the only comfort you have is in a bottle." I force myself to look him in the eye. "Or in my body."

"What's wrong with a husband taking comfort in his wife?" He steps closer to me, and I fight the urge to shrink away. "That's what you were made for."

"That isn't true, and you know it."

He cups my chin. "True or not, you didn't stop me." He leans down to whisper against the shell of my ear. "Because you enjoyed every second of it."

My breath hitches and I remind myself to breathe, but it's too late. Amory knows he's won this argument. He knows he's thrown me off, with just that little gesture.

More importantly … he knows he's right.

Embarrassment works its way through my body and into my heart, it squeezes away whatever dignity I had left and leaves me squirming in shame. Amory knows me just as well as I know him. And that haunts me.

I try my hardest to show him the man I know he can be.

But he does the same thing to me. Peeling back the layers of my heart to reveal the woman I've always been.

The one whose heart begins to race at the sound of his stern voice. The woman who enjoys his overbearing dominance. The wife who finds freedom in submission.

Amory had taken me roughly. But I had not stopped him. I hadn't uttered a word in protest. He had taken something I hadn't offered—comfort that wasn't his—but I had taken from him too. I had watched as the warmth drained from his eyes, had fed on it, consumed his chilled passion and used it to extinguish the burning lust I could not control.

We're a demented pair. Like vampires who can only feed on each other.

A tear runs down my cheek as I realize just how right Amory is. I was made for him.

But he was made for me too.

He surprises me by leaning down and kissing my cheek. "It won't be like this forever. I won't be the Jägermeister forever."

I look at him, daring him to make that a promise, but he doesn't. He can't.

"How long?" I ask—no—I *demand*. "How long will it be this way?"

Amory walks away, heading toward his wardrobe to get dressed. "As long as it needs to be."

That isn't good enough. But I suppose it's better than it could be. I could have been saddled with Conrad—a man who isn't afraid to raise his hand to his wife, not even in front of others. I could have been given to Wolfgang, a man who killed his own fiancé with his bare hands. But I married Amory. This is my cup, and it's filled with so many things—anger, bitterness, vengeance, blood.

I plan to drink every drop.

Because if I don't, Amory will. And he won't survive that. The man I first married, the man who showed me what it means to be loved, will never return if he drinks from those bitter waters. It has to be me.

If there is one thing I was made for, it was to stand by Amory's side. To never give up on praying for his salvation. That's what it means to be a wife. That's what it means to love.

"Go get cleaned up." Amory's voice drags me from my thoughts. "I don't want to be late for the funeral."

A dark part of me wants to laugh. We're in the middle of a gruesome mafia war. My father-in-law is dead, as well as his brother. I should feel afraid that Amory is next. I should feel worried that no one is safe. But I only feel numb. I suppose that's what happens when you kill the little girl inside, and finally grow up.

Amory is the Jägermeister now. I am the Mistress of the German mafia now. We learned how to be married. We learned how to love. But just when I'd begun to understand this chapter of our lives, just when I'd mastered the art of clipping thorns, we sprouted weeds. *What now?* I ask God in my heart. *What on earth am I supposed to do now?*

I feel His answer in my bones—in my marrow—as clear as the sound of Amory's voice as he once again tells me to get ready for the funeral.

Now, you start over.

Finish the series…

Starting Over

(Fall 2022)

Keep scrolling to enjoy a free sample of *Starting Over*!

More books by Valicity Elaine & TRC Publishing!

Christian Fantasy

Cross Academy

The End of the World series

The Scribe

Christian Science Fiction

I AM MAN series

Christian Romance

The Living Water

The Woof Pack (Coming Soon)

Christian Children's Fiction

Too Young

ACKNOWLEDGEMENTS

I thought writing *Withered Rose* was a challenge, but I think *Clipping Thorns* proved to be its own achievement. I'm so happy you've stuck around this long! Just one more to go and the story is over…

I mentioned before that I am not a fan of romance. This project is my attempt to write something I'd like to read and see more of in the Christian romance market.

It's been quite a journey, as much as I have enjoyed myself, I sincerely look forward to finishing this trilogy. Let's end this strong in the final installment, *Starting Over*. In the meantime, feel free to busy yourself with some of my other books! Like I said, I don't enjoy romance, so here are a few Christian fantasy adventures for you to enjoy.

Cross Academy

I AM MAN

Sign up for my monthly newsletter to stay updated on new releases, sales, and updates! See you soon.

The Rebel Christian Publishing

We are an independent Christian publishing company focused on fantasy, science fiction, and YA reads. Visit therebelchristian.com to check out our books or click the titles below!

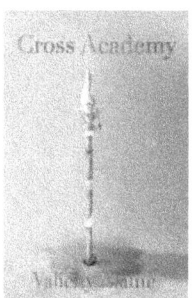

I ΔM MΔN

Valicity Elaine

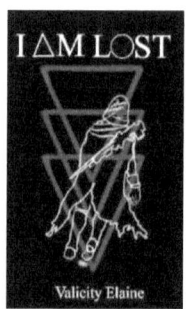

I ΔM LOST

Valicity Elaine

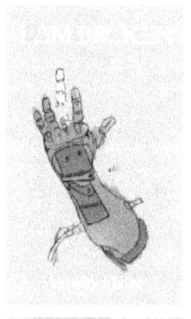

I ΔM FREE

Valicity Elaine

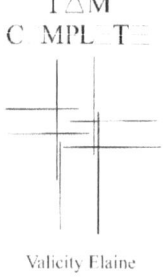

I ΔM
COMPLETE

Valicity Elaine

THE FLYING

A. BEAN

PATCHES

Valicity
Elaine

The I Word

Valicity Elaine

Original Author's Notes

This book was originally published as an episodic story on Kindle Vella. Please enjoy the original author's notes below.

Chapter One

One of my goals for this story is to toughen Rosa up lol I love her as she was in Book One, but I am tired of teary-eyed innocent ladies being tossed around by the wind. I want to take a stab at writing a strong female lead, I pray I get this right.

Chapter Two

Both of my sisters hate Eliana XD I wonder if you hate her too? See you in the next chapter.

Chapter Three

Even though Olivia doesn't love him, I was incredibly excited to write about her wedding with Marco. She is such a lovely bride and character. Hopefully, we'll see more of her in the future. Hopefully we'll see more of Aldo too XD

Chapter Four

So far ... I'm really liking this new 'tough' version of Rosa. She isn't hard as steel, but she is certainly stronger. A rose with thorns XD

Chapter Five

I am so excited to get into Amory and his discovery/exploration of the Faith. His salvation is two books in the making so far, but I wanted to take my time. I wanted to do this in a realistic manner. Prayerfully, it's turning out alright. Oh ... and I'm totally digging the steam between Amy and Rosa XOXO

Chapter Six

I don't really know what else to say except that I did a lot of praying before writing this scene and I believe what God gave me was enjoyable. My goal was to present love in its purest form, the way God intended it to be, between a husband and a wife. I hope you found this chapter entertaining and *tastefully* steamy, haha. See you in the next chapter. XOXO

Chapter Seven
Who else thought it was sweet that Amy suggested they pray together? XOXO

Chapter Eight
I'm honestly sad to see Amory end his alliance with the Morenos because of how much I enjoyed Emilio. One of the things I've always loved is culture. Exploring the different mafias can sometimes be dark but the language, physical descriptions, food, and even the decor of their homes stemmed from their cultural backgrounds and I loved portraying that. Now a part of that will be ending haha, maybe we'll see more of the Morenos and their Spanish culture later on? We shall see.

Chapter Nine
Obviously, these two have some changes to make and things to work out in their relationship. Marriage isn't always bright and beautiful, but with God in the midst, I know it can certainly become as such. Even though these characters are fictional, I find myself cheering for them as they learn through their mistakes and work through their issues.

Chapter Ten
I honestly have no idea how I would have handled this situation... I feel it is very easy to read this series and think of Rosa as a weak character, but I must admit, in many ways, Rosa is much stronger than I am.

Chapter Eleven
I've been waiting for the war to finally begin... Now that it's here, I'm kind of stunned. This story somehow turned into a

bit of an action thriller XD I hope you enjoy!

Chapter Twelve
Oh boy... What are we going to do with these two? XOXO

Chapter Thirteen
For some reason, this chapter was quite sad to me. I feel like this was a conversation our couple needed to have, but there was never any intention for it to end in tears the way it did. Hmm... Sometimes the story gets ahead of me lol but God leads the way, so I guess this is how it needed to go! See you in the next chapter XOXO

Chapter Fourteen
You know, I have personally never liked Hans, but I feel like his brutal personality was a real driving force in this chapter. If there was ever a time where I was happy to have him in the book, it was today XD

Chapter Fifteen
Rest in peace, Ja'meek Williams...

Chapter Sixteen
I love writing Rosa's POV because she brings in the spiritual aspect of the book. Her faith in God honestly inspires me, which is strange because God blessed me to write her character, haha! But I love doing Biblical research for her chapters, working in the Word and applying a message to her journey. It gives meaning to her struggles and I think that makes the series come alive. Being able to relate to a character on a spiritual level is an amazing thing. Christian fiction is so awesome XD

Chapter Seventeen
Amory *seems* to be on his way to salvation, but I feel like it's going to be a painful journey. Some people must be broken before God can put them together. How much will Amory face before he finally gives in to the Voice of God? We shall see

XD

Chapter Eighteen
Poor Morgen... He and Conrad have slowly become favorite characters of mine. But this is war. Blood will be shed. I hope you're prepared.

Chapter Nineteen
Do you think Volkov will honor the two-day grace period???

Chapter Twenty
This is one of my favorite chapters. So many unplanned things happened! Morgen was NOT supposed to survive and the Rosa lookalike was not supposed to become a major player. I'm excited about what's to come. Already looking forward to Book III!

Chapter Twenty-One
Ahh I love Rosa's chapters for the chance to work in more of my faith... I couldn't wait to write this one. I hope you enjoyed it XOXO

Chapter Twenty-Two
Do you think Amory will learn to trust God? I think that's a lesson some of us end up learning the hard way lol

Chapter Twenty-Three
Is anyone else excited about Rosa's glow-up??

Chapter Twenty-Four
I loved this chapter and was honestly tempted to end the story here. But we've got to end the way we started! With little miss Rosie XOXO

Chapter Twenty-Five
Thank you Jesus and thank YOU so much for sticking with me through yet another novel! This book was just as fun and exciting as the last and I can't wait to get into Book III! Keep

your eyes peeled for Starting Over, the last installment of the trilogy. It will be here before you know it!

Keep scrolling to read a free sample of *Starting Over*!

Free sample of Book III, *Starting Over*

Chapter One

In the silence, I clamped my hand over my mouth to muffle my own cries. Salty tears streamed down my cheeks as I heaved into my palm, snot dribbling over my raw knuckles. My sore shoulders shook with each sob, my broken ribs ached each time I drew breath. I was broken. In mind, body, and spirit. But as much pain as I had already endured, I knew there was more to come.

The stone floor was cold beneath my bare feet. I adjusted my position, trying to sit as close to the wall as possible while avoiding the puddle of urine I'd left just off to my right. There was a tooth on the floor, not far from me. I wouldn't kid myself by thinking it belonged to one of the men who'd attacked me. As I worked my jaw, swollen tongue fishing around in my bloody mouth, I found the hole in my gums where the lost tooth had once been. Oberon had probably knocked it out. He had thrown the first punch when I was dragged into the room.

My own uncle.

My sobs turned to whimpers as I heard footsteps approaching my dark little room. The quiet solitude had broken my mind—crippling every thought, filling them with fear in its silent aguish. I was stuck in a dimly lit room with no windows and only one giant, metal door with a massive crank to let me know I was locked inside. I had no idea how long I'd been in the room, but I had used the bathroom three times— once when I'd been punched so hard, I couldn't help myself— and twice because I just couldn't hold it any longer after the men had left.

Three days, I reasoned, wiping at my puffy eyes. They hadn't fed me, hadn't let me bathe, hadn't even treated any of my injuries. But they made sure to check on me every five hours. I kept track of every hour in my head, ticking them off on my bloody fingers after counting to 3600—the number of seconds in an hour. When they checked on me for the third time and still hadn't brought any food or bandages with them, I realized they weren't checking to help me recover, they were making sure I hadn't died.

The footsteps drew nearer, just outside the door now. I gasped and scooted even closer to the wall, trying to hide in the shadows. The movement sent fire through my behind, rubbing brush-burns against my naked bottom, but I kept struggling. As if I could get away.

When the door opened, the creak was loud enough to swallow the shamefully feminine squeal of fear that escaped me. I was huddled in the corner, hands up in defense of the burning light streaming in, my swollen eyes peeled open as wide as they could.

There was a man standing in the doorway. It wasn't until I heard his rumbling baritone that I realized it was my father.

My fear nearly tripled.

"Amory," he said calmly.

I choked out a sob.

Klaus, Onkel Oberon, a General named Elias and another named Adolf, a bodyguard named Otto, and a grunt called Jürgen entered the room behind my father. Screams echoed around us—it took me a moment to realize they were coming from me.

I wasn't afraid of another beating; it was the sight of Jürgen that sent a chill up my spine. He was only a grunt, but he had been the most brutal. He had been the one to strip me naked in front of all the others. He had been the one to hold me down. But he hadn't punched me. He hadn't kicked me. His hands brought gentle touches that sent talons of fear clawing down my body.

The other men had watched it happen, expecting me to fight back, but I'd been too weak after two days of brutal violence. It didn't hurt as much as it shamed me. Humiliated me. But that was the point of all this. To break my mind and body.

That day had been so normal. At fifteen, I'd ridden my bike out to Staten Island to meet up with Giovanni. There was a guy there who would sell us cigarettes to smoke while we watched pretty Russian girls toss rocks into the canal. But when I got there, I realized Gio had brought his kid sister along so we couldn't bum smokes off anyone—not in front of her, at least. Gio had said his father would kill him if Rosa came home smelling like smoke. So we'd walked the docks without any cigarettes and whistled at the Russian princess when she walked by with her body guard.

Sofia Volkov. She had been pretty even as a girl. And she'd had a pretty older cousin named Dominika.

That day, Dominika had tagged along with Sofia, walking a few paces behind her cousin during their little stroll. Sofia was wearing a white dress that made her look like an angel, but Dominika…

Dominika was wearing a red blouse and a tiny little matching skirt I'm positive her Uncle Mikhail knew nothing about. Neither Gio nor I could keep our eyes off her. We followed her along the docks, whistling and shouting at her until she finally turned and gave us a seductive smile. Gio, ever the flirt, had dared her to come over and give one of us a kiss. She had shaken her head but when her cousin and her guard had turned away, she held a finger to her lips and then flashed us.

I had almost peed myself, standing there staring at Dominika with her shirt up and her pale breasts right there for me to see. It was the first time I'd seen a naked girl in person. Gio too. Neither of us had any idea how to react except to stare and stumble over ourselves as she lowered her shirt and sauntered away, giggling the entire time.

We tried to follow her, but as soon as we crossed the crowded streets, their guard started yelling and we had to take off. Three Wolves chased us all the way to the ferries—I had to carry Gio's kid sister as we tore through the crowd, laughing and howling. When we boarded one of my father's boats, Gio turned and mooned the guards who'd been chasing us, and we shouted the lyrics to a Russian song as we waved at them while the ferry pulled away.

When I was snatched out of my bed that night, my first thought was that I was being punished for what'd happened with Dominika. She wasn't a mafia princess, but she was high-ranking enough for us to be whipped for looking at her body without her father's permission. But as I stared up at my father and the six German men he'd allowed to beat me, I realized what this really was.

Uwe Jäger pulled up the legs of his pants before he squatted in front of me, looking right into my battered face as he said, "Do you want the pain to stop?"

I nodded. "*Bitte, Vater.*"

"I'm going to ask you a question," he said calmly, "if you answer correctly, I'll tell them to leave you alone."

Just to mess with me, Elias stepped forward and I realized he was holding a bat. My ribs ached at the sight. Not even a day ago he had taken that bat to my body, like I was a criminal—not the son of the Jägermeister. But I was fifteen. I wasn't some innocent kid anymore. I was a man. At least that's what this whole thing was supposed to make me into. A mafioso. A Hunter.

I was being initiated.

Jürgen smiled down at me from over my father's shoulder. I inched backwards, trying hard not to cry anymore. But it was hard to focus on Vater when Klaus was wrapping a chain around his fist and Otto was staring at his razorblade, inspecting it. My skin stung as I watched him, remembering each time he ran the knife over my back and chest. I would have scars for the rest of my life because of him.

"Amory," Vater's voice brought me back.

I blinked at him.

"*Ja?*"

"My question," he said slowly.

I nodded.

"You're fifteen now. Old enough to join me in the business. When you're older, you will replace me, son. You will run the entire German mafia. But first you must be initiated. You must start at the bottom of the barrel. As a grunt. And when you are ready, you will wear the crown."

I nodded again, wincing as I swallowed.

Vater leaned toward me, his dark hair falling into his face. The light from the hallway made shadows dance along the concrete walls, a pillar of darkness covered half of my father's face as he gazed at me. His stare was intense, regarding me like he was looking at a stranger. Not his own child.

I resisted the urge to shiver as I stared back. I didn't want him to know how afraid I was.

"Do you accept this position?" Vater asked softly.

My mouth opened to answer, but no words would come.

Vater sighed into the silence and pushed to his feet. Klaus took a step—I started screaming again.

"Wait—Vater, wait!"

Uwe watched as Klaus came closer, chain in hand. The sound of the links rattling together was oddly reminiscent of the sound of chattering teeth. I wanted to scream—I already was screaming. Shamelessly. Loudly. And scooting away like I was a mad, feral animal.

Oberon slapped me so hard, I thought he loosened another tooth.

"Please!" I squeaked, throwing my hands up in surrender.

Vater calmly slid his hands into his pockets. "Do you accept this position, Amory?"

The mafia was ruled by Uwe's command. I wouldn't be able to escape him or his beatings if I said yes. But I had a greater fear of what would happen if I said no.

"I—I…"

I wet myself.

I couldn't help it. I hadn't even known I'd had to pee; I only felt the sudden warmth bloom in my bladder and then it was running down my dirt-stained legs, puddling around my feet.

Elias laughed.

My father sighed again.

I scrambled back and took a deep breath. "I accept this position!" I had no idea if it was too late or not, but I was willing to agree to anything if it meant Vater would call off his men.

They all stopped moving toward me and glanced back at my father. The silence that stormed through the room left me dizzy and weak in my pee-streaked knees.

Very slowly, Uwe pulled his hands from his pockets and turned to leave. He spoke over his shoulder as he reached for the metal door. "Bring him."

They dragged me naked through the halls of the warehouse and then shoved me into the back of an SUV. I passed out during the ride; I don't know if it was because of nerves, exhaustion, or injury, but when I woke, I realized I was in a bed with my wounds finally wrapped and a bowl of soup waiting on my bedside table.

A primal sort of hunger overcame me as I spied the bowl. I ignored the screaming pain in my bones and muscles as I crawled across the bed and took the soup in my hands. I didn't bother with a spoon, just drank the salty chicken broth right from the bowl, enjoying the warmth as it trickled down my chin and neck. When I finished, I burped and wiped my mouth with the back of my hand, immediately feeling lightheaded and sluggish at the same time.

There was a water bottle on the little table, I grabbed it and twisted the cap, hands trembling as I raised the drink to my bruised lips. Half of it spilled down my chest, making me realize that I was naked from the waist up. Someone had finally given me a pair of underwear to hide my shame. But the flesh that was exposed was hidden by a different sort of cover.

Scars. Wicked carvings going through my chest and over my back. Thick, bulging scabs bubbled over recent wounds. Every move I made left me wincing as I looked down at myself. I was ugly. Grotesque. But I didn't mind. I'd been initiated. That meant I was entering an ugly world. There was no room for beauty—only ashes.

I reached up to scratch my head and realized they'd shaved my head. That must have happened while I was passed out. Every new grunt had their hair removed, though I wasn't sure if it was out of punishment or convenience. Half of mine had been ripped out from Onkel dragging me by my hair. The rest had been matted with blood.

As I ran my hand over my smooth scalp, I wondered how the rest of me looked. My face, my back. Probably just as bad as the parts of me I could see.

The door to my room opened to let Uwe inside. He was followed by a pretty woman wearing a white dress and low heels. She looked older than me, probably late teens or early twenties. I wasn't sure.

Vater closed the door, the sound of the lock sent a tendril

of fear brushing over my heart.

"Amory," he said evenly, "welcome to the German mafia."

I nodded.

"Thank you, Vater."

"You survived the initiation."

I nodded again.

"But there is one more test."

My eyes flicked to the woman who only smiled at me. I didn't know what to make of the look on her face—was she encouraging me? Comforting me? Mocking me?

Vater spoke again. "You let Jürgen turn you into a little girl." His voice was dark, like the whole thing was all my fault.

I lurched forward as the memories of Jürgen's hands on me replayed in my head. I wanted to vomit, and I'm sure I would have if I hadn't slapped a hand over my mouth. I'd just gotten my first meal in three days, and I had no idea when I'd get another. I didn't want to waste my food.

Vater straightened his shoulders, making himself look taller. "I don't have any daughters."

I swallowed, trying to control my breathing, trying to ignore the clammy feel of Jürgen's hands ghosting over my body, touching me in places that were forbidden, in ways that were sinful. The pain wasn't half as bad as the shame, the fact that my father and uncle had watched. The fact that all I'd done was scream and cry. I had brought shame to Vater. I should have fought back. But I'd been too weak.

Vater jerked his head at the woman, never taking his eyes off me. "It's time to prove to me you aren't a little girl."

The woman stepped forward and slipped down the straps

of her dress. It fell to the floor at her feet; she stepped out of it and gracefully removed her heels. When she stood upright again, that odd smile was on her face—it was the only thing she was wearing.

Every hair on my body raised. I felt my muscles stiffen. I felt my mouth fall open.

"Vater," I exhaled.

He snapped at the woman. "Get on the bed."

"*Vater*," I said again.

He took one large step forward and suddenly his hand was around my throat. "You *will* take her," he hissed in my face. "Or you will never leave this room."

With a shove, he released me to fall back into the covers. I stared at him in shock, wishing for the days when he would have whipped me for looking at a girl inappropriately. Now he wanted me to lay with one right in front of him.

I had no fanciful dreams about the first time I'd have a woman. I wasn't waiting for marriage—or even thinking about it. And I wasn't interested in finding my soulmate. I wasn't even sure if I had a soul. I secretly hoped I didn't … because I was sure Vater would have taken that from me too.

No matter what I'd imagined of my first sexual experience, I hadn't guessed it would play out like this. As some sort of twisted gang initiation.

This is the part of mafia life they never mention. In the cool movies, in the dark thriller stories, in the dirty little romance novels you read at night. They don't tell you how you're beaten and raped and then forced to sleep with someone you don't know. They don't tell you that the men who hurt you are your own relatives and friends. They don't mention that the goal is to survive initiation, but while you're being initiated all you wish for is death.

Waking up alive seems like a curse once it's all over. Because that means it was all real. It wasn't a dream, or even a nightmare. It's reality and there is no escape.

The mattress sank with the weight of the woman as she crawled over to me. I ignored her, keeping my swollen eyes locked on Uwe.

"Vater…" I tried once more.

His voice was a growl and his fingers twitched as he glared at me, aching to reach for the gun holstered at his hip. I believed he would shoot me if I disobeyed his order. So I swallowed and steeled myself for the command I knew was coming.

"Prove that you're a man, Amory. It's time."

Chapter Two

I stare down at my father's lifeless body, blinking rapidly as my memories recede to the dark pit I'd kept them locked in for so long. I can't recall the last time those thoughts surfaced in my head. I don't remember the last time I relived those three dark days.

I don't want to.

The scars on my back and chest have been enough of a reminder. I've lived with them for over fifteen years now. I've seen the horror of my flesh every time I've looked in the mirror, felt the ache of the knife splitting my skin all over again each time I stepped into the shower. Over the years, I've tried to cover them with tattoos. Hired an excellent artist who's treated me well, but even she had a hard time coming up with designs to make me look suitable whenever I undressed.

The man responsible for these scars is in a coffin now. So is his brother.

Now I'm supposed to conjure up some tears and tell the onlooking crowd that he was a good father and that I miss him so very much. I can't find the words. I can't think of *anything* to say as I stand at the podium in the church—not even a lie.

I could swallow my dark memories, smother them with a reminder that it was all just tradition. Something Vater himself went through when he was fifteen, as well as Onkel and Klaus and Elias too. Even Jürgen was initiated the same way, probably worse since he was just a Hunted grunt.

But that didn't make it alright. Not while it was happening and not afterwards, when I was given my reward for surviving.

Vengeance

Two years after those horrible three days, I was assigned my first execution. The German way is to release the man who'd been sentenced to death and hunt him down yourself.

I spent three days prowling the streets of Brooklyn, searching for the man my father had saved especially for me. Because of what he'd done to me.

I had smiled as I'd pulled the trigger and ended Jürgen's life. But there was no joy in the act. No redemption. No satisfaction. Just a raw, potent hatred that seemed to grow each time I pulled the trigger after that night.

It swells in my chest now as I stare down at Uwe's corpse.

Dressed in a three-piece suit with his hair combed away from his aged face and his eyes glued shut.

I want to spit on him, but that would cause a scene.

My father was not a good father. He was an even worse husband. And he was a terrible human being in general. I have no kind words for him, not even at his own funeral … but I do miss him.

That's the sad truth that sends shivers over my scarred back. I miss my father. From the moment I saw his car go up in flames I've felt a hollow ache in my chest. Because, even though he was a crappy guy in every other area of his life, he was an excellent Jägermeister. He was a respectable mafia boss. And he was the best mentor I had in this dark life.

I need him. Now more than ever.

How am I supposed to take over the Hunting Grounds? How am I supposed to get us through this war that is rapidly spiraling out of control?

I've been an underboss for a couple years now. I've been ruling in my father's stead long enough to have the trust of the men standing guard in the cathedral. But I don't trust myself. I have no confidence in my decisions. It was my decision to ignore the warning Voice of God that got my father killed. It was my decision to cover up Wolfgang's crime that started this entire thing.

I'm thirty-one years old now, but I suddenly feel like that fifteen-year-old kid who peed himself and cried out to his father for help. Except my dad is dead now. And there is no one to call off the men who want my head. There is no one to say the word and end my suffering. Not anymore.

Someone in the crowd clears their throat and I realize I've been standing at the podium for longer than normal. I grip the sides of the wooden stand and swallow; the sound is picked up by the mic and sent echoing through the grand sanctuary. I wait until it dies down before I try to speak.

"Uwe Jäger was my father."

Christina sniffles and my eyes snap to her. She's crying, has been nonstop since she heard the news. My heart breaks for my mother. Breaks for the woman who should be weeping tears of joy because her abuser is finally dead. But Mutti has always been too kind for her own good. She loved Vater, despite all his shortcomings. Without thinking, I glance over at Rosa whose eyes are also red and weepy. I absently wonder if she loves me despite mine.

Not even an hour ago, I'd had her in my bed. It hadn't been sweet. It hadn't been loving. But Rosa hadn't complained, not until the very end. She'd laid there and taken everything I'd given. Accepted my pain for pleasure. Took my misery in exchange for ecstasy—as fleeting as it was. She didn't deserve what I'd given her. She didn't deserve *me*. But this is the hand we've been dealt. This is our cup. I vow we'll drink from it together.

. . .

Starting Over will be available on Amazon as an eBook and in print in October 2022! Join our newsletter to be notified of its release! Thank you so much for reading XOXO

www.ingramcontent.com/pod-product-compliance
Lightning Source LLC
Chambersburg PA
CBHW070548260626
47161CB00002B/542